DOGMA OF WAR

DOGMA OF WAR

THE ELVEN PROPHECY™ BOOK SIX

THEOPHILUS MONROE

MICHAEL ANDERLE

DISRUPTIVE IMAGINATION

Copyright © 2021 LMBPN Publishing
Cover copyright © LMBPN Publishing
A Michael Anderle Production

LMBPN Publishing
PMB 196, 2540 South Maryland Pkwy
Las Vegas, NV 89109

Version 1.02, October 2021
ebook ISBN: 978-1-68500-401-9
Print ISBN: 978-1-68500-402-6

THE DOGMA OF WAR TEAM

Thanks to our JIT Readers

Diane L. Smith
Dorothy Lloyd
Jackey Hankard-Brodie
Zacc Pelter

If We've missed anyone, please let us know!

Editor
The Skyhunter Editing Team

CHAPTER ONE

I soared over the canopy while Clarence bounded through the forest below. Bears can smell people from almost a mile away. If anyone encroached on our outpost in the Canadian forests, he knew it. I followed his lead, utilizing the powers of aether and air so I could spy on the intruder from above.

I think it's only one person, Clarence said, licking his sharp teeth. He'd just finished devouring a fish from a stream. What kind of fish was it? No clue. Short of catfish or fish sticks, my ability to identify different kinds of fish was limited. He spoke to me the same way my cat Agnus did. I could hear his thoughts. That meant we could communicate some distance apart.

"One person?" I asked, also utilizing my newfound ability to speak to Clarence. "No one wanders this deep into the forest alone."

I touched the blades I had strapped to my waist. One of them was a common blade. The other contained Aerin's soul. The drow princess had given her life, according to the dictate of the Elven Prophecy, and trapped her soul in the blade. When I wielded it, she lent me her skill. It was more like she took over.

The problem? Anyone we killed with that blade had a fraction of their soul added to hers.

We'd acquired a second drow blade to take care of any killing in the future. So far, we'd only taken down a few elves with Aerin's blade. While none of them were complete persons, too many souls crowded into the blade, and eventually, they'd overpower Aerin's influence. Like Clarence and Agnus, she spoke to me through a connection of our minds. Any time I touched the blade, I could hear her, and she could read my mind in turn.

It may be a scout, Aerin said. *If it is, we'll have to kill him.*

I sighed. "I don't want to kill, Aerin. We should try and capture him first."

This is war, Caspar. Eventually, lives will be lost.

I snorted. "Yeah, well. So far, I've mostly avoided that. We can win hearts and minds through nonviolence. Once blood is shed, things will change."

"Just ahead," Clarence interjected. "It smells like an elf."

I grinned. I hadn't realized until I'd met Clarence that elves had their own scent. Layla, my elven wife, always smelled amazing. I credited her Herbal Essence shampoo with that. Of course, she said I always smelled like a man. I don't think that was a compliment, though.

If it's an elf, Aerin said, my hand still firmly gripping her blade, *we can't let him go. If he reports our location to Brightborn, it'll just be a matter of time before government bombers blast the whole area to kingdom come.*

I nodded. *As I said, I intend to capture him. He won't report back to Brightborn either way.*

Stop, Caspar! Clarence shouted. This one has magic.

I sighed. Most elves had magic. So far, I hadn't met one who could match me. Most of them could only wield one element. A few had two. I had all five: air, water, fire, earth, and aether. In a battle of the elements, it was like a complex version of rock-paper-scissors. If my opponent wielded fire, I'd use water. If they wielded water, I used earth. If they churned the earth, I could usually counter it with air. With aether, I could endure anything anyone wielding air could throw at me. Almost everyone could wield aether at some level. But there wasn't much anyone could do with that to hurt me. Aether was comparable to what one might call soul. It was the power typically used, as I'd discovered, to control and focus all the other elements.

Because I drew my power not merely from the elements, but the elementals whose spirits I'd absorbed, if all else failed, I could usually counteract any kind of magic with the same kind. I was stronger. Throw a tornado at me. I could unravel it with air. Shake the earth. I could tame it. I could fight fire with fire and water with water.

If push came to shove, I also had access to fairy magic. The residual power that had remained within me after Trixie, the fairy queen, briefly possessed me meant I could teleport myself, or my enemy or anything else, to any place I could clearly visualize.

So far, the only time I'd had to resort to killing was when I was trapped in a spire equipped with magical dampeners.

In the forest, we were in my domain. All the elements thrived there, which meant my power was more acute than it was in the city or within the confines of a building. No matter what this elf could do magic-wise, I'd be able to handle it. I had plenty of options depending, of course, on which element the elf happened to wield.

I hovered in mid-air before slowly lowering myself to land behind a black spruce. It was the most common tree in the area. They didn't have broad canopies, so I could have spotted the elf from above. However, I was hoping I'd see him before he saw me.

The elf held a bow in his hands. Not an ornate bow like Layla's. It was plain, hewn from wood. He knelt, placing his hand on the ground. He wore a long brown cloak. His hands were wrapped in burlap. Long dark hair fell from beneath a green cap.

His pointed ears gave it away; he was an elf, but he didn't look like any elf I'd encountered before. The New Albion elves, who came to Earth with Brightborn, dressed in elaborate gowns. Their weaponry was decorated with ornate carvings and jewels.

I touched Aerin's blade. "What is this guy? He doesn't resemble any elf I've ever encountered before."

I don't know, Aerin replied. *He has to be with Brightborn. I can't imagine...*

"You can't imagine what?"

Nothing, Aerin said. *It's a crazy idea.*

I shrugged. "I'm used to crazy at this point."

Maybe he's not from New Albion. The drow remained on Earth for centuries undetected. What if this elf... What if he belongs to another race we didn't know about?

I pinched my chin. "Or perhaps that's just what he wants us to think."

I hate to admit it, Caspar. But I think in this instance, you're right. We need to talk to him. Find out the truth.

"So what do I do, just walk up to him and introduce myself?"

No, if you're right and he is one of Brightborn's legionaries in disguise, he might attack you before you can react.

"I have an idea," I said, lowering myself to the ground as I continued eying the elf from a distance.

I placed my hand to the ground and drew on earthen magic.

The second I did, the elf fixed his eyes on me. I opened the earth beneath him, creating a small sinkhole. Unless he could fly, which the New Albion elves generally couldn't do, he'd be stuck long enough that I could approach him from above. According to Brag'mok, the warrior-giant who first started training me in the art of combat, it was always good to maintain higher ground over one's enemy.

The elf didn't so much as scream. Strange, I thought. I was prepared. I had all five elements ready to go just in case he tried something funny.

I approached the sinkhole until something grabbed me by the ankle. I looked. A tree root had burst from the ground and wrapped itself around my leg.

It continued to spiral its way up my thigh. I grabbed Aerin's blade and let her take over. She chopped at it. But then another root grabbed hold of my arm.

I channeled earth magic. At least I tried to. But it didn't respond.

"Why isn't my magic working?"

Try fire! Burn it off!

I brought fire to the forefront of my mind. But again, I couldn't release it. "What the hell!"

"Clarence!" I shouted. "I need your help!"

Already on my way!

I glanced at the sinkhole as the tree roots tightened around me just in time to see the elf pull himself over the edge. He rose to his feet and dusted off his cloak. He cocked his head, furrowing his brow, as he stepped toward me.

Clarence blasted between the trees with a roar.

The elf raised his hands, a subtle green glow enveloping his arms. Clarence stopped, sat down, and whimpered.

The elf barely paid my grizzly companion any mind. He focused on me as he took small steps toward me. He cocked his head slightly.

"*Awina kiya?*"

I grunted. I didn't have a clue what he was saying. "Do you speak English?"

"*Tanite oci kiya?*"

I shook my head. "I'm sorry. I don't understand."

The elf placed his hand on his chest. "*Nisihkason Mingan.*"

"Your name is Mingan?" I asked.

The elf smiled. "*Eha!* Mingan!"

"I'm Caspar," I said.

The elf nodded. "*Awas*, Caspar."

5

I shook my head again.

The elf brushed his hand across the front of his face. *"Awas!"*

"Go away?" I asked.

"Awas!"

I pointed to my leg. "I don't know how I can go away. You have me tangled up in these roots!"

The elf laughed, clutching at his belly. Then, he raised a hand. Green magic flowed out of his fingertips, and the tree roots around my leg slithered off and retreated to the ground.

"Thank you," I said.

The elf nodded. *"Awas,* Caspar. *Awas!"*

I nodded, turned, and reached out to Clarence in my mind. "I think he wants us to leave."

He does, Clarence replied.

I scratched my head as I walked up beside the bear. "You could understand him?"

Of course. He was speaking something similar to Cree.

"So he isn't a New Albion elf, then?"

Definitely not. His people have lived in these forests for centuries. That's how I know his tongue.

"And I'm just learning about this now?" I asked.

Why would I think to mention it? These elves are no threat to you or our friends.

"How many more are there?" I asked.

Hard to say. Hundreds. Maybe thousands. They travel much. Sometimes, I go years without meeting one. Then, it seems, they appear in great numbers.

"That's strange," I said.

Clarence nodded and growled. *Yes. Very unusual. But now that we have seen one, I suspect many more will show soon.*

CHAPTER TWO

Aerin didn't have any clue that elves lived anywhere in Canada, much less elves who could wield magic like that. It was the strangest thing. It was as if the trees themselves silenced me at his command. When those roots had been wrapped around me, it wasn't that I didn't have magic. I just couldn't release it, almost like the elementals whose power and essences coursed within me refused to comply. Like they were heeding a higher authority.

What did he mean when he told me to go away? Was he telling me to leave him there at that moment? Or was he trying to tell all of us, presuming he knew we were settled in the forest nearby, to leave the area? If that was what he wanted us to do, well, I didn't know where else we could go.

Brightborn would surely have scouts watching the North Pole since we'd been there before. We couldn't go anywhere within the reach of any major governments. Brightborn effectively had most governments, at least the larger ones, wrapped around his little finger.

Of course, we had the support of the people. We'd produced several videos since we went into hiding. Periodically, we'd use fairy gates to teleport somewhere we could upload them to the

Internet. I couldn't do it myself. We had to rely on Trixie and the other fairies. While I could portal anywhere I could visualize, they could open gateways to just about anywhere. Then, if the fairies didn't want to hang out, I could easily create a portal to take me back to our fortress in the forest. Usually, I took Jag with me. He was the tech wizard. Often Layla went along. Mostly so she could watch my six—and by that, I don't mean stare at my butt, although my posterior had gotten rather taut as of late. We were more concerned that someone might recognize us and report us to the authorities.

For the most part, we had widespread support amongst the people who opposed their governments' alignment with Brightborn. However, there were others who were convinced that we were the terrorists they painted us as. Since neither those who supported us or those who opposed us wore uniforms, we couldn't trust anyone when we went into the cities.

It had been three months since we first set up camp in the northern part of Quebec. We'd used elven technology combined with my elemental acumen to create large, tree-like spires that reached the height of the trees around us. We could have made them taller, but we were trying to remain inconspicuous. After all, the governments looking for us had satellites. Our spires blended into the landscape. We put out our fires every night. We were careful.

Between the giants, the drow, and the elven resistance, our numbers were just south of three hundred. Hardly enough that we could counter one, much less all, of the world's military forces. However, we were too many to stay hidden forever.

Unlike our previous stay at the junkyard ranch, we weren't just biding our time. I wasn't willing to wait for Brightborn to make his next move. We were training and planning for the inevitable war.

Three hundred against the world's governments? We didn't have a chance. Not by strength of arms alone. But if we could all master our abilities, our various magics, we could certainly give Brightborn's elven legion a run for its money. Take them out, take out Brightborn, and we'd save the world from his tyranny. Of course, we'd probably all be bombed out of existence later. To the President of the United States, to Canada's and Britain's Prime Ministers, Brightborn was a savior. Once we took him out, if we succeeded, we'd be the world's most wanted. If we weren't already.

I heard the clanging of metal from a hundred yards away. With three different races, not counting the two humans—Jag and myself—each group had its own fighting style. The elves excelled in ranged attacks with bows. They fought, generally, with spears in close combat situations. Not all of them had been a part of Brightborn's legion. Some of them were civilians. Nonetheless, I'd learned that all elves served at least one term in the royal legion. At least, they used to on New Albion. They all had basic fighting skills. Since their style of combat most closely resembled that of Brightborn's legions, they were an invaluable asset.

The giants had spent their whole lives fighting elves on New Albion. They had their own tactics for countering the elves— getting them into a close combat situation where the elven spears were at a disadvantage against broadswords and axes in the hands of giants who were roughly three times the size of any elf.

The drow had never been to New Albion. They fought with sleek, single-edged swords like the two I carried. All of the drow —Aerin's father, Elrand was the only exception—were female. Don't let any misogynistic misconceptions deceive you, however. They were lethal. Their blades were enchanted with elemental power and they were agile fighters, more than capable of handling themselves against elves and even giants.

I chuckled as I saw Gronk, one of the leaders of the giants, sparring with Rina. He was quadruple her size, easy. But she was so quick that she managed to dodge all his attacks. With her blade covered in burlap for safety's sake, she struck him a dozen times, and he didn't manage to hit her once.

Good thing, because even with the sharp edge of his ax covered similarly, with his strength, a single blow could still be quite painful.

"*Dreg snaffit!*" Gronk shouted, slamming his ax into the ground as Rina stood behind him, her hands on her hips chuckling.

I always got a kick out of giant curses. I didn't have a clue what the words meant, but I imagined it was close to dagnabbit, dadgummit, or use of the Lord's dreg-snaffit name in vain followed by a dammit.

"What's wrong, Gronk?" Rina asked. "Can't catch me?"

"You're like flies, the lot of you!" Gronk shouted, shaking his head. "Why can't you just stay still and fight like a man?"

Rina chuckled. "Why do you think our men don't fight? They'd never survive. Maybe if you learned to fight like a woman, you'd stand a chance!"

I glanced at the perimeter of the sparring ring that had been roped off between trees. Layla was smiling wide and laughing, amused by Rina's display of girl power.

Clarence had already made his way back to Layla. She had a way with animals. The first time she'd met Agnus, albeit in part on account of Agnus hoping to seduce her with his feline friskiness, she had him won over in a matter of moments. She'd spoken to Clarence almost right away. It had taken me weeks to be able to connect to the bear. So long as I was the only one around, they were fine with me. We got along great. Since Agnus was my cat, despite his stubbornness and incessant antics, he loved me. But when Layla was around, well, I didn't rate.

I sneaked up behind Layla and goosed her.

She turned around with death in her eyes.

I held up my hands. "Sorry. Couldn't resist."

Layla chuckled. "I'm just glad it's you. Not one of those giants."

"Has a giant been harassing you?"

Layla snorted. "Not overtly. But the way some of them look at me, you'd think they'd been harboring secret elf fantasies all their lives."

I shrugged. "Who hasn't?"

Layla grinned. "It's just a little strange since, you know, our races were mortal enemies back on New Albion."

I snickered. "Sleeping with the enemy is a thing, you know."

"Not like I'd ever do that! Can you imagine? They must be huge!"

I cocked my head. "His thing would be too big? *That's* the reason you wouldn't sleep with a giant?"

Layla grinned, grabbed me by the shirt, and kissed me gently on the lips. "And because I've got a man."

"What's your man gotta do with me?" I asked, with a bit of rhythm to my cadence.

"I'm not tryin' to hear that, see," Layla shot back.

I chuckled. "I'm surprised you caught that reference."

"Bad nineties rap. I suppose when I came to Earth all those years ago to study your culture, I had to start somewhere."

"Makes sense. If that's the sort of stuff you shared with your dad, no wonder he's trying to conquer us."

Layla snickered. "You'd be surprised. When I first brought back a Discman loaded with *Please Hammer Don't Hurt 'Em*, he listened to *You Can't Touch This* on repeat for months."

"And here I thought your father and I had nothing in common?"

Layla rolled her eyes. "Let me guess; you rocked those parachute pants back in the day."

I nodded. "Who didn't? I mean, when I wasn't wearing my tight-rolled jeans and Reebok Pumps."

"When all this is over, we have to go meet your mother. I bet she still has old photos."

"Oh, she does. Albums upon albums chock-full of pure embarrassment. Just wait until you see my mullet phase. Eclipsed only, perhaps, by my bowl cut."

Layla giggled. "Here I was, thinking you had Vanilla Ice hair."

I nodded. "Yup, yup. Had that phase, too."

"That's awesome!"

I grinned. "On a more serious note, do you have a second to talk?"

Layla squinted. "Yes. Aren't we doing that?"

"I mean in private."

Layla grabbed my hand. "Yeah, of course. Everything okay?"

"I'm not sure," I said. "I don't want to alarm anyone."

Layla followed me into the spire where we stayed and into our quarters. Agnus was curled up on the floor, snoring. I'd say "sawing logs," but since we lived in what was basically a giant log, I figured that would make for a poor and destructive choice of words.

"Are you aware of any other elves other than the drow who lived on Earth after your people fled to New Albion?"

Layla scratched her head. "Not really."

"No, or not really?"

"No," Layla said. "It's possible that there were some other than the drow who stayed on Earth, I suppose. Perhaps they went elsewhere to flee persecution."

I nodded. "I met one in the woods."

"Today?"

"Yes. He didn't speak a lick of English. Clarence said he spoke a dialect of Cree, an indigenous language around here. He also said he wasn't the first he'd met. Said that they tend to disappear for years at a time and then, once one shows up, they appear in droves."

"You're sure he was an elf?" Layla asked.

I sighed. "Well, he had the ears, and he could wield magic."

"What kind of magic?"

I shook my head. "I don't know. But he commanded the trees. They wrapped me in their roots, and I couldn't unleash any of my power. It was like whatever he did silenced my abilities."

Layla furrowed her brow. "How strange. I've never encountered anything like that."

"It was almost like back at the North Pole when we were in the spire and my abilities were squelched by Aelfrich's dampeners."

Layla shook her head. "But this elf, if that's what he was, used magic to do it, right?"

"Yeah. He had a green glow in his hands. A lot like earth magic."

"The dampeners kill every magic all around," Layla said. "It's a technology created from the elements native to New Albion. Call it anti-magic. It's not common. Very difficult to mine. If anything, what you're describing is the opposite of that. It's not so much anti-magic as a kind of magic that cancels out whatever you can do with elemental power."

"I agree," I said. "I had that same thought. It was almost like when I was trying to invoke the elements, the elf canceled it out. Like a veto, or as if his command over the elements came with a higher authority."

"And Clarence said more of them will likely come?"

"That's what he said. More than that, I'm pretty sure he was telling me to leave. To go away."

"To leave the forest entirely?"

I bit my lip. "I'm not sure. Clarence couldn't tell, either. The elf wasn't specific. But he clearly said to go away."

Layla shook her head. "But if we left, where would we go?"

I sighed. "I don't know. I don't think we should leave. If these elves truly do wield a superior kind of power, they could be great allies."

"I can't disagree with that. But if they don't want us around, how could we convince them to join us?"

I scratched the back of my head. "I don't know. If they've remained in obscurity for centuries, they clearly don't have much interest in human affairs. Why would they care if some elf king they'd never heard of was trying to take over human governments?"

"I don't know. But if Clarence can communicate with them, or at least translate for us, we should try and talk to them. At the very least, perhaps we could learn a few tricks from them that might come in handy to stop my father."

I nodded. "I agree. Clarence might also come in handy trying to find them. Though, if what he said is true, I imagine they'll find us sooner rather than later. If they haven't already."

I felt a paw on my leg. I ignored it for a second. Big mistake. The claws came out next.

"Damnit, Agnus! That hurts!"

"I have to poop!"

I shrugged. "Then poop."

"I'm not using that box. It hasn't been cleaned in a week."

I sighed. Acquiring litter was a chore, as difficult as it was to get *any* supplies. It meant traveling to a city, buying what we needed while remaining unrecognized, and using a giant fairy portal to send it back. The last trip, we'd forgotten fresh litter. I was trying to skimp on what we had to stretch it out until we made the next supply run.

"Just use it for now. We'll make another trip in a day or two."

Agnus hissed. "I'm not pooping on my poop! That's disgusting. Every time I go to bury it, I have to dig my paws into nastiness and usually just churn up more turds."

I sighed. Some of this was my fault. Back when we still lived in an apartment and had most of the luxuries of the technological era, Agnus had one of those electric self-cleaning litter boxes. I'd spoiled him. Now the chickens...or the turds...were coming home to roost. "You could just go outside."

Agnus looked up at me with a blank stare. "Do I look like an animal to you?"

I snorted. "Well, yeah. You do."

"I'm a semi-divine creature. The Egyptians had their shit straight. They worshiped us as gods! Tell me, Caspar, as a religious man, would you ever tell your God to go take a poo *outside*?"

I shook my head. "I don't think God poops, Agnus."

"Of course he does!" Agnus insisted. "After Jesus rose from the dead, he ate fish, right?"

I nodded. "Yes. After he appeared to men on the road to Emmaus."

"You've read the book, Caspar. Everyone eats; therefore, everyone poops."

"Jesus didn't ascend into Heaven until forty days after the resurrection," I said. "I'm sure he expelled his bowels before that."

"You don't know!" Agnus said. "Either way, whether it was in Heaven or on Earth, he pooped. You believe that Jesus is divine, right?"

I sighed. "Yes. I do."

"Then you believe that God, and other gods, like me, must poop. We deserve to defecate with sanctity and reverence!"

I sighed. "I told you, Agnus. We'll get you more litter next trip."

"If we were short on toilet paper, would you wait until tomorrow or the next day to go get more?" Agnus demanded.

I nodded. "Yes. I would. Given our situation, I'm not going to risk my life and everyone else I'm responsible for toilet paper."

"What's the difference if you go now or go tomorrow? Look, Caspar. My little bitty butthole is pulsing right now. Look at it."

"I don't need to look at your butthole, Agnus. I can take your word for it."

"I said *look*!" Agnus said, turning around and sticking his tail end in the air.

I winced when I saw it. "Holy crap, Agnus. You really have to go!"

"Holy crap is right," Agnus said. "My crap is always holy, and I need to dispose of it appropriately!"

I sighed. A mysterious elf was lurking in the forest. I needed to learn more about what they could do. I had bigger issues to address. And now I had to make an early supply run to get my cat fresh litter? Who ever said that being the chosen one was supposed to be a dignified life?

"All right," I said. "We need time to get a list of needs together. If I'm making a trip, I'm getting everything at once."

Agnus turned back to me and nodded. "Just make it snappy, Caspar. Or else."

"Or else what?" I asked. "Your butt will explode?"

"And in this way, I shall smite you," Agnus said.

CHAPTER THREE

Making runs to the city was always an ordeal. Inevitably there'd be someone, no matter how diligent I was about asking in advance, who would be upset that I made the trip and they didn't get their items on the list.

Still, certain items were essential. I didn't need to ask. On my last run into town, I had bought so much Axe body spray that the cashier asked me if I was fixing to party like it was 1999. I tried to explain it wasn't for me. She didn't believe me. It wasn't like I could tell her that I lived with a horde of giants who smelled like feet.

At least now, they smelled like feet *and* a subtle, sweet fragrance with a hint of spice. That's how the scent was described on the can, minus the feet part. Of course, when a giant uses half a can at once, there's nothing subtle about it. The "hint" of spice was like being smacked in the face with bricks if bricks were made of potpourri.

Of course, that was just one item on the list. Lots of food, mostly nonperishable stuff. I usually brought back some rotisserie chickens and frozen pizzas. They'd all get eaten right away. But it was nice to have meals that didn't come in cans periodically. Without an oven? I fire roasted those babies. Agnus wouldn't eat them. He said eating pizza cooked using magic that came from my body was like eating food cooked over a lit fart. His loss.

I bought as much in bulk as I could. I teleported whole pallets back to the forest. The challenge was to get the pallets somewhere no one would see me. It was tempting to just shoplift it all. How easy would that be with my abilities? But I had plenty of money, thanks to the seemingly unending bank account in Aerin's name that I could access. Also, I still had standards. I maybe wasn't a minister anymore, but I hadn't given in to the dark side of the force, either.

This time I bought a whole pallet of scoopable cat litter, enough to last a lot longer than we needed. Especially since we only had one cat. But I didn't want to have the same problem ever again. Hell, with this much litter, Agnus could have a fresh box every day, and we'd probably make it months.

Layla was with me. She usually came along to watch people while I took care of business. If anyone recognized us we'd hightail it out of there via fairy portal and try our chances at another place.

"This mustache tickles," I said, tugging at the fake Tom Selleck 'stache we'd glued to my upper lip.

" You think it tickles?" Layla asked. "You should try kissing yourself."

I cocked my head. "How would I go about doing that?"

Layla smiled. "Not impossible. I mean, if you just kiss in mid-air and the only thing your lips are touching are themselves, isn't that like kissing yourself?"

I scratched my head. "No. That's just kissing air. But say we discovered a parallel dimension, and I met myself for the first time. Since I'm a narcissist, I would totally fall in love with my other self. Then, theoretically, I could kiss myself."

Layla chuckled. "First, you're not a narcissist. But maybe the other dimension's version of you is. In that case, if the other you tried to kiss you, you could sue yourself for sexual harassment."

"I suppose, either way, if you sue yourself, you always win."

"Presuming trans-dimensional currencies are exchangeable, of course," Layla said.

"I wonder if the other dimensions version of me would also have this stupid mustache on?"

Layla smiled. "You know why we have to do it. After all those videos we've released, too many people would recognize you otherwise."

"I'm just not sure a mustache alone is enough."

Layla shrugged. "If Clark Kent can deceive everyone into thinking he's not Superman by wearing glasses, surely a mustache will hide your true superhero identity."

"Then why don't you wear one if they're so effective?"

Layla laughed. "The whole idea is to avoid people's attention. I think a woman with a mustache would do the opposite of what we're trying to do."

I sighed. "Yeah, yeah. Fair point."

"What the hell?" Layla said.

I turned to see Layla's eye had caught one of the televisions on display. Her father was on the screen. The caption at the bottom of the screen read: King Brightborn addresses the United Nations.

I reached over and pressed the volume button on the screen. The store had them all turned down for obvious reasons.

"The problems that plague this world cannot be solved without true unity. We will never stop rising global temperatures if every nation acts independently. When only one nation refuses to participate in agreements to reduce emissions, it places those who do agree to make drastic changes at a competitive disadvantage. The world's governments, the nationalism that separates peoples, is a broken system ill-equipped to address the global challenges of our day.

"There are voices out there who would have you doubt my goodwill for this planet. People who tell lies about what I did on my former world. The truth is, war did destroy my home. I fought, and my people fought, for centuries against hordes of orcs who sought to prevent us from coming to your world, who hoped we might never arrive to redeem your planet. Their intentions were clear. To bide their time until you destroyed or weakened yourselves so you might be more easily conquered. For this reason, they and their allies—including, much to my regret, my own daughter—continue to oppose my efforts and attack my credibility.

"They follow a false Messiah, a discredited minister. He performs wonders meant to deceive you. But you will know him by his fruits. He has sown division. His actions have turned friends and family against one another. The protests of those who have chosen to believe his lies have led to destruction and needless rioting and violence.

"Consider what fruit has resulted from my arrival in this world. The President of the United States is working with the Presidents of Russia and China. The Arab world has come to the table with Israel to pursue a common hope. To save this world. The one known as Caspar Cruciger leads a movement of division and destruction. What I promise is a future unified in healing and hope."

"What bullshit," Layla said, shaking her head.

"But people are eating it up," I said.

Layla cocked her head. "We need to be careful about how we're mixing our metaphors."

I shrugged. "I don't know. People are eating his bullshit. He's literally spooning it into their mouths."

Layla raised one eyebrow. "Literally?"

I snorted. "By literally, I mean metaphorically."

"Is that like saying by bad I mean good?"

I shrugged. "Michael Jackson pulled it off."

Layla sighed. "I swear. My dad could *literally* serve bull shit on a plate and convince people it's caviar."

I nodded. "That's what makes this so dangerous. As passionate as the people are who follow our videos and protest the government's actions, the other side is just as convinced that they're right, that your father is here to save the world."

"But once he shows his true colors and the folks who defend and embrace him realize the truth, it will be too late," Layla said.

I knew she was right. "Right now, he has the bully pulpit. Our videos stream online. It's great. But he's on the major news networks. It's much easier to discount what people find on the Internet as a conspiracy theory."

"The problem is if we find his legion and attack, it will only add more credibility to his false narrative."

I nodded. "But if we don't attack soon, or at least do *something*, he'll only get stronger and more untouchable. With the support he has now, even if we figure out how to portal to wherever he goes, he'll be surrounded by secret service protection."

"Along with his elite legionaries," Layla said. "But he's garnered the world's support by making false promises. Things he can only bring about through magic. What if he couldn't use magic anymore?"

I cocked my head. "You're suggesting we learn more about the mysterious Cree elves?"

Layla nodded. "It might be our best chance."

"Right now, your father looks like a savior. But the world has seen politicians before who can't or won't keep their promises. If we can reduce him to another lying, power-hunger politician, we might have a chance."

Layla huffed. "It's ironic, you know? The prophecy said that the chosen one would unite all peoples. He's trying to make you look divisive. As if he's the real unifier."

I nodded. "But he unites only to consolidate his power. It's interesting. Even Jesus, who urged the people to be one, even as he and his Father were one, also told them that he came not to bring peace but a sword. To turn a man against his father, a daughter against her mother, and the like."

"How do you reconcile those values?" Layla asked.

I sighed. "I don't know. But I think we have everything we need here. I'm going to send you back with all the crap we bought. I'll be there shortly. I'd like to pay an old friend a visit."

Layla cocked her head. "Who are you going to see? Your AA sponsor?"

I shook my head. "I don't want to put him in danger. I don't have a place I could teleport where I'd be sure to meet him in private. I'm going to go see Philip."

"The bishop who took your place as the minister at the Church of the Holy Cross?"

I nodded. "He's supported me despite everything, and he always has good advice. I won't be long."

Layla kissed me on the cheek. "All right, let's get this stuff back to the forest. Be careful, Caspar."

CHAPTER FOUR

It wasn't my intention to leave Layla with the responsibility of changing Agnus' litter box while I went to seek Philip's counsel. Though, you know, if it happened to work out that way, I wasn't going to complain.

Cat urine is probably one of the most detestable substances on Earth. It might not be quite as vile as radioactive waste, but it's certainly close. The last time Agnus pissed in my laundry basket—a display of vindictiveness for feeding him Science Diet rather than tuna—I had to wash those clothes three times on hot to get out the smell. Based on the current condition of Agnus' box, well, if someone *else* had to deal with it, yes, even someone I love, I wasn't going to complain.

Love is funny that way. Layla and I would probably give our lives for each other. Genuine love is selfless like that. But selflessness reaches its limit when it comes to common chores like cleaning the cat box.

After sending Layla and several pallets full of supplies back to our forest hideout, I created a fairy portal, visualized the chancel in the sanctuary at Holy Cross, and teleported myself into my old church.

"Well, hello, Pastor," a voice said from behind where I appeared.

I turned toward the altar, where one of the members, Doris, was setting up for the Lord's Supper. It must've been a Saturday. Having been in the forest for so long, I'd lost track of the days of the week.

I smiled at her. "Doris! I'm sorry if I startled you."

Doris laughed. "You saved my life before, Pastor. I've been following your recent activities. Jesus healed the sick. He once appeared behind locked doors."

I snorted. "I'm no Jesus, Doris."

Doris laughed. "Oh, I know that. But based on the New Testament, he had a track record of choosing unlikely figures to further his purposes, does he not?"

I nodded. "He certainly did. Common fishermen. Even a tax collector."

"And a pastor without a place to preach," Doris said. "He still works in mysterious ways."

I smiled. "How have you been?"

Doris grinned back at me. She was a frail woman. She had all the aches and pains that normally accompanied the elderly. But she always had a peace about her, a contentment, a faith that I always envied. "How can I complain?"

"Is Philip around?" I asked. "I'm looking for a little advice."

Doris shook her head. "He's making his rounds at the nursing homes. I believe he'll be going straight home after that."

I nodded. "Darn. Well, I suppose timing is everything."

"Tell me, Pastor. What is on your mind?" Doris asked, stepping down from the altar and taking a seat in the front row of pews.

I took a deep breath and exhaled as I sat beside her. "I feel like I've been called to unify people. But all I'm doing, it seems, is ripping the world apart. I was just telling Layla..."

"She's your new wife?" Doris asked.

I nodded. "She is."

"She's quite beautiful."

I tucked my chin and smiled wide. "Yes, she is incredible."

"Sometimes things must end that other things can begin," Doris said.

"Like my ministry here?"

Doris nodded. "You have another calling, but your service here, the things you preached and taught, continue to live on."

"The thing is, I know that Jesus also told his people to be one. But in another breath, he said he came not to bring peace but a sword. I'm struggling to reconcile those two values."

"What do you think makes for real unity?" Doris asked.

I shrugged. "I don't know. A common hope, perhaps? A shared purpose?"

"I agree," Doris said. "A lot of people can come together, hold hands, and sing Kumbaya. But unity is only as strong as whatever binds people together."

I stared ahead at the altar where Doris had set up the Lord's Supper. "You know, the early Christians called the Lord's Supper *koinonia*. It's the Greek word that we translate as communion."

"But when the Corinthians came together, even around the Lord's table, they were not unified in heart. There were divisions among them. Thus, Paul chastised them. He told them it was no longer the Lord's Supper that they ate."

I nodded. "That's true. The meal lost its meaning because their unity was a sham."

"The crowd that shouted 'crucify him' on Good Friday was unified, too."

I scratched my head. "I suppose they were."

"I don't think those crowds are any more evil or sinful than the rest of us," Doris said. "They were deceived by the lies their chief priests told them. They were misguided. They wanted a savior, but only one who saved them on their terms."

I shook my head. "I'm not the savior. I'm not the Christ."

"Neither is that elven king," Doris said.

I sighed. "Still, it seems that he's creating more unity in the world than I am. He wasn't wrong. I don't know if you heard his speech earlier."

Doris shook her head. "I didn't. I was here, getting the church ready for tomorrow's services."

"He wasn't wrong. He has brought people together. He's brought world leaders together who are adversaries at heart."

"When the truth is revealed, their unity will fail," Doris said. "They are not unified in heart. They are only unified by fear and desperation."

"I agree," I said. "But am I offering them anything more than that?"

Doris grabbed my hand. "So far, you aren't."

I bit my lip. "What do you mean?"

"I've seen the videos you've put out. You've told everyone about the horrors Brightborn was responsible for in his world. The atrocities he committed. The people who are following you, you must ask, are they following you out of fear or faith?"

I sighed. "I don't know. I really don't."

"Do you know what I always liked best about your sermons?"

I snickered. "My bad jokes?"

Doris chuckled. "Well, they certainly are that. But what I liked the most about your sermons, at least those you preached the last few years, was that you didn't rely on fear of judgment, Hell, and all that to try and motivate people to change their lives. You always gave us a positive reason to follow the Lord. Don't get me wrong. Fear can be a motivating force to a point, but all it does is move people to avoid whatever it is they're afraid of."

I smiled. "I suppose I just always wanted to encourage people to follow our faith out of love of God because it's an adventure, a privilege even, to get to know God like that. Not just because God's way is the default alternative to judgment, Hell, and damnation."

Doris squeezed my hand. "Then why is it that every time you and your friends put out another video, the whole point is how dangerous the elf king is? I get it. He's a monster. But at least he's winning people over with a vision for the future. All you're offering is fear about what future he might bring. You're offering a chance to resist and return to the status quo."

"Not totally. I mean, I showed people how I could grow trees, whole forests."

"An intriguing message, to be sure. But again, you followed that up with more fear-mongering. That's not you, Pastor. I know it isn't. So why is it that's what you're sharing with everyone?"

I sighed. "That's a good question. Maybe it's because when I'm talking about my faith, I have intimate experience with how God can change my life. My sobriety is nothing short of a miracle if you ask me. I've learned that walking in faith is a better way to live. I trust God to lead the way. Maybe this is different because all I'm asking people to do now is follow little old me."

Doris smiled. "If you want people to follow you, you need to believe you're worth following."

I nodded. "I suppose I need to give them a reason to want to follow me. Not just a reason to oppose Brightborn. But that's the problem, isn't it? Who am I, really? Why would anyone want to follow me?"

Doris scratched the back of her hand. "Why would anyone want to follow a carpenter's son from Galilee? Why would anyone want to follow a rag-tag group of disciples who claimed their crucified rabbi had risen from the dead?"

I considered my answer. "They had a message. Something bigger than themselves that they could hold out for hope. Jesus preached the coming of the Kingdom of God. The disciples, on account of Jesus, preached the forgiveness of sins and eternal life."

A glow spread across Doris' face. Nothing magical. More like the kind of pride that beams from a parent's face when they see their child take their first steps, do something selfless, or graduate from school. Funny, because all these years, I'd been her pastor. But the hard truth is that I'd learned more about faith from little old ladies like Doris than all the professors at the Seminary. When I came to Holy Cross, I had arrived with my education, imagining that it qualified me to lead them spiritually. In truth, I think I was sent to them to grow a heart of faith to match my mind.

I had to go through things—alcoholism, my divorce, and all I'd endured since the elven prophecy became a part of my life, including losing my ministry, to get to the place I was at now. Yes, I was still as rough around the edges as ever. I didn't have a clean faith. It was a little messy. I was more than a little messy. But it was *real.* Might it be that everything I'd gone through was put before me because I couldn't get to the destination without taking the journey? Perhaps my path wasn't ever meant to be a smooth highway. It was rocky. But it was the path I had to take.

I didn't see it at the time. However, now that I was on the other side of those trials and tribulations, I was grateful for them.

I had to have faith that the trials I was enduring now could be faced with gratitude, too. I didn't see the big picture yet. But that's what faith is about. The question was, how would I package that in a way that would persuade people to follow a path, not just because it was not Brightborn's way, but because the vision I have is better, more desirable, more hopeful?

I needed to give people a reason to follow us, not just to resist Brightborn but to rally around a cause that would persist even when we defeated the elven king.

The problem? I didn't have a clue what that vision was. Without a clear vision, I was like a blind man leading a movement of the blind. It was no wonder many people, including government leaders, followed Brightborn. His vision might have been a lie, but he *had* a vision. It's easier to follow an illusion than it is to step into darkness and trust that the vision will materialize along the way.

CHAPTER FIVE

I returned to the forest without any problems. It was always a risk going to the city. Chances were high that someone had spotted us even with my Tom Selleck lip caterpillar. It wasn't altogether a bad thing if someone did report us to the authorities. If we were seen in St. Louis, the government would focus its efforts to find us in the area. Sure, they knew I could travel vast distances. At least, Brightborn knew I could. But so long as we get in and out of the city without incident, even if we were recognized, it meant that most efforts to find us would be focused in and around the city.

Still, I didn't have any reason to believe that was the case. No one had said anything to us. Eventually, I figured, they'd find us. Until then, we had a relatively safe base of operations.

I made my way to our quarters in our spire. Layla wasn't there. She was probably busy distributing supplies. Agnus greeted me with a head-butt and a purr.

I reached down and scratched him behind the ears. "I take it Layla already changed your box?"

"I have something to show you," Agnus said.

I continued petting Agnus, running my hand down his back.

His hindquarters perked up as I reached his tail. "What is it, buddy?"

"Follow me."

I never knew what kind of surprises Agnus had tucked up his metaphorical sleeves. However, I could be reasonably sure that it would be unexpected.

Agnus led me to his litter box. It was mostly clean, except for one massive turd. The thing was probably close to eight inches long, a good half-inch in diameter. "Good Lord, Agnus. Did you do that, or did Brag'mok use your box?"

Agnus looked up at me. "That was all me."

"Damn!"

"Impressed?"

I snickered. "Strangely, I have to admit I am."

"I did *that* all by myself!" Agnus exclaimed with pride in his voice.

I chuckled. "You sure did."

"Now, scoop it."

I snorted as I grabbed a plastic bag and a scooper. "I might need a shovel."

"I feel like an all-new man!"

"Cat, you mean?" I asked, depositing the turd into the bag and tying it shut.

Agnus shook his head. "I'd call that a man-sized dookie."

The bag was heavier than I expected. "I could give this to Jag. He could do some curls with this shit."

"Glad to be of ass-istance," Agnus shot back.

I laughed. "See, I'm not the only one with bad puns."

"Hard to beat a good poo-pun," Agnus said, nuzzling my leg again.

"Indeed," I said, still smiling. "I better go help Layla with the distribution…and get rid of this log."

"Why don't you frame it?"

"I'm not framing your poop, Agnus."

"Come on! It was a real accomplishment."

"I'm not disputing that," I said as I stepped out of the room. "But dude, saving turds is a little strange. Besides, it smells."

"Fine," Agnus said. "But take a picture for my posterior's sake."

I chuckled. "Don't you mean for posterity's sake?"

"I mean what I said," Agnus said.

I smiled. "I'll make sure we snap a photo before I toss it into the compost."

"You didn't forget my tuna, did you?"

"We have plenty of tuna. No worries, Agnus. I wasn't about to risk incurring your wrath."

"Good boy," Agnus said. He turned and sauntered back into our quarters.

I shook my head as I walked down the ramp that spiraled around the interior edge of the spire. The ramp inclined steadily around the spire, leading to various openings where folks lived. Jag lived next to us about a quarter turn down the ramp. I peeked inside and found Jag doing pushups.

"Hey, man," I said. "Have you got your phone? I need you to take a picture of this."

"Of what?" Jag asked, sweat beading on his brow.

I tossed the bag to him. It landed where his nose nearly tapped the ground with every pushup.

Jag recoiled back on all fours before leaping to his feet. "What the hell is that?"

"Agnus made it. He's proud of it. I promised him we'd take a picture."

Jag shook his head. "That damn cat."

I smiled. "He's a handful, that's for sure."

"Did you get my whey?" Jag asked.

I nodded. "I did."

"Isolate, not concentrate, right?"

"Yes, I got the whey isolate you requested," I said. "Layla's distributing supplies now if you'd like to join me."

Jag nodded, then grabbed his phone off the wooden platform that he used as a bed and opened the bag before taking a quick photo.

He tossed the bag at me. I grabbed it out of mid-air, thankful that the shit inside didn't go flying out of it in flight. The last thing I needed was for that...*thing* to get free. I half suspected it would come to life, like Mister Hankey the Christmas Poo, and attack us.

Jag followed me down the ramp the rest of the way and outside. I deposited Agnus' latest contribution to the community compost pile and wadded up the bag to add to the trash pile. What we could burn, we did. What we couldn't, we buried. Not the most eco-friendly effort, but given our situation in the middle of nowhere, it was the best we could do.

Layla was in a small clearing just east of the spires. Everyone knew to stay clear of the area when we were doing a supply run. It prevented any accidents when transporting the pallets and piles of wares via a fairy portal. If we dropped the stuff into a person, it would be problematic. Pretty much the whole community was huddled around as Layla distributed the items to their respective owners. Most of it was community supply. We had a hut made with the same technology and magic we'd used to construct the spires. It resembled a small silo. After the goods meant for specific people were distributed, we'd move the rest into storage so we could manage consumption and minimize the trips we'd have to make for more supplies.

Jag approached Layla, and she handed him a five-pound plastic container of whey isolate protein. He smiled like a kid on Christmas Day as he took it with both hands and examined the label. With a subtle nod, he confirmed that we'd picked up the right stuff. I'd always thought that whey was whey. Apparently, I was wrong. He had to have the right stuff. Without it, well, we'd mess with his gains. Heaven forbid he lose a quarter-inch from the oversized arms he affectionately referred to as cannon one and cannon two.

I reached into the pile of supplies we'd bought so I could help. "Who ordered baby powder?" I asked.

"That's mine," Brag'mok said, approaching me and extending his hand.

I gave him the bottle. "Why do you need baby powder?"

"Helps with chafing," Brag'mok said. "Thanks for that, by the way."

I nodded. I grabbed more items, distributing them each to their intended recipient. It was a fairly efficient process, all things considered. It didn't usually take long. This time was no exception, especially since Layla had a head start. We disbursed the remaining special orders in a matter of about ten minutes. What was left was mostly food and Axe body spray.

"How'd it go with Philip?" Layla asked as she handed a can of hairspray to one of the drow warriors.

"He wasn't there," I said. "Had a good talk with Doris, though."

Layla smiled. "How's she doing?"

"Well," I said. "She had some insights I think will help if I can figure out how to apply them."

"What kind of insights?" Layla asked.

I shrugged. "Just some spiritual wisdom. She thinks we've been too negative with our messaging. We need a positive message. People need a reason to follow us, something that will make them want to embrace our movement, not just protest Brightborn."

Layla nodded. "Sounds like good advice. The prophecy was never about thwarting Brightborn, you know. It was always about uniting the peoples."

I nodded. "Yeah, we just need to come up with something compelling."

Layla grinned. "I'm sure you'll find some inspiration sooner or later."

"Hopefully sooner rather than later," I said. "After Brightborn's speech, we need to do something. The longer this stretches out, the more the world embraces his leadership."

"I think we need to send the fairies out again," Layla said. "His legions have to be up to something."

"I agree. I'm sure whatever it is they're planning isn't good."

"How are you going to give the people a more positive message if you're focused on fighting the legion?" Layla asked.

I sighed. "I don't know. But we have to stay the course. Hopefully, I can come up with a stronger message and get a clearer vision for the future when we know what your father is up to."

Layla smiled. "Well, we should get the rest of these supplies into storage."

"Where's Clarence?" I asked. "Surprised he isn't here at your side."

Layla shook her head. "He's been a bit aloof ever since you encountered that elf in the woods. I think it rattled him."

I nodded. "When the elf looked at Clarence, it was like he was under a spell. He was charging the elf then, all at once, he cowered. Strangest thing."

"We should probably talk to him about it. He's out looking for food right now."

"Looking for food? Is that what he told you?"

"Yeah. Is that strange?"

"Well, he just ate when we were out on patrol. But he does eat a lot."

Layla nodded. "A grizzly can eat up to ninety pounds a day. Since we interrupted his hibernation, it makes sense."

"You're right," I said. "Still, something in my gut tells me that it has something to do with these mysterious elves."

"You think he'd seek them out on his own?" Layla asked.

"I don't know," I said, casting air magic to transport the extra supplies via a controlled whirlwind into the silo. "I think we should probably check on him. Just to be sure."

Layla nodded. "I'll get my bow. We should go into the woods armed. Just in case."

We jogged back to our quarters. Agnus was tongue-bathing himself in the corner, seemingly oblivious to our entrance. Layla grabbed her bow and the quiver of celestially charged arrows. She'd acquired that ability from the two rings the drow had protected for years. They had been meant for me. Long story, but I'd had to give them to her after she'd been attacked by a dagger infused with the same kind of magic. It had been the only way to save her. Now, her arrows were lethal. If the trauma of the arrow strike didn't kill someone, the magic within them would kill them later.

If we did happen to run into another one of those elves in the woods, I was glad she had them. I certainly didn't want to get into a battle with the indigenous elves. However, since they could suppress my magic, it was a good idea to have a backup plan in case they weren't as friendly as we hoped. I grabbed my two blades. Again, if push came to shove, I might need Aerin's abilities to fight. Her insights might be valuable as we tried to sort out who these strange visitors were. Not to mention, if I had Aerin's blade on my person, she'd be aware of what happened. Aside from Layla, she was the only one who knew about the elves.

CHAPTER SIX

I decided not to fly this time. It was better for Layla and me to stay together. I could fly with her on my back, but it took a lot more energy. Sure, I could channel a ton of magic. So far as I knew, the quantities were virtually unlimited, but channeling magic also took a toll on my body. I'd pass out from exhaustion, so I had to exercise moderation. Ironic since as a recovering alcoholic, moderation has *never* been my forte. Not with booze. Not with my spending habits. Now, not with magic.

With a tendency to overexert myself, magically speaking, I had to restrict myself. When magic wasn't necessary, it was best to exercise an alternative. In this case, it meant walking with Layla rather than flying. I flew when patrolling before, but then I didn't *expect* to run into anything supernatural. This time, there was a good chance I might.

I don't know what it is. There's something I find incredibly alluring about a woman with a weapon. I suppose I've always been attracted to women who look like they could kick your ass. Think Michelle Rodriguez from the *Fast and the Furious* movies. In our case, Layla *could* kick my ass. Every time we wrestled, she won. Of course, I wanted to get pinned. Though it's not the act of getting my ass kicked by a woman who excited me. It was the look, the air of confidence Layla exuded. The recognition that she was a force of nature not to be reckoned with. Intimidating, yes, but sexy as hell.

Layla had spent her whole life training as an elven princess warrior. I'd spent most of my life playing World of Warcraft. We both won a lot of battles. The difference was that she couldn't respawn if she died in one. For that reason, I followed her lead in situations that involved real-world battles. At the moment, of course, we weren't looking for a fight. However, until we knew the intentions of these indigenous elves, we had to be ready for the possibility.

The fallen pine needles on the path crunched beneath our feet as we made our way through the trees. It was early evening. Not quite dark yet, but it would be soon. I hoped we'd find Clarence before nightfall. If not, I could use low-level magic to illuminate our path, although we'd be more visible to the other elves if they were lurking.

I reached out with aether, hoping to connect to Clarence. Layla did the same. Chances were better, given their relationship, that she'd find him before I did.

"Any luck?" I asked.

Layla shook her head. "Not really. I thought I sensed him up ahead. If he was there, though, he didn't respond."

I sighed. "I'm telling you. That elf had some kind of power over him. If he's out there, and he's not responding, there's a good chance they are nearby as well."

Layla nodded as she pulled an arrow from her quiver and set it in place on her bow. "Hopefully, you're wrong. I suspect you aren't."

"Try not to shoot them if you can avoid it. If there is any chance of an alliance with these elves, I'd rather not spoil our chances with a preemptive attack."

Layla nodded. "Obviously. It's just good to be prepared."

I smiled. "I know. I was a boy scout. That was our motto."

We continued our way toward where Layla thought she sensed Clarence. I didn't have the same feeling for whatever reason. Not a total surprise. While I was more powerful overall, when it came to animals, her magic was more focused.

We climbed over a small hill and saw Clarence standing on his hind quarters at the edge of the creek below.

"Clarence?" Layla asked as we moved up beside him.

No response.

"You all right, buddy?" I asked.

Again, nothing. His eyes were fixed ahead as if he was in a trance. His shoulders rose and fell as his chest expanded and contracted. He was breathing normally. Otherwise, he was completely non-responsive. Almost as if he'd gone catatonic. Except his body remained erect.

I surveyed our surroundings. I didn't see anyone. Not at the moment, anyway. But that didn't mean no one was there. There were enough trees, boulders, and other forest debris that if someone was trying to hide from view, they'd have plenty of options for cover.

I glanced into the creek. It was flowing heavily following the latest rainstorm. In this condition, it could probably be classified as a small, shallow river. The current was moving quickly, rippling around the rocks that littered the bed of the creek.

I cocked my head, and I drew on the element of water. I felt a familiar sensation within the stream. I'd sensed it before, at the confluence of the Mississippi and Meramec rivers back in Missouri. I knew the ley lines ran near here. I'd traveled through them when I came here the first time. It made sense. But what I detected wasn't *just* a ley line. It felt like the portal that used to connect Earth to New Albion.

"I think I know what's happening," I said.

"What is it?" Layla asked.

"There's a gateway here. Do you think it leads to New Albion? If it does, that would explain the origin of these elves."

Layla scratched her head. "I've never met any other elves on New Albion who resembled those you described. Then again, we only inhabited a small part of that planet. There were parts beyond the lands we'd imbued with earthen magic that were uninhabitable. It's possible, I suppose, that there were other elves on the planet. In places we'd never explored. A civilization that was, perhaps, parallel to our own."

"That would track," I said. "Clarence said these elves appear here at certain times and then disappear completely."

Layla shrugged. "We could go into the portal and find out."

I shook my head. "If all those elves have the power that the other one did, it would be too risky. There's no telling what we'd find ourselves in the middle of when we emerged on the other side."

Layla nodded. "You're right. But at least now we know where they're coming from. If more are coming, this is where we can meet them."

I glanced at Clarence. "I wish I knew what was going on with him."

"It's almost like he's been hypnotized," Layla said.

I sighed. "He must've known something was up. I'm not sure he left our camp to go hunting. He was looking for something."

"I agree." Layla ran her hand along the grizzly's back. "Whatever it was, though, he didn't tell me. Why wouldn't he say something about it?"

I shook my head. "I don't know. If we can get him out of this trance, maybe we can ask him."

"I'm at a loss," Layla said, still running her fingers through Clarence's fur. "Maybe Aerin has an idea what happened to him."

I shrugged. "I can ask."

I placed my hand on the hilt of Aerin's blade. "Hey, Aerin. Any idea what's going on with Clarence?"

It's certainly interesting. We never wielded magic like that, as you know. But my father might be able to help.

I nodded. "Thanks, Aerin."

"What did she say?" Layla asked.

"She thinks Elrand might know more. We probably should bring him in on this issue, anyway. If anyone knows more about magic, how it works on Earth, and whether there might be other elves who've been on Earth intermittently over the years, it's him."

CHAPTER SEVEN

Elrand stayed mostly to himself. He'd lived alone for several years. He was an outcast, exiled from the rest of the drow for refusing to submit to their laws that prohibited the use of magic beyond enchantments.

The laws were meant to protect the drow from fairy interference. Since fairies could detect magic, and the drow revered their purpose to await the arrival of the chosen one, the rule had allowed them to avoid any conflicts with the fairies or anyone else that might thwart what they believed was their holy purpose.

Elrand disregarded all that. Aerin had been given no choice but to exile her father as a result. As luck would have it, he'd left the home of the drow in India and come to Missouri. Why Missouri? To get closer to the ley lines, the portal between worlds, where he could practice his magic in obscurity. Mostly, he exercised his skills within a stone circle. The stones helped shelter his magic from detection by the fairies. They also allowed him to access elemental powers beyond those he innately possessed. He'd already been a great help. It was Elrand who'd helped us evoke the Furies and, ultimately, overthrow the

Unseelie fairies who were in league with Brightborn. His efforts had helped us to bring the Seelie fairies from New Albion. As a result, the Furies had placed the Seelie court in charge of Earth and imprisoned the Unseelie in the fairy realm.

It was no small contribution. When Brightborn had the Unseelie in his back pocket, he had been able to teleport anywhere. He had used them as a magical alert system. Now, with Trixie and her Seelie court, those abilities belonged to us.

Brightborn knew as much. If he used magic now, he either did so in a way similar to what Elrand had done with stone circles, or he did it to send us false messages with respect to his whereabouts.

We found Elrand meditating in his quarters. He lived in the same spire I did rather than with the other drow. He was the only male drow in our camp, and since the rest of the drow were matriarchal, he didn't want to live with his kinswomen. He didn't want to be treated like an inferior. He refused to be their bitch. Not to mention, despite his vast contributions to our cause, the other drow still viewed him as an outlaw, a renegade. They didn't talk to him much, if at all. He didn't talk to them, either. He'd lived in solitude for years. He was content to do so now, although he was aligned with our cause and stayed near and ready to help whenever we needed his insights and aid.

We brought Elrand with us to the creek, where Clarence still stood in his trance. The sun was barely hovering above the horizon, though we couldn't see it with the trees all around.

"You say when this elf cast these roots on you, you couldn't wield magic?" Elrand asked after listening to my explanation of recent events.

I nodded. "Right."

"And this elf has harnessed the mind of the grizzly?"

I waved my hand at Clarence. "Well, judge for yourself. He's staring at that river like a ten-year-old at a video game screen, and he's almost just as non-responsive."

Elrand nodded. "Step aside, son."

"Son?" I asked.

"You were married to my daughter, were you not?" Elrand said with a chuckle.

"And he was married to me!" Layla piped up.

Elrand smiled. "I'm aware of the peculiar situation you three were in together. But that does not change the fact that, in a way, Caspar is my son."

I nodded. "It doesn't matter. I'm honored by it."

Layla grunted. "All right, so what are you going to do?"

Elrand ignored Layla's question. Instead, he pointed his finger at the ground and traced a line all around us. He stepped to the bank of the creek, and with his finger, completed the circle.

"What are you doing?" I asked.

"I'm establishing a circle for our ritual," Elrand said. "We are without stones at the moment. So, this circle will have to do. The circle is a profound symbol for all rituals. It represents the cycle of life. The seasons which, in turn, reflect the pattern of our lives."

"Isn't life more like a hill?" Layla asked. "You peak at some point, then you go over the hill and follow the slope downward until you die."

"If a hill is perfectly round, I suppose you will have nearly outlined half the circle. But there's more to life than that. Every year we see the seasons. We see the birth of new life in the spring. We see the maturity of the world around us through summer. Then, when we reach about your age, Caspar, we turn to autumn."

I snorted. "I'm in my autumn years?"

Elrand grinned. "You're only entering that season. You have many years before you enter winter. That's when we go dormant. But a healthy tree's roots continue to grow even in the winter. When winter ends, when we pass through the season of death, the cycle ends and then repeats."

"Are you talking about reincarnation?" I asked.

Elrand nodded. "That is how I see it, but perhaps you might see it as resurrection. New life. All magic, even the elements, have their origin in the greater mystery of life itself."

"That's what you think these elves wield?" I asked. "Life magic?"

"The term is insufficient, I suppose. In the west, when we speak of life, we speak of it as if death were its antonym. In truth, death is but a part of life."

"So this magic you speak of is what, exactly?" I asked.

"Awen," Layla said.

Elrand nodded. "That is correct."

I bit my lip. "I thought that's what I drew on before I knew about the elements. It's just earth's magic, right?"

"Awen is much more than that, son. It is the creative principle of all things. It is the magic behind the mystery of all existence. It is the mystery, the inspiration, that flows from a poet's pen or through a musician's symphony."

"You can wield this stuff?" I asked.

Elrand smiled. "As can you. It flows in all of us, Caspar. Some of us are more in tune with the source than others. That is why these elves have a power that overtakes your own. The elementals are creatures, after all. It is Awen that gives *them* power."

"All right," I said. "So, what are we doing here?"

Elrand smiled. "Enough talking. You'll see soon enough."

Layla and I looked at each other and shrugged simultaneously. Elrand stepped into the middle of the imaginary circle he'd drawn with his finger before. He raised one hand over his head in the direction of the setting sun.

"May there be peace in the west," Elrand said, making a quarter turn clockwise, "and peace in the north. Let there be peace in the east and peace in the south."

Completing his turn around the circle, Elrand extended his hands into the air. "May there be peace in the whole world!"

When he spoke, the river in front of us started to swirl. The rapids were no longer moving downstream. Rather, the current was drawn into the heart of the circle, where a green glow emanated and expanded until the whole circle Elrand had cast became a swirling cone of energies all around us.

"What is this?" I asked.

"It is drawn from the source!" Elrand said.

"From the earth?" I asked.

Elrand shook his head. "From the source that precedes even Earth. From the cauldron of the goddess, where Awen was born."

I bit my lip. I wasn't one to judge another's beliefs, but I was a thorough monotheist. I didn't believe in goddesses. Still, I did believe that God was bigger than I could possibly imagine. As such, who was I to limit Him to any particular definition, myth, or identity? I had to try and keep an open mind. Ultimately, I couldn't deny that whatever Elrand was doing was working. The magic that swirled around us had the same flavor and same color as that which had coursed through the mysterious elf's hands.

Elrand laughed as the cone of magical energies spun faster around us. "It's beautiful!"

"You haven't done this before?" I asked.

Elrand shook his head. "Never! I only read about it. But this has proven my hypothesis. This portal, whether it leads to New Albion or somewhere else, I cannot say. But the power that flows through it is pure Awen."

As the energies spun faster, Clarence dropped onto all fours again and looked at me, then at Layla.

What are you doing here? Clarence asked.

"We were going to ask you the same thing!" Layla said. "You're awake!"

Of course I am. Was I asleep?

"The sun has set, Clarence."

But it was still mid-afternoon when I came out here? When... Wait...

"What happened, Clarence?" Layla asked.

There were elves.

"The indigenous elves?" I asked.

Clarence nodded. *They were there, yes. But there were others. Two others. They were lurking in the forest. I pursued them. Then I found one of the other elves. He touched, and that's the last thing I remember.*

"Greetings," a deep voice said behind me.

I turned. The elf I'd encountered before stood there.

Layla gripped her bow, but the elf wasn't threatening us. I raised my hand to steady my wife's trigger happiness. "You speak English?"

"I do not," the elf said. "But where we stand, it is not a language at all we speak. We commune in the mystery of Awen."

I grunted. "I'm sorry. Mingan, was it?"

The elf nodded. "Yes, and you are Caspar, are you not?"

I nodded. "I am. This is Layla and Elrand."

"It is an honor," Mingan said.

"The honor is truly mine," Elrand said.

"Who are you, exactly?" Layla asked. "Where did you come from, and why did you attack Caspar before?"

"Attack him?" Mingan chuckled. "It was he who attacked. I simply pacified his assault. Why have you not heeded my warning?"

"You told me to go away, right?" I asked

Mingan nodded. "There are those who would do you harm. I warned you that you might flee and evade their assault. They seek to do you violence, and these lands are sacred. Blood should never be spilled here."

"The other elves," I said. "Brightborn's elves. They are here?"

Mingan nodded. "They are."

"How do you know about this?" Layla asked. "I grew up on New Albion. I never met anyone like you there before."

"I am not from your world," Mingan said. "I was born in this one, long ago."

I snorted. "How long ago?"

"For me, but a lifetime. For you, it has been more than a thousand years since I was born."

"So you're saying you're old?" I asked.

Mingan cocked his head. "What is old? What is young? We are all but traversing the circle of time."

"Through the seasons of life," Elrand said.

Mingan nodded and smiled at Elrand kindly. "Quite so, friend."

"So, where did you come from, then?" Layla asked.

"For our people and your ancestors, we druids call the place Annwn. If you can call it a place."

Layla scratched her head. "I know of Annwn. It's where all life began."

"Like the Garden of Eden?" I asked.

"Some have called it such," Mingan said.

"So if you came from the ancients, you must know of Taliesin, the druid who preserved the elven prophecy."

"Yes, Caspar. He lives with us in Annwn, still."

"He's still alive?" Layla asked, raising her eyebrows.

Mingan laughed. "He is. But that does not mean he has never died."

"Winter has turned to Spring," Elrand said.

Mingan nodded. "It is as you say."

"And you leave this Annwn place and come here at times?" I asked.

"We come every Samhuinn," Mingan said. "That we might observe the festival of the fall, even as we come to do the same for the festivals of Yule, Imbolc, Ostra, Beltane, Litla, Lughnasadh, and Mabon."

"So you weren't from this part of the world originally," Layla said.

Mingan shook his head. "I have been born many times and in many places."

"But you spoke an indigenous language before. My bear, Clarence, he said it was a dialect of Cree."

Mingan nodded. "It is the language I learned to engage the peoples who once dwelled in these lands. But I know many languages."

"But not English?" I asked.

Mingan shook his head. "Not English."

"You said you came to warn us of an imminent attack," I said. "You told us to leave."

Mingan nodded. "Yes. As I said, these are sacred lands. Should blood be shed here in violence, the consequences would be profound."

"I don't understand," Layla said. "What consequences?"

"We continue to return here to celebrate each of the festivals I mentioned before," Mingan said. "This is not merely a religious observance. By doing so, we keep Earth's magic alive and well. But these sacred lands must remain in peace if the Earth, herself, will remain at peace."

I bit my lip. "So you wanted us to leave to protect the land from a catastrophe that would somehow unsettle the Earth?"

Mingan nodded. "Our time runs short, druid."

I cocked my head. "You called me a druid. Why?"

"What you wield, the power you hold, it is the power that only a druid can wield. What Taliesin intended for you, Naayak, is to make of the whole world what this land preserves."

"To bring peace to the whole Earth?" I asked, glancing at Elrand.

"It is the blessing over the earth that was spoken here that called me," Mingan said. "But time is short. Those who would pervert this place with bloodshed draw…"

Mingan gasped as an arrow struck him in the chest.

"No!" I screamed, running to Mingan. I caught him as he fell.

"It is done," Mingan said. "Do not waver from your purpose."

I pulled the arrow from Mingan's chest and pressed my hand to his wound. I visualized it closing and healing, but nothing happened. "Why can't I heal you!"

"It is my time," Mingan said. "The cycle must continue. Even as this land passes through the season of death, so you must bring back the time of Spring, the season of rebirth. But to do that…"

Mingan's voice faltered as he tried to speak. Two elves bounded into the magic that encircled us. As they did, the magic dissipated.

One of them lunged at Elrand with a spear. I grabbed Aerin's blade. With it, she guided my hand as I swiped the elf's spear just before it hit Elrand.

I grabbed my second blade. "You've got this, Aerin."

She did. With fury, I wielded both blades. Her blade blocked the elf's second attack. The second blade, the one not enchanted, sliced the elf's throat.

Layla and the second elf struggled with one another. She couldn't shoot him at close range.

"You must come with me," the elf said.

"Never!" Layla screamed, kicking the elf in the chest.

As she did, I found my opening. With Aerin's skill flowing through me, I charged the second elf and sliced my second blade across his back.

He buckled and fell, blood pouring from the wound. His body convulsed on the ground. I kicked him over. I screamed with fury as I jammed the sharp end of my second blade into his neck.

My heart thumped in my chest. The adrenaline coursing through my body was addictive. It wasn't Aerin somehow controlling me that did it. It was me. My stomach churned even as I felt a thrill come over me. I hated that I'd just killed someone. Two more elves, in fact. But as much as I despised it, a part of me felt…satisfaction.

"This cannot portent good things," Elrand said. "Blood has

now been shed here thrice. Whatever it was that Mingan feared has come to pass."

"It's too late to stop that now," Layla said. "If there were two legionaries here, there will be more. We must return to the camp and prepare ourselves for war."

CHAPTER EIGHT

It didn't take much convincing. All I'd had to do was tell Gronk to ready the giants for battle, and he'd had them mobilized in a matter of minutes.

"We have to protect this land," I said as Layla strapped on her cloak and black leather armor.

"I agree," Layla said. "If my father's legions find that portal, there's no telling what they might do."

I nodded. "It's more than that. We can't let them take this land. I don't know if it's too late for that. But Mingan made it clear that I needed to bring peace to the world, to make the whole world what these lands used to be. Somehow we'll have to access that portal to do it. There are other elves back in that place.—what was it again?"

"Annwn," Layla said.

I shook my head. "Hard to say. Ahh-nun. What is that? British?"

Layla giggled. "Welsh. It's a part of our legends. The ones we were taught as elves descended from the ancient druids."

"It's like the Christian Garden of Eden?" I asked.

"Sort of," Layla said. "That, or like Heaven. It's where the dead reside before they are reborn. It's sort of like a combination of both Eden and Heaven, I think. The origin, the source, of all. Also, the place where we rest when our spirits depart our bodies."

I nodded. "The Bible describes the new creation, the heaven-on-earth at the end of times, like a sort of Eden restored."

"That makes sense," Layla said. "In the stories we were taught, the ancient druids also believed that Annwn had a sacred tree."

"Like the Tree of Life in Genesis?" I asked.

Layla nodded. "We were taught that the tree had three branches. The tree of the spirit bull, the All-Father, and maker of all things. The branch of Taranis. Then, there was the branch of Hu-Esus, the perfect man who was said to one day emerge from Annwn and guide the rest of us in the idyllic path. Finally, the branch of Beli, a spirit of fire and aether, dwells in all of us. It is he who guides us to the great tree even as all three branches are united in a single trunk—both rooted in the earth and stretching toward the skies."

I bit my lip. "That sounds...familiar. We didn't ascribe so much to the Tree of Life in my religion. But that symbolism, there's a lot of overlap there with what I believe."

Layla nodded. "Perhaps our beliefs have a common source."

"We usually focus so much on what makes our beliefs different, as if we're trying to make a case that no matter how similar things are, they can't be compatible. Like how other religions have similar accounts to Noah's flood. Or, when it comes to the tree, how the Nords believed in Yggdrasil. Rather than try to find the golden thread that connects these mythologies, we were always taught to try and prove that ours was the truth, that the others were diabolical forgeries."

Layla nodded. "That's unfortunate. There's so much beauty in seeing the connection."

"Be that as it may," I said. "This is what we have to face now—this mysterious Edenic world. Somehow I'm supposed to bring a taste of it back to Earth. But how?"

Layla scratched her head. "I'm not sure. Somehow we need to get to Taliesin if he's there. He'll know what we need to do."

"Can't do that if the legions are fighting us here," I said.

"You heard what Mingan said. We can't allow more bloodshed here."

I sighed. "Then what do we do?"

"We must leave this place," Elrand said, stepping into our quarters.

"Leave?" I asked. "And let the elves take it over?"

"If you protect these lands, the elves will know that there is something here you're guarding."

"How do we know they don't know that already?" I said.

"If we leave, we'll figure that out pretty quickly, won't we? You can come back here at any time. If the elves leave when we leave, we'll know that they are here only for us. They don't know the truth about the magic that flows through these forests."

"But if you're wrong," Layla interjected, "we'll be handing my father access to Annwn."

Elrand shook his head. "I'm not wrong. If your father knew of this place, he would have come here long before you ever did."

"Where else would we go?" I asked.

"Somewhere you're sure they'll check," Elrand said. "The battle is coming one way or another. There isn't a place in this world where the world's governments cannot reach in hours."

"I hadn't thought about that. If the legion fights us here, and they call in human reinforcements, this whole land could be bombed, defiled even more. The gateway to Annwn might be destroyed."

Elrand nodded. "Which is why you must lure the elves away from here. Lead them to a place where you are comfortable, a land you know, where you'll have every possible advantage."

I looked at Layla. "Are you thinking what I'm thinking?"

Layla's eyes widened. "Caspar, you aren't considering returning to the junkyard ranch, are you?"

I nodded. "It's perfect. We know the place well. We're close to the ley lines where my magic is the strongest—"

"All of our magic is stronger there," Layla interjected. "It benefits the elven legion as well."

I shook my head. "Not as much as it does me. It's also far enough from the city that if we have to fight, we can reduce unnecessary civilian casualties."

"But it's close enough to the city, too. Remember how the people of St. Louis support you."

I nodded. "A lot of them do."

"Most of them, I'd say," Layla insisted.

I chuckled to myself. "The giants aren't going to like this. They've been itching for a battle for months. Now, we have them battle-ready, and we're about to pull the plug and tell them we're going to cut and run."

"It's not exactly like we're retreating," Layla said.

I sighed. "I know. But they won't see it that way."

"Of course they won't," Layla said. "They are prideful warriors. One thing about giants, they *never* retreat. It's a part of what makes them so difficult to face. It's also a weakness. A strategic retreat allows an army to regroup, re-strategize, and live to fight another day."

"A weakness your father was known to exploit, I suppose."

Layla nodded. "It's likely what led to their downfall on New Albion. Honestly, it's a wonder that the giants that are left survived at all."

"Perhaps you should talk to them," Elrand said, nodding at me.

I shrugged. "Couldn't hurt. Either way, I think you're right, Elrand. We shouldn't fight this battle here. If this land holds the secret for our ultimate victory, any more bloodshed here could be catastrophic."

"I'll come with you," Layla said.

I raised my eyebrow. "When have the giants ever respected what you had to say?"

Layla shrugged. "I get it. I'm an elf princess. But I know how they think. I might be able to help."

I sighed. "All right, well, here goes nothing."

CHAPTER NINE

The giants were armored—mostly with parts of old cars they'd refashioned into breastplates, greaves, shields, and the like back when we were at the junkyard ranch.

They stood at attention in perfect lines. It reminded me of my time in the high school marching band. At the time, I'd held a trumpet. These giants held large broadswords and axes, and they didn't have feather plumes connected to their hats or gaudy pants that were designed to provide a constant wedgie to the wearer.

Gronk and Brag'mok stood in front of the group. Targigoth, their high priest, stood just behind them.

"I need to talk to you," I said, approaching Brag'mok. "All of you."

"We're prepared for war!" Gronk said.

I nodded. "I can see that. But we can't fight here."

Gronk huffed. "We can score a quick victory. We know these forests. They don't."

I nodded. "We've acquired some new information about this place. These lands are sacred."

"Sacred?" Targigoth asked, approaching us. He was significantly smaller than Brag'mok and Gronk, but he still towered over me by about two feet.

"There's a gateway here to another world. To a place that an ancient elf we recently met in the woods calls Annwn."

Targigoth scratched his head. "Are you certain?"

"I am," I said with a nod.

"Then we must protect this place at all costs!" Brag'mok added.

I shook my head. "Too much blood has been shed here, already. If Brightborn doesn't know the truth about this place already, we can't risk that he or his elves will discover it."

"But the horde is ready!" Gronk protested. "Brightborn will learn nothing if we defeat the legion here and leave no survivors."

"My father is too clever for that," Layla said. "He wouldn't send a legion here if they were certain to be slaughtered. The elf we met, the one from Annwn, says that Taliesin lives in the otherworld. We have to keep the war as far from this place as possible."

"I agree with the princess," Targigoth said.

"You what?" Gronk asked, one hand on his hips, the other gripping the handle of his ax.

"Annwn is the source of all the magic here," Targigoth said. "According to the legends, it was from Annwn that life first sprang. It is the connection of the earth to that realm that preserves the mystic power of this world."

I nodded. "And the elf, before he was killed—"

"Wait," Brag'mok said. "Someone killed this elf from this other world?"

I nodded. "Two of Brightborn's legionaries came after us. I don't think they knew who the elf was. But the blood that was shed has already tainted these lands. He said we must leave, that I must find a way to revive this land, to bring peace and love to the rest of the world."

"And how are you going to do that?" Targigoth said.

I sighed. "I don't know. But I do know we can't fight a battle here."

"Now that my father knows we're here," Layla said, "he'll unleash more than his legion on us."

"I doubt he intends to attack us with his legion at all," I added. "They're here to scout us out. It's only a matter of time before the human armies start bombing us."

"Then blow them out of the sky!" Gronk said. "We can't fight them unless they're on the ground."

I shook my head. "It's too risky. If they drop bombs on this place and it destroys the gate to Annwn, there won't be any chance left for me to restore it, much less spread whatever that place represents to our world."

"Then where would have us go?" Brag'mok asked.

"Back to the junkyard ranch."

"But they'll look for us there!" Gronk said. "They could bomb that place as well as they would here."

"Maybe," I said. "But if they drop bombs there, so close to the city, people will know about it."

"With so many people in St. Louis already supporting our cause," Layla added, "they'll have to at least think twice about doing something like that."

Brag'mok nodded. "It is one thing to bomb us up here, in the middle of a Canadian forest, hundreds of miles from the closest city. It is another thing entirely for the US government to drop bombs on its own land. Especially since other people live not far from where the ranch is located."

Gronk grunted. "My men crave battle. We will not sit tight and wait for the humans and Brightborn to make a move."

I bit my lip. To crave battle—why would anyone crave battle? But it had barely been an hour since I drove my blade into that elf. I knew what he meant. There was something to a fight, to battle, that was almost addicting. It was the closest thing to euphoria mixed with shame that I'd experienced since my drinking days. I hated war. I abhorred violence. But a part of me relished in it. I didn't like it. At least I recognized it.

"When do we leave?" Brag'mok asked.

"As soon as possible," I said.

"We can't leave yet," Layla said.

"Why not?" I asked. "We can have Trixie make a big enough portal for everyone."

"We need to make sure that whatever of my father's legion might be nearby sees us leave."

"So we engage them!" Gronk said.

"Yes," Layla said. "But we don't kill anyone."

Gronk huffed. "How do we engage them without killing them?"

"Very carefully," Layla said.

"They'll shower us with arrows the second they see us!" Gronk said.

"I can take care of the arrows," I said.

"What about all the supplies we just brought back?" Layla asked.

"We'll move everything to our training grounds. We'll all gather with the supplies, and Trixie can teleport us all together. Once the elves are in pursuit and we can be sure they'll see us leave."

"What if you're wrong?" Targigoth asked.

I shrugged. "Wrong about what?"

"What if Brightborn's men already know the truth of this land?"

I sighed. "If they do, they won't leave. The fairies will let us know. They can check for us to make sure."

"So we march," Gronk said. Then he grunted. "And then we run."

"It's not a retreat," I said. "There's no dishonor in this. Consider it a strategic maneuver. We're drawing the enemy to another battlefield, one that works in our favor."

Gronk snorted and nodded before he turned to leave.

"Let us know when you're ready," Brag'mok said.

I nodded. "I will. And thank you."

"For what?" Brag'mok asked.

"For trusting me on this," I said. "For helping me persuade Gronk."

"Were it not for Targigoth's insights, I'm not sure anything could have stayed his hand," Brag'mok said. "It's not merely that the giants are hungry for battle. Remember, our people lost everything."

"I get it. They want revenge," I said.

"We want *justice*," Brag'mok said. "There's a difference."

"Sometimes there is," I said. "Right now, I'm not so sure it's easy to tell one from the other."

Brag'mok rested his hand on my shoulder. "It might look the same from the outside looking in. But when you're in the midst of war, the warrior knows the difference between a battle fought in rage for revenge and one fought with resolve for justice."

I pressed my lips together. "I suppose that's right. Layla, would you get the drow together and have them gather the rest of the elves of the resistance? We need everyone ready to go as soon as possible."

"Got it," Layla said before kissing me on the cheek and walking back toward the spires.

Brag'mok stayed there, standing in front of me. He cocked his head, staring at me with wide eyes.

"What?" I asked.

"You've killed recently," Brag'mok said.

I scrunched my brow. "What do you mean?"

"I can see it in your eyes," Brag'mok said. "Any seasoned warrior can see it in the face of someone who has just taken a life."

I bit my lip. "Surely you've killed a lot of elves through the years."

Brag'mok nodded. "I have."

"And when you kill, do you get crazy eyes, too?" I asked.

Brag'mok laughed. "I didn't say you have crazy eyes, Caspar. There's nothing crazy about the thrill of a kill when at war. No matter how many lives I take, even if they be elves, each kill changes me. One cannot take another life and remain the same."

I sighed. "This isn't the first time I've killed. There was Hector. There was Fred."

"But you were not in a battle at the time," Brag'mok said. "It settles on the soul differently when you kill in the thrill of a fight, does it not?"

I scratched the back of my head. "You'd think it would be easier. You know, since it was unavoidable. It was kill or be killed. I guess it was easier, but it was more than that."

"You took pleasure from it," Brag'mok said.

I took a deep breath. "Don't tell anyone that. But, yeah. How fucked up is that?"

"War is fucked up, Caspar," Brag'mok said. "There's no such thing as a non-fucked war. What you felt, and still do, many warriors experience. It's why many warriors will not speak of their battles with civilians. At least, that's the case amongst our kind."

"Humans, too," I said. "A lot of soldiers who've been to war won't talk about their experiences except with other soldiers."

"Because only a warrior can understand another warrior, Caspar. If we spoke of what it felt like at war, if we admitted in times of peace that we missed it, craved it, even, no one who hasn't been to war could possibly understand."

I shook my head. "I haven't even been in a proper battle yet."

"What is a proper battle? There's nothing proper about any war."

"You know what I mean," I said. "We were attacked by two elves. We fought. That was that. But this time, it wasn't Aerin controlling me. Sure, I might have drawn on her abilities. But *I* did it. I'm the one who plunged my sword into that elf's flesh."

"And you liked how it felt."

I sighed. "Even as I was disgusted by it."

Brag'mok nodded. "That is how it is for me, with every kill. I'd say it gets easier, but that would be a lie. It is good that you feel these things."

"How is that good?" I asked, cocking my head.

"Because when you feel the kill, the thrill and the horror of it, you remain human, even as I remain a giant. When we grow numb, when we can kill without any emotion, that's when we lose ourselves."

"You've seen that happen?" I asked.

Brag'mok turned and looked off in the distance at Gronk as he stood by his men. "I have. Such warriors, those who've long since lost themselves, can be deadly on the battlefield. But they are also dangerous."

"You're talking about Gronk?" I asked.

Brag'mok nodded. "I do not mean to alarm you. He is bound to duty as much as anything else. But you don't want to become like him, Caspar. Even if every enemy were killed, he would never find peace."

"How can I find peace like this? When I feel these things?" I asked.

"I don't know," Brag'mok said. "But at least when you feel it, when you recognize it, you know that your humanity is intact. Then, I suppose, there's always hope you might one day find serenity again."

"Serenity," I said. "That's a loaded word for me."

"How so?" Brag'mok asked.

"It's a part of the prayer we speak at the beginning of every AA meeting. God, grant me the serenity to accept the things I cannot change. The courage to change the things I can. And the wisdom to know the difference."

Brag'mok smiled, his lower incisors still overlapping his upper lip. "You've fought a war already, Caspar. A war within yourself. A battle with addiction."

I nodded. "I suppose I have."

"Then you know that the true battle, even in a war, is not with the enemy," Brag'mok said. "To win a battle is not always a victory. You must also win the battle in your soul if you are to truly win the war."

CHAPTER TEN

I moved our supplies from the silo to the training grounds as the elves of the resistance and the drow gathered around. We didn't have the space at the junkyard ranch for everyone. We could create more spires, I imagined, but we weren't going there to make ourselves at home. We were going there to fight.

Ironic, I thought, that to protect this land, we had to abandon it.

Technically, we were going home. It didn't feel like it. Of course, nowhere had felt like home since my apartment. I was always waiting for the shoe to drop. The next hard right turn that would force us to abandon where ever we'd temporarily settled.

Maybe I was getting ahead of myself. We had to lure Brightborn's legions, wherever they were, into a skirmish. No one could die. No blood could be shed. However, we needed them to chase us just in time to see us leave.

I wasn't sure it would work. I didn't have any idea how many legionaries might be nearby. If we had them outnumbered, they would be wary of pursuing us. One of the elves who attacked us before had urged Layla to come with them. They were here for her and probably to scout us out so Brightborn could alert the militaries so they could bomb the bejeezus out of us.

The giants were ready to march, even if only to "retreat" back to the fairy portal. I needed the fairies twice. First, to scout out and identify the numbers and locations of the legionaries in the area. Second, to open the fairy portal to send us back to the junkyard ranch.

Trixie took off with three other fairy companions. I didn't know any of their names. They stayed mostly to themselves, usually in the trees surrounding our forest outpost. It wasn't that they were excluded in any way. These fairies hadn't known any non-fairy allies for most of their lives. On New Albion, the elves had hunted them to try and seize their powers. The giants weren't their enemies, but it wasn't surprising the two races didn't have any real relationship. The giants weren't exactly known for their hospitality, and the fairies were mostly content to remain to themselves.

Trixie was nothing if not efficient. She flew like a hummingbird. All the fairies did. They could dart around at crazy speeds then, still fluttering their wings, hover in mid-air. Since they could portal wherever they wanted to go in an instant, once Trixie found the elves, she'd be able to tell me seconds later.

The elf resistance emerged from their spire, with Aelfrich still bound in leather straps. Aelfrich was a loyalist who'd deceived me when I'd gone to the North Pole. He'd led me to believe that *he* was the leader of the resistance. He'd taught me how to make a spire of ice and magic at the pole. The plans for the spire were contained in a crystal. All I did was provide the crystal with the requisite magic needed to construct the spire. It was all a trap. Little did I know that the whole thing was engineered to function as a prison instead of a refuge.

If it wasn't for Aerin's blade and me allowing her to take control, we never would have been able to fight our way out. Not with magic. The place had inhibitors in place to prevent it.

In the end, we'd taken Aelfrich prisoner. He hadn't divulged much since we returned to the forest. Mostly because he didn't know much about what Brightborn was doing since we'd thwarted his previous plans. But we couldn't let Aelfrich go, either. We didn't want him to divulge our location.

Now the elves knew where we were, he was little more than an extra mouth to feed. He didn't have any useful information, and even if he did, he wasn't talking. Still, it wasn't hard to figure out what Brightborn was up to. He was using a combination of deceit and magic to convince the world's leaders that he could save the planet from climate change. Maybe he could. But his aid came at a cost—the acquisition of power. Brightborn allowed the world's governments to retain their autonomy. He pretended he wasn't interested in ruling, only coordinating the world's powers for the betterment of the planet and humankind. However, he'd established a one-world government under his emperorship. He was the king of kingdoms. The ruler of rulers. The president of presidents. If any single nation dared to defy him, he'd rally the rest to force them into compliance.

Climate change wasn't Brightborn's real concern. It was a tool, a political cause he could use to bring the nations into compliance. After all, if a single nation defied his one-world rule and refused to comply with his dictates, it would complicate his purported agenda. Before Brightborn, issues like the reduction of carbon emissions were a difficult sell for many nations. So long as a few developed nations continued pumping smog into the atmosphere, they had a competitive economic advantage over the nations who were making the necessary changes. Under Brightborn, all nations had to comply or face the wrath of the larger world empire. To exercise such wrath, if it were needed, Brightborn also required a supreme command of every nation's military.

The problem was, once he had that power, he'd never cede it back to the nations. Once the climate problems were solved and the nations were all united under his rule, there wouldn't be much need for militaries anymore. Not once all the threats—like our resistance and other popular uprisings around the world—had been squelched.

Yet, Brightborn was effectively making the case that he needed the control of all the world's militaries so he could end the resistance. Then, so he promised, the world would know a peace it had never before realized.

Peace by way of violence to me was a lot like achieving purity by way of fornication. It was a contradiction, hypocrisy of epic proportions. But it also meant we had no choice. If we wanted peace, we had to fight back. After all, once our resistance was removed and all the world's uprisings had been squashed, Brightborn would assert his authority to the point of tyranny.

Virtues like equality, liberty, and justice weren't the values that would govern his rule. Elf supremacy and the reduction of humanity to servitude was his ultimate agenda. He'd stop at nothing to see it through.

That meant we had no choice but to fight.

CHAPTER ELEVEN

Trixie showed up in a flash of golden light and a shower of what looked like glitter—sparks of fairy magic.

"Find the elves?" I asked.

"We did," Trixie said as the other fairies who'd gone with her appeared in a similar magical fireworks display.

"How many are we talking about?" I asked.

"Not many. Maybe fifty elves. Not enough to defeat our army."

I nodded. "Then we'll have to play this smart. They won't want to pursue us if they know we outnumber them."

"Do we need them to pursue us here?" Layla asked. "We know they're here for me."

I bit my lip. "What are you suggesting?"

"My powers can allow me to teleport, too. They won't catch me. But if they think I'm alone, they might follow me far enough to at least see us leave."

I sighed. "I don't know. Why would they think we'd flee if we do have the advantage?"

Layla shrugged. "For the same reason, I suspect, that they haven't attacked us yet. They have reinforcements coming."

"Military reinforcements," I said.

Layla nodded. "They won't be able to catch me. But they won't attack us here until the other armies arrive. Still, they want me. They won't attack even with a human military force if they think I'm with our army."

I sighed. "Because your power still offers them a weapon. If you channel it into a stone circle."

"Exactly," Layla said. "My father has convinced the legions that *I* am the chosen one of the elven prophecy. Even if the legion doesn't know he just wants to wield my power, they'll believe I need to be saved and separated from the rest of our army for the sake of the prophecy."

"Then I'm coming with you," I said.

Layla shook her head. "You can't. If they see you with me, they'll back off. They know what you can do."

"That didn't stop the two elves who came after us before," I said.

"Because they thought they were taking us by surprise," Layla said. "You might be powerful, but they could still take you down."

"But they won't kill me," I said. "We're soul-bound. If they killed me, they'd kill you."

"That doesn't mean they couldn't incapacitate you. Use magic to heal you just enough to keep you alive but unconscious."

I grunted. "I hadn't thought of that."

Layla put her hand on my arm. "Trust me, Caspar. This is the only way."

I sighed. "All right. But if you get into trouble, I'm coming after you."

Layla smiled. "I know you will. But it won't come to that. I'll be fine."

I nodded. "Fair enough. But I'll be watching from a distance. I'll fly through the tops of the trees where they won't see me."

"What about the giants?" Layla asked.

I smiled. "They're itching for a battle, and they outnumber the legion. If the giants can engage the elves, without killing any of them—"

"How in the world are you going to prevent them from killing anyone here?" Layla interjected.

"We just need to get them close together. Then the fairies can portal all of them to the fields near the junkyard ranch. It isn't every day that we have a chance like this. We should take advantage of it."

Layla nodded. "Not a bad idea. It means the giants won't have to swallow their pride and retreat. They'll get what they want. Just make sure that some of my father's legionaries are left behind alive so they can tell my father that we left. Otherwise, he'll only send more military to these lands. They'll scorch the place trying to flush us out if they can't fight us right away."

Gronk smiled wider than I'd ever seen the usually grumpy giant grin when I told him the plan. He loved it. No need to retreat and they'd get to satisfy their hunger for battle. He also agreed that it was smart. We might not ever get another chance like this to *outnumber* Brightborn. But if we eliminated a good contingency of his legion, there was a better chance we'd have more opportunities to outnumber him in the future.

Since I could heal our wounded back at the junkyard ranch, we could probably minimize the casualties on our side.

I went in full camouflage, floating from tree to tree behind Layla as she made her way through the forest. Trixie was at her side, guiding her to the elves. I kept a good distance. I'm not good at estimating distances, but I stayed close enough I could see Layla, but only just. The way I saw it, especially since she was actively hoping to be seen while I was doing my damnedest to remain hidden, there was little chance anyone would spot me.

Layla had her bow loaded and ready. The purple glow of the celestial magic that coursed through her arrows only increased the likelihood she'd be spotted. Hopefully, she wouldn't need to take a shot. If she did, though, she'd aim for the leg, maybe the upper shoulder. She'd avoid any vital organs that way, and if push came to shove, we'd portal the elf out of there before the magic spread. A technicality, perhaps, but at least that way, no one would die on these lands. Presuming things went according to plan.

Having Trixie along was a big help. Not only could she take us to where the elves were camping, but she'd know if anyone was stalking us from a distance, and she'd know it if anyone unleashed any magic.

As luck would have it, we were moving the opposite direction from the creek and the ley line where the portal to Annwn was. If it was still there. Bloodshed had tainted the land already. What impact that would have on the viability of the portal was uncertain. Mingan had died before he could explain much of anything.

Layla turned and raised her hand to signal that I should stop. She'd come upon the elven camp. The trick was to be seen without it looking like she was *trying* to be seen.

She shot an arrow into the camp. She didn't often miss. This time, she missed on purpose. Just barely. The elves gathered around a fire in the center of the camp stood up and pointed at the arrow. They could see the purple magic radiating off it, and they knew what that meant. There was only one person who wielded *that* kind of power.

They dropped their roasting sticks and grabbed their spears. So far, only a small number were in pursuit. We needed to get the attention of the rest. They had a number of tents in their camp. Nothing distinctly elven. The green canvas suggested that these were military-grade tents. I hovered around the perimeter, careful to stay hidden behind the foliage. Since the majority of the trees in the area had needles rather than broad leaves, it wasn't as easy as it could have been. Still, while my camouflage was of the thrift-store variety rather than the military-grade stuff that the elven legion had acquired, camo is camo. So far, no one had seen me.

I needed to flush out the rest of them and lure them all back to our camp, where the giants would engage them in close combat. There were a few ways I could do it. I could use the earth and shake the ground beneath them. Since we weren't near a fault line and earthquakes weren't common, they'd probably know it was me. However, we were trying to give the impression that Layla was here alone and that they had a chance to try and grab her without incurring my elemental wrath.

I had to think of something I could do to alert the rest of the camp, to startle them, without being obvious about the fact that I was the one behind it all.

Burning their tents might work, but tents don't spontaneously combust. I'd have to somehow manipulate the fire they already had, make it look like it had spread accidentally. I could try and flood them out. Unfortunately, we were uphill from the stream, and that would be suspicious. I could bring a wind storm upon them. However, I imagined they'd focus on trying to keep their tents up. I could give them a big enough gust to make that futile, of course, but that would take a lot more energy than it would to stoke a fire.

After all, I'd have to keep my magic constantly channeling to blow the wind that hard. Wind doesn't produce itself. Fire only required me to use enough magic to cause it to catch on the tents. After that, well, magic wasn't required. Nature would take its course. It was the smartest option. There was a good chance I'd need all the magic I had to pull off the relocation job I'd planned, especially since the elves wouldn't jump at the chance to face the giants in close combat. I'd probably have to figure out a way to *make* it happen.

Of course, once they were close enough to our outpost, I'd be less concerned about them identifying me. We just needed to get them to move our direction so that we could engage the legion, portal them to *our* battlefield near the old junkyard ranch, and leave enough behind that they could report to Brightborn what had happened. So he'd know that we were no longer in the Canadian forest.

Trixie buzzed around me. "Is Layla all right?" I asked.

Trixie nodded. "Yup! She wanted me to let you know she has three elves in pursuit. Said that would be enough if we wanted to revert to the original plan. They'd see what would happen. Even if we don't get the whole legion trapped."

I shook my head. "This is the best chance we have to outnumber our enemy. Tell her I'm going to try and flush out the rest of them. Well, not flush them out, literally. I'm going to use fire rather than water."

"You got it!" Trixie said. I loved the fairy. She was an immense help, don't get me wrong. But she was *always* chipper. Even when passing along tactical plans in the middle of an operation. The enthusiasm in her voice as my heart raced in anticipation of what might happen next was mildly jarring.

The sweat beaded on my brow as the heat that came with evoking fire filled my frame. It struck me that back when I was in school, this ability might have come in handy if I'd ever needed to convince the school nurse that I had a fever.

I extended my arm, clenched my fist, and rather than channeling fire directly, I connected my will to the campfire in the middle of the camp. I drew a trail of flames from the fire across the dirt to one of the tents. It looked like it had caught on gasoline rather than igniting on account of my magic. Until the flames reached the first green canvas tent.

At first, it didn't catch. But once the flames caught the canvas, it didn't take long before the whole thing was ablaze. I sent a gust of wind. Not so much that it would strain me, just enough to stoke the flames enough that they caught another tent on fire.

The elves were fleeing. A few of them who had an affinity for water magic tried to gather some moisture from the air to stop the flames. It wasn't enough, especially since I was keeping the flames burning hot through my magic.

I didn't want them to see me, but I wanted them to pursue me —an unknown person who'd set their camp ablaze.

A few of the elves were already chasing Layla through the forest. I led the others in the same direction. To these elves, I was nothing but a vandal, someone who had caught their tents on fire and thought I could escape without consequences. They didn't know who they were chasing. If they did, they'd probably turn and run the other way. The elves knew what I could do. They'd be foolish to try and take me on directly.

It wasn't long before the whole rest of the legion was on my tail. If Trixie's count was exact and three elves were pursuing Layla, I had forty-seven highly trained elven legionaries on my ass.

I had to move fast. Aether could make sure of that. But it was a balancing act. I had to go slow enough that they'd catch an occasional glimpse of me in the distance but fast enough that they couldn't get close enough to identify me.

I had to believe they knew where our outpost was. If we kept moving in that direction, they'd figure it out that whoever I was, I came from our camp.

An arrow landed in a tree trunk beside me as I fled ahead. I evoked the power of air, forming a small cyclone around me strong enough to divert any arrows that might strike me. In theory, anyway. It's not like I'd had much chance to test it out. Besides, it had been a few years since I'd taken physics. All I knew is the smaller I made the cyclone, the faster the wind would have to turn. A larger cyclone could divert an arrow better over a longer spread of space. It wasn't just a question of force and velocity. The drag on the arrow had an impact too, a lot more math than I could figure, even with the aid of a calculator. I say that to say this—I wasn't a hundred percent certain my little tornado would work.

Still, it was the best solution I could come up with while running through the woods with a legion in pursuit. If they all started firing arrows, my best protection was to remain a moving target. To give them just enough of a visual to know I was ahead of them but not enough that they could get a good aim on me.

Another arrow whizzed past my left ear.

I grunted. I had to try something else. I invoked earth. I called to a stone, a boulder about twenty feet to my left. I forced it to move parallel to me. There was enough brush that I figured it wouldn't be easy to tell for certain that the boulder wasn't me. All they'd see was a disturbance, some motion, and hopefully be more distracted by the mysteriously rolling rock instead of me.

Between the wind I was casting, making the boulder roll, and the natural exhaustion that accompanied running, I was reaching my limit. Hell, running alone probably accounted for most of it. The extra energy it took to cast magic was enough to test my already less-than-impressive level of cardiovascular endurance.

I turned the wind I had spinning around me into a tailwind. I didn't want to fly. Then it would be obvious to the elves behind me who I was. But if I could use the wind to help propel me forward, I hoped I could avoid total exhaustion. Or, one of those nasty side cramps that usually hit every time I went for a run.

The elves were getting closer. It took everything I had to land in the middle of our training grounds. Layla had arrived just before I did...

She had an arrow in the back of her leg. Elven arrows were nasty. The arrow heads weren't just triangular, meant to pierce flesh, but on the back-side, on either side, they were barbed. They were also strangely ornate, not merely functional. Crafting arrows in elf culture was an art. While most of Layla's arrows were rather plain—she hadn't had the time to give them the TLC that she used to—most elves spent time engraving their arrows with ornate designs, floral patterns, and elven letters.

The three elves who pursued her were at the perimeter of the grounds, trying to avoid engaging the larger contingency of giants, drow, and the resistance who were gathered and ready for transport.

"We're ready," Gronk said.

I nodded, placing my hand on Layla's leg and, drawing on aether, visualizing her wound closing after I removed the arrow from her leg. She winced in pain. Pulling out an elf arrow sucks. The back end of the arrowhead tears at the skin when you remove it. Nothing I couldn't heal. But it hurt like hell.

"You all right?" I asked.

Layla nodded, springing back to her feet. "Good as new. Damn, that hurt, though."

"We need to get everyone else out of here," I said. "There are almost fifty elves pursuing us."

"I can stay back with you until we're ready to take the giants," Layla said.

I shook my head. "Go with the drow and the resistance. Get them ready to assault the elves from the flank when I bring them with the giants mid-battle to the fields."

"All right. Just be careful. Remember, no bloodshed here."

"To avoid that, we'll have to move fast. So, make sure to get everyone in position right away."

Layla nodded. "We've got this."

I smiled before calling Trixie. She took care of portaling the drow and the resistance back to Missouri, along with Jag, Elrand, Layla, Agnus, and Clarence. Presuming they cleared the field quickly, I'd be able to portal the giants there myself.

Gronk raised his ax and shouted. Brag'mok did the same. The rest of the giants followed suit.

I grabbed Aerin's sword and raised it into the air. "Woohooo!"

Brag'mok looked at me, raising one of his bushy eyebrows. "Woohoo? That's your battle cry?"

"Look, I don't know how to roar," I said. "It's the best I can do."

The giants took off, charging through the woods. The sooner

they could close the gap between themselves and the elves, the better. It would eliminate the elves' advantage of a ranged assault.

I could barely keep up, especially after I'd just run from these same woods. Thankfully, the elves weren't far.

When they saw the giants charging, they lobbed arrows through the woods. Only a few hit. Most of them hit trees or were blocked by the giants' shields. Those who did get hit didn't suffer any mortal wounds. I glanced over at one of the giants who took an arrow to his shoulder. He snapped it off and charged forward, yelling with even more vigor than before.

"Remember!" I yelled, trying to keep up with Gronk and Brag'mok. "No killing! Not until I've portaled us all back to the battlefield!"

They kept yelling. I'd have to trust they heard me. They knew the plan.

We closed in on the elves. They'd retreated into a close formation, now wielding spears rather than bows. Rather than attack head-on, the giants formed a circle around the elves. The elves turned outward to guard themselves against the attack. They were outnumbered. They knew it. On the inside, with nowhere to run, they were at a decided disadvantage.

One of the elves started to evoke fire. I could see it in his eyes. I knew the sensation. He was going to try and blast all of us.

I doused him with water.

Then another elf broke ranks as I started forming a fairy portal over us. He charged me. I saw his magical spark, his arrows in his quiver. They had the same unique carvings as the arrow that struck Layla.

Anger boiled up within me. I was pulling the portal down over all of us, but this elf was determined. Brag'mok raised his broadsword to block the elf's attack.

The elf—he must've been an assassin by the way he moved—slid under Brag'mok's blade and came after me with his spear-point.

I gripped my second blade, and utilizing Aerin's abilities, I swung around, catching the elf under the chin. Blood gushed out all over the ground. No bloodshed. But damn…what else was I supposed to do? And it felt good.

I pulled the rest of the portal over us, and we reappeared in the middle of the field near the junkyard ranch. The elf's bloodied body lay at my feet.

CHAPTER TWELVE

I swung both blades around with a rage, a fury, a thrill like nothing I'd ever known. We were back in Missouri. The thick, humid air. The familiar smells. The air had a distinctly unique odor on account of the different plant life that thrived there. Now it was mixed with the scent of battle. *That* was new to me. Blood mixed with sweat. Any other time I would have found it repulsive. Now, combined with the scents of home, it was intox-icating.

I'm not sure if it was the blood of the elf at my feet, the scent rising to my nostrils, or if I'd bitten my tongue, but I could taste blood in my mouth as I pivoted on one foot and sliced my second blade across another elf's abdomen. His blood sprayed out of his wound, hitting me in the face. I licked my lips.

I didn't know what had come over me. I wasn't in the frame of mind to question it. I buried my doubts and thrust my fist forward, channeling a torrent of flames at two elves as they were about to jump with daggers in hand on Brag'mok's back. I screamed as I forced more magic into my assault until their bodies were completely consumed and all that remained was ash.

Another elf came at me with his spear. I blocked it with Aerin's blade and sliced his neck with my second.

I sheathed my blades. I looked around. Bodies were scattered all around. Elves. Not a single giant had fallen. A few were clutching at wounds on various parts of their bodies. I'd deal with that later.

I thrust my fist to the sky and roared. The giants followed suit.

Just like that, we'd taken down fifty of Brightborn's legionaries. It was one small victory in a larger war that now included most of the world's militaries. But it felt good.

I looked beyond the fog of the battle, mostly due to the smoke of my flames and the dust caused by the fight. Layla stood there, her hands at her side and her hand over her mouth.

I approached her, my blood still pumping from the battle. "I know what you're thinking. 'My husband looks sexy covered in blood.'"

Layla scrunched her brow and stared at me, biting the inside of her cheek. "No. That's not it."

I shrugged. "Then what is it?"

"I've… It's just… I've never seen you lose control like that. Full of so much rage."

I smiled. "I'm fine. One of them hit you with an arrow. Maybe I got a little angry. But we did the job, Layla."

Layla nodded. "We did. But you also spilled more blood on sacred lands."

I scratched my head. "Maybe I portaled his corpse out of there in time. Either way, it was just one kill. Surely the sacred lands will understand."

"And it was just one bite from the apple… You know, in your Bible, back in Eden."

I chuckled. "I see what you're doing. This was different. We had to fight to get them off the land, and we did."

"You didn't have to kill him there. You could have injured him enough to give you the time to cast the portal."

I grunted. "Whatever. It's done."

Layla nodded. "It is. We'll have to deal with whatever consequences there might be later. But I'm worried about you, Caspar."

"I'm fine," I said, taking Layla's hand and grasping it between both of mine. "Maybe I got a little lost in the heat of the moment."

Layla bit her lip. "It doesn't bother you? That you just killed people?"

I snorted. "I don't know. It's not hitting me the same way it did before. It felt different since he was attacking us, I guess. Maybe that's it. Or maybe it'll hit me later once I crash from the adrenaline surge. But I don't feel much of anything about it right now, and we don't have time to talk about it."

Layla placed her hand, the one I wasn't holding, on top of both of mine. "I suppose you're right. There's no sense settling in here. We need to get ready, prepare ourselves for another battle. Once my father learns what happened, he'll strike back hard. I don't think he'll be coming after us with spears and arrows next time."

"Everyone back at the junkyard?" I asked.

Layla nodded. "Trixie is putting the veil back in place."

I cocked my head. "I thought she couldn't do that anymore."

Layla shrugged. "There was something about the land in the Canadian forest that prevented it. At least, that would be my guess. No matter, our old base is sufficiently hidden again."

"Won't make much difference," I said. "They'll know to come looking for us here now. It may just buy us enough time for the next battle."

"Then we'd best get ready," Layla said. "We don't have enough lodgings for everyone."

I sighed. "I realize that. But we aren't making a home out of this place. If push comes to shove, we'll make some more spires to shelter us from the elements."

"The farmhouse is still intact," Layla said. "Why don't you come and rest a little? You've been casting a lot of magic."

I shook my head. "I don't want to rest. I want to keep fighting."

"Caspar," Layla said, her eyes wide with concern. "This isn't you."

I shrugged. "Who am I, anyway? What if this always was me? I just never knew it until now."

Layla shook her head. "That's the adrenaline speaking. Give it some time, rest a little, and you'll start thinking clearly again."

"I don't know if I've ever thought more clearly," I said. "There's only one way to end this."

"You can't win in an all-out battle with the whole world and their militaries, Caspar."

I shook my head. "Maybe not. But we can sure as hell fight our way through whoever stands between us and your father. Once he's gone, this hell will be over."

Layla cocked her head. "Just hours ago, you were talking about how we needed to avoid killing people. About how you needed a positive message to rally the support of the people. Now, you're talking about assassinating my dad."

"Think about it," I said. "If he's out of the picture, the rest of the alliance under his one-world government will fall apart."

Layla dropped my hands. "You aren't an assassin, Caspar. That's not what you were chosen for."

I snorted. "Yeah. I was chosen to unite the peoples. But what the hell does that even mean? What is unity, anyway? Holding hands and singing Kumbaya?"

"I think the prophecy predicts something a bit deeper than that, Caspar."

"Is unity even possible?" I asked. "People pretend to get along. They work together when they have common goals. But at the end of the day, everyone's selfish. They're all looking out for themselves. It's just a matter of time before those who are unified today find themselves at odds with each other's interests tomorrow."

"Which is why the prophecy chose you, Caspar. Not just any brute could do what you were chosen to do."

I snorted. "Then I'll preach a sermon or something. I'll give the world the greatest TED Talk ever seen. People will love it. Once I've killed your father. Once we've destroyed our enemies."

Layla sighed. "You know who you sound like right now?"

I shrugged. "Who?"

Layla narrowed her eyes. "My father."

CHAPTER THIRTEEN

The farmhouse was infested with field mice. That meant that Agnus got to have some fun. If anyone knew what the thrill of the hunt was like, it was him. When Agnus detected a mouse, he released the strangest meow. It sounded like *he* was the one dying. In truth, it was something like a war cry. He lowered his head, staying close to the ground, keeping the mouse in his line of vision.

He didn't always kill them right away. He liked to play with his prey. Torment the mouse a little just because he could. Eventually, he'd end the rodent's terror. He wouldn't eat the mouse. Instead, he'd take it in his mouth to me. Drop it down in front of me and look up with me as if to say, "Yup. I know. I'm a badass."

Then, he'd saunter off, cool, calm, and collected, leaving his victim for me to deal with. Like a boss.

It had been a regular routine when we were living in the farmhouse at the junkyard ranch before. This was the first time he'd completed a stalk and kill since we returned. I had a new appreciation for it. It wasn't about food. It was about getting in touch with something primal, something carnal, something usually suppressed by his typically refined feline routine of sunbathing and licking his junk. In a world where his food was served to him on a platter—tuna fish not caught in the ocean but purchased in a can at a grocery store. The hunt put him back in touch with his true nature, the animal, the hunter within.

For once, I related to what Agnus was doing. I didn't often understand why a house cat would bother hunting a mouse and never attempt to eat it. What was the point? That was exactly it. There wasn't a point. It wasn't about a meal at all. It was all about the hunt and the kill.

It wasn't practical. At least not to the person looking at it from the outside. For my whole life, I'd abhorred violence of any sort. Then, all this prophecy started, and I had killed. The first few didn't overtake my conscience, although I hated it. But now, it was like with every kill the reptilian mind, the primal thrill of the kill was more awakened.

I still had a conscience. A part of me hated it even as I craved another battle. But it was getting easier. Not just to kill but to ignore whatever moral qualms I still harbored about what I was doing. This was war, after all. I had my reasons. Those reasons had nothing to do with how I *felt* about the battle, but it was certainly better since fighting was the only option to get *something* out of it, some kind of thrill or pleasure, rather than being constantly overwhelmed by guilt and shame.

I'd experienced the same thing when I was drinking—the ability to rationalize away or dismiss my conscience whenever it objected to my behavior. Only then, my actions had been purely selfish. Now, I was doing something worthwhile. I was fighting for the world. History had its share of war heroes. People rallied behind the image of power. Perhaps that's what Doris had meant. People needed something positive to follow, a hero to believe in. Someone who takes action, taking names while kicking ass.

Whatever the case, fighting was something I could do. Restoring the land? Healing the world? Well, first, I didn't even know how to begin with that. Second, why clean the mouse turds out of your cabinets *before* you kill the mouse? I'd do what I could to save the world, to restore whatever paradisaic vision that the ancients envisioned. Call it Annwn. Call it Eden. Whatever it was, there was no sense bringing it back so long as Brightborn and the world were allied against it. I had to beat them down first; I had to catch the mouse before I cleaned up its mess even if that meant, analogous to the farmhouse at the junkyard ranch, I had a whole infestation to deal with.

I knew Layla was worried about me. It wasn't like my morals had changed. I was still *opposed* to violence. But I'd tasted it, and part of me liked it. Again, not a surprise. I'm sure a part of me would like sleeping with a thousand women, too. A lot of sins are pleasurable. Still, the thrill of the battle at least helped me get through my moral barriers, to overcome my qualms with what had to be done.

Martin Luther, the protestant reformer, once said that there are times in life when we have to "sin boldly." What he meant was that the world is so broken, so fucked up, that sometimes the best you can do is approximate righteousness. Sometimes, you are forced into a situation where sinlessness is impossible. There are times when you have to get your hands dirty. Does that mean it's not sin? Not at all. I still believed that killing was wrong and that even in the context of war, it was evil precisely because God didn't create us to kill or even to die. God created us to live, to thrive.

But in this broken world where people *do* kill, where death is an inevitability, I had to believe that God could redeem even the actions of a sinner like me. I had to sin boldly but believe more boldly still. I had to trust that despite myself, God would save me.

I watched from the floor of what used to be my bedroom. My popped and deflated mattress lay in the middle of the room like the world's ugliest floor rug. At least if I sat on it, I wouldn't get splinters from the well-weathered wooden floors.

Agnus was crouched low to the ground as he stalked the latest intruder. He was having the time of his life. "Get him, boy!"

"Shush," Agnus piped back. I was either going to scare his prey or he found my encouragement patronizing. Probably some of both. After all, he was much more efficient at killing mice than I could ever be, even with mousetraps. Hell, most of the traps I set usually got outsmarted by the mice. The peanut butter or cheese I set as bait would be gone after the trap was sprung, no mouse inside.

There was a small gap between the flooring and the base molding. Based on the condition of the floors, I'd imagined that these were the original. The staples in the floor suggested that at some point, someone had put carpet in. At a later date, probably due to moisture, it was ripped out. The baseboards were likely added after the installation of the carpet. They sat about a quarter to half an inch over the floor, just enough for a mouse to squeeze through.

Agnus knew the mouse would have to come out eventually. Presumably, in that section of the wall, the rodent would be trapped between two studs. I guessed they were probably eighteen inches apart. Of course, I had no clue what might be behind there. Likely the wall on the opposite side of the bedroom, the wall on the left-hand side of the foyer.

Agnus took a few quiet paces back.

I heard a squeak.

The mouse darted out from under the gap in the wall. Agnus pounced, catching the creature between his teeth. The mouse shrieked. Then it didn't.

Agnus sauntered over toward me. He dropped the mouse right in my lap.

"Merry Christmas."

I cocked my head. "It isn't Christmas. Get that thing off of me!"

Agnus shrugged. "I just had the thing in my mouth, and you're grossed out that it touched your pants? You'll be fine. Don't be such a pussy."

I snorted. It wasn't the first time that Agnus had called me that. It still struck me as ironic. "Why do you kill those things anyway? You don't eat them."

"Something to do. It's my nature."

I nodded. "I get that. I'm beginning to wonder if our natures aren't that dissimilar."

"Don't flatter yourself," Agnus said. "Humans bow in the shadow of feline superiority."

"Right. Which is why you need me to open cans of food for you. Tuna that was caught by humans on the ocean somewhere thousands of miles away."

"My point, exactly," Agnus said. "An entire civilization, bent to the will of the cat, going to great effort to deliver delicacies to us. You imagine yourselves superior. We allow you to think as much. It keeps you working, slaving, producing those things that serve our comforts."

I snorted. "I don't think people fish the oceans for tuna just for cats. Fishermen catch tuna so we can make tuna casseroles and tuna salad sandwiches."

"An expression of our mercy as cats that we allow you, you pitiful creatures, to indulge in the finest of earthly pleasures," Agnus said.

I smiled. "I see. If you'd prefer we be oblivious to the fact that you're using us as slaves, why'd you just tell me, then?"

"What are you going to do about it now that you know the truth?"

I shrugged. "Probably nothing, Agnus."

Agnus nodded. "Thus, there's no harm in revealing these things to you. But now you know, you might worship me more fully."

CHAPTER FOURTEEN

We had the junkyard ranch well fortified, employing magical defenses. I wasn't the only one who could wield air magic. About a fourth of the elves from the resistance had the ability. Between us, we could probably stop most air strikes. A bomber, helicopters, even a missile fired at us; if we caught it in time, we could probably blow it off course.

That was the trick—catching it in time. It wasn't like we had radar. If a missile came at us and we weren't ready, it could still hit us. That meant constant patrols, not just on the perimeter to stop ground-based attacks, but elves with air proficiencies had to survey the sky.

I didn't know how successful that would be. Even with patrols, we'd have to be lucky to catch a missile on time. I didn't know how fast a missile could travel. Probably pretty damn quick. Even with several elves on the lookout, we couldn't watch every inch of sky surrounding the junkyard ranch at all times. Since we were in the heart of the country, they could attack from all sides.

We needed a better strategy. I called together a meeting. A leader from each of the races. I insisted that Brag'mok accompany Gronk. He and I knew each other and, more than once, he'd settled Gronk's hair-trigger nerves. Rina represented the drow, although I had Aerin's blade at my side and could consult her expertise at any time. Illarion, a youthful elf Layla had grown up with, headed the elven resistance and represented their interests and insights to my makeshift military council. Layla had been coronated, in defiance of her father, as the new queen of the elves. Layla knew her father better than anyone else, but she insisted that Illarion be involved. He'd led the resistance before she assumed the crown. They trusted him. He knew their interests, their concerns, better than she did. She'd vote. But she'd given him a vote, too, and would likely defer to his judgment.

I also had Elrand and Jag in the room. Elrand had insights into what was possible with magic that were beyond what the rest of us understood. Jag was the only human fighting for our cause, apart from me. He was in tune with what was happening in the news, what Brightborn was up to, and how the popular resistance protesting the government's alliance with Brightborn was faring. Mostly because he was more than an amateur body-builder—he was also tech-savvy. As a member of the former elf gate cult, he also knew a lot about how Brightborn had worked long before he came to Earth to sow seeds in the government to make it more likely to cede him the authority he'd now managed to acquire.

"I'm not comfortable with our position here," Gronk said. "We're vulnerable."

"Agreed," Rina added.

"I think we can all agree with that," Illarion said. "Since, thanks to the valor of the giants, we just wiped out fifty of Brightborn's legion, I fear we have little time to figure out our next move."

"It would be best to move first," Gronk said. "If we wait to react to what Brightborn does, it will surely be to his advantage rather than ours."

"Agreed," Layla said. "My father is, if it is his only virtue, a brilliant military strategist."

"We learned on New Albion," Gronk continued, "that any time we met Brightborn in battle on his terms that there'd be an unpleasant surprise of some kind waiting for us."

"Honestly," I said. "If we just sit here, I don't think he'd even need to resort too much in the way of strategic brilliance. As soon as he learns we're here, he'll come after us with the full force of the US military."

"We need to find a place to fight that would cripple their efforts," Rina said. "Somewhere the US military wouldn't fight, or would only be able to fight with limited means."

"How about in the city?" Jag asked.

I shook my head. "I don't want to put any civilians in danger."

"A protest is scheduled at the Federal courthouse downtown today," Jag said. "Twitter is all abuzz about it. They're expecting ten thousand people or more."

I snorted. "That's a lot of people. But it's not as big as it could be. I don't know how that helps us."

"I'm texting with Dwight now," Jag said. "He thinks we should join the protest."

I bit my lip. Dwight was a Marine. I'd say ex-Marine but if you asked him, he'd tell you once a Marine, always a Marine. He'd joined our cause after Brag'mok kidnapped him to commandeer his eighteen-wheeler. He worked for a trucking company as a post-military career. More than once, he'd used his rig to help us gather supplies back before I'd regained my ability to wield fairy portals. He'd seen enough "strange" after Brag'mok kidnapped him that he was curious about what we were up to. He'd joined the elf gate cult before it fell apart when its former leader, Fred, betrayed us. Now, we had many civilian followers. Our Internet broadcasts all went viral. It was a challenge now that the government was working to take us down every time we went live, but we still managed to get a few videos out.

"If we made an appearance at the protest," Jag said, "Dwight insists it would help embolden the movement. With more and more people buying into Brightborn's bullshit, if we want to maintain the popular support of our movement, we need to do something to show them that we're still fighting."

I sighed. "I don't know. It's a risk."

"He has a point," Rina added. "Would your military really attack civilians?"

I grunted. "Not with bombs. But whether it be the military or the police, we've seen the authorities get violent with protesters in the past."

"We can watch the perimeter," Gronk said. "Anything they try to throw at us, we can handle. We can protect the humans."

"You were telling me before, Caspar," Layla added. "We needed to give the people something positive to believe in. Something more than fear of what Brightborn's rule might mean."

"I don't know how marching with them will provide that," I said. "It is a very different thing to protest tyranny and fascism than it is to rally for freedom and liberty."

"Is it?" Layla asked. "If people saw us still standing strong, still fighting the fight on their behalf, it would surely inspire them."

I sighed. "I suppose if there's anything that might sway the US government, it would be the people. At the end of the day, the government is run by politicians all concerned with re-election."

"Not all politicians support the President's alliance with Brightborn," Jag said. "The house minority leader has already drafted articles of impeachment."

I shrugged. "I'm not sure what good that will do. The President's party holds both houses of Congress."

"All I'm saying is that Brightborn doesn't have the whole US government in his back pocket like he'd like the world to believe," Jag said. "The best way to weaken the President's position is to encourage the popular movement that opposes the alliance."

"I think this is wise," Gronk said. "As eager as the giants are to fight, we must choose our battles wisely. If the government publicly attacks its own citizens in their hope to take us out, it won't look good."

I nodded. "Sometimes, the pen is mightier than the sword. I just don't want to see anyone get hurt."

"What does Aerin suggest?" Rina asked.

I placed my hand on the hilt of Aerin's blade and listened to her advice. She agreed with Jag's proposal.

"She believes that this is our best move at this point. If we fall in battle here, which is likely, more people will be hurt in the long run if our forces are defeated."

"But what do we do after the protest?" Brag'mok asked. "If all goes well, we still need a place to hide."

"We cannot return to the forests in Canada," Elrand said. "It does not mean we cannot hide in other forests. There are more caves in this state than anywhere else in this country. I know of a place."

"We hide in a cave?" I asked.

Elrand nodded. "At the very least, it would buy us some time and provide shelter."

"What about Aelfrich?" Illarion asked. "We can't bring him with us to the protest."

"I agree," I said. "Dragging a hostage through a protest wouldn't be great optics."

"He's of no more use to us," I said. "We should execute him."

Layla turned and stared at me. "Caspar! That's not what you're about. It's not what *we're* about."

"What's the difference," Gronk said, "between executing a war criminal and slaying an elf in battle?"

"We're not murderers!" Layla shouted.

"It's not murder in war," I said. "It's just war."

"That's nonsense, and you know it," Layla said, shaking her head.

I sighed. "What choice do we have? The last thing we can

allow is for another powerful elven mage to get free. We've done damage to the legion. He was a leader among Brightborn's loyalists. If we freed him, it would embolden the legion."

Layla rolled her eyes. "I didn't say free him."

"So long as he's in our captivity," Gronk said, "we must devote resources to guarding him and ensuring he does not escape. We cannot afford to have any of our number wasted on guarding an elf who is no longer of use to us."

"Then we put it to a vote," I said. "All in favor of executing Aelfrich, raise your hand."

I looked around the room. Gronk raised his hand. Rina did, too. So did Illarion. I raised my hand as well.

"Those opposed?" I asked.

Only Layla and Brag'mok raised their hands.

"What about Jag and Elrand?" Layla asked.

"I have no opinion on the matter," Jag said.

"I am not here to make such decisions," Elrand added. "My role here is to provide counsel on matters pertaining to magic."

"It doesn't matter," Gronk said. "The leaders of each race voted in favor of execution. Those are the only votes that count."

I nodded. "Then it's decided. Aelfrich will be executed. The method should be decided by the resistance."

Illarion nodded. "We'll take care of it."

"Handle it quickly," I said. "Then prepare the rest to join the protest. Jag, when is this march supposed to start?"

"Within the hour," Jag said. "We have little time to spare."

CHAPTER FIFTEEN

I tried to put my arm around Layla as we left the farmhouse. She shrugged me off. "Babe, what is it?"

"You know what," Layla said. "This is wrong, Caspar."

I nodded. "I know. But there's nothing right about anything we've had to do lately."

Layla rolled her eyes. "At the very least, allow me to perform his last rites."

I shrugged. "What are the last rites?"

"Just a prayer," Layla said, "words that are said when an elf is dying. We can at least grant him that."

I snorted. "Fine. But make it quick."

Layla nodded and jogged over toward Illarion as he circled around the back of the farmhouse to the fields where the resistance was gathered. It was also where they held Aelfrich. She was right; this wasn't a good thing, no matter how it was justified. But Gronk also had a good point. We couldn't continue to devote any of our number to guarding him. We were at a numerical disadvantage, not only against Brightborn's legion but against the whole freaking world and their armies. The only alternative to executing the elf was to free him, and that would mean Brightborn gained a powerful sorcerer who'd been watching us for months. Aelfrich didn't know what we were planning, but he'd have information, even if it wasn't enough to make the difference in the war, that he could give to Brightborn. He could report on our abilities, our capacity to wield magic, he might even know something about our interests in the Canadian forest.

Bottom line, he had to be dealt with. We couldn't afford to keep guarding him. We couldn't afford to set him free. What other choice did we have?

The least I could do was allow Layla to perform the last rites that elves gave to their dying. At the end of the day, Aelfrich was a soldier, and he was loyal to his king. He was following orders. We were at odds because of this war. There were no two ways about it; he was dead. If it made Layla feel better about what had to be done, it was a small concession to grant.

While Illarion and Layla took care of Aelfrich, I sat down with Jag to go over the plans for the protest. They were meeting on the streets near St. Ensley's, the old church where the defunct elf gate cult used to meet. We'd renamed the place in honor of the former fairy king who'd died fending off the Unseelie court. Trixie had avenged his death eventually. It was also the church where I'd completed the trials that resulted in me mastering the five elements and absorbing the elemental spirits into my body...or spirit...or whatever part of me formed their current residence.

We hadn't done much at St. Ensley's in months. It was too risky. However, the place was still a monument to the popular opposition to the alliance between the US government and King Brightborn.

Since the building was sealed, I could easily portal us inside and meet the protesters on the church steps. According to Jag, Cecil was giving a speech before the march.

Cecil had brought his daughter to me when I was still a minister at Holy Cross. He'd asked me to heal her—she'd suffered from spina bifida and was bound to a chair. Against my better judgment at the time, I did it. Last I knew, Cecil's daughter was doing great. He was one of my most vocal supporters. Not just because I'd healed his daughter. Cecil genuinely believed in what we were doing. It would be good to see him again.

The plan for the march was fairly straightforward. They would go from St. Ensley's and march across downtown St. Louis to the Federal Court building. There, they'd have a rally and a few speeches before gathering again at the Arch. Why the Arch? Well, it wasn't the monument itself, the "Gateway to the West," that they were rallying to. It was the trees I'd grown there as a demonstration of what my power could do that they were gathering around.

At the time, the idea was to undermine Brightborn's idea for reversing global warming by showing that we could plant trees and grow them using my abilities. It would take a trillion trees to do it, but some scientists believed that if so many trees were planted, they would effectively counteract the effects of climate change by removing more carbon from the atmosphere than humans were creating. No one had ever taken tree planting as a solution to climate change seriously before because it takes time to grow trees, and a trillion trees are a lot to plant. Not to mention, to overtake the loss of trees from deforestation, which remained a problem all over the world, we'd probably need to plant even more than that.

Could I do it? Sure. It would take pretty much everything I had to make it happen, but it was possible. It wasn't a vain hope. It was a hope meant to offer an alternative to Brightborn's agenda. The government had since gone to great efforts to attack what I'd proposed. It was, however, something positive. Exactly the sort of thing Doris said I should be offering in order to rally support. So far, while the numbers of our supporters were waning as the propaganda against us put forward by the media swelled, the trees stood as a reminder that there was a solution, there *was* hope, and that people didn't have to turn over their freedoms to an otherworldly tyrant to realize it.

We had a plan. We were ready to go. But where the hell was Layla? How long could it possibly take to say a few prayers, or whatever the elven last rites entailed, and kill a guy?

I stepped out of the farmhouse and went around back to where Illarion and the elves were gathered. I found Illarion and Layla were standing just off the side from the rest of the elves, talking to one another.

As I approached, they looked at me and stopped talking. Illarion put his hand on Layla's shoulder. She looked at him. They both nodded.

"What is going on?" I asked. "Is Aelfrich dead?"

Layla bit her lip. "Not exactly."

"What do you mean, not exactly? How can someone be *not exactly* dead? He's either dead or he isn't!"

"We let him go," Illarion said.

"You what!"

"It was best," Layla said.

"But we voted!"

"I changed my vote," Illarion said. "So you no longer had the majority."

I sighed. "Why in the world did you let him go?"

Layla grabbed my hand. "This thirst for blood, or whatever the hell is going on with you...it's not *you*, Caspar."

"How am I supposed to know what is or isn't me?" I said. "If I'm doing it, it's me!"

Layla shook her head. "I know your heart. This isn't coming from your light. It's coming from your inner darkness."

I snorted. "Inner darkness?"

"Everyone has a darkness," Illarion said. "Even you."

"It's true," Layla said. "We all have dark thoughts, things we think but never act on. Ideas that terrify us, that come from a monstrous place we usually suppress."

"So you're saying I'm becoming a monster now?" I asked.

Layla shook her head. "I'm saying we all have a monster inside of us, deep down. The only way the darkness can come out is if the light isn't shining. Darkness can never overcome the light. You need to find your light again, Caspar. Before this…whatever it is that battle is bringing out of you takes over completely and you lose yourself in it."

I sighed. "We still shouldn't have let him go."

Layla shrugged. "He wasn't talking. That doesn't mean he doesn't know anything."

I raised one eyebrow. "What are you implying?"

"Trixie is following him," Layla said.

"He is going to lead us to Brightborn," Illarion said. "The fairy will tell us how we can find him."

I sighed as I scratched the back of my head. "I hate to admit it, but you're right. This probably was a better idea than an execution."

Layla smiled. "You think?"

I snorted. "If you want me to tell you that I was wrong and you were right, I said this was *probably* a better idea. We don't know for sure how it will pan out."

"I don't care if you tell me I was right," Layla said. "At the very least, this gives us a chance. A way to maybe end this without an all-out war with the entirety of humanity."

"Presuming, of course," Illarion added, "that Aelfrich knows where Brightborn is."

I nodded. "And that wherever he is, Trixie can take us there."

"The question is, Caspar, what are you going to do once we find him?" Layla asked.

I bit my lip. "If one man, one elf, has to die to prevent a war, then even if it costs me my soul, it's the price that will have to be paid."

CHAPTER SIXTEEN

Trixie was busy tracking Aelfrich and, by proxy, Brightborn. Hopefully. No matter. I could portal us into St. Ensley's. It was an old church, but there weren't any pews left in the place. The large atrium, what had once been a sanctuary, was where I'd faced off with each of the five elements.

There was plenty of space. I imagine, back when the church was a real church, it could have seated a thousand people. Like many older church buildings in St. Louis, the once-thriving congregation had dwindled into nonexistence. It was a trajectory that my own church, Holy Cross, was on. It was a mostly-white congregation in a neighborhood that was ninety percent black, and they didn't do anything to change, to engage the community around them. I'd tried to get them involved in a soup kitchen. A joint effort with a neighboring Methodist church. Not so that they could play the role of the community's "white saviors," but so that they could get to know people in the community, to spend time listening to their stories, engaging people from a different walk of life.

Still, it was an uphill battle. Despite my best efforts, the congregation was still duty-bound to following denominationally approved liturgies and singing old hymns that favored minor chords and lacked any discernible melody. Sure, the words were solid. The content of the songs was wonderful. Beautiful, even. But most of the people spent so much time figuring out the notes to sing that they didn't pay a lick of attention to the words.

It was counter-cultural even to members who grew up in our denomination. And they wondered why the local community didn't take any interest in our services. That is, until I healed Cecil's daughter.

My parishioners believed it was a miracle. Especially Doris. After all, I'd healed her of a stroke. I wasn't sure. It was this magic, this elemental stuff that I'd only started to be in tune with after I was stabbed by the Blade of Echoes, that had done it.

Where does the power of God come from, anyway? If God can work through any kind of power, even the power he wrote into the elements of his creation, why couldn't we call it a miracle? Regardless, my denomination tended to be skeptical. The officials had believed that what I was doing was demonic, not divine. I could have quoted scripture at them, citing the story of when the scribes and Pharisees accused Jesus of casting out demons in the name of Satan. How foolish would that be? A kingdom divided against itself cannot stand. Why would the devil cast out his own? Why would a devil inspire me to heal an old lady of faith from a stroke or a young girl of spina bifida? The former I'd healed out of desperation. I didn't even know what I was doing at the time. But the latter, Cecil's daughter, I'd healed out of compassion. Not because I wanted to spark a movement, a personality cult, and certainly not because I was in league with the devil. I had a way to help. I didn't understand it. But I could do it. So I did. How couldn't I? What does it mean that Jesus commanded us to love our neighbors if we aren't to use the gifts we've been given to do it?

All of that felt like it had happened a lifetime ago. Even St. Ensley's had a thin layer of dust over the surface of everything. Not that I was inclined to play the maid.

I ushered everyone to the perimeters of the room as first the drow, then the other elves next, finally the giants entered the portal. We had to clear the opening of the portal to make room for everyone else. Otherwise, we'd end up with a multi-body pile-up. More people than football players fighting for a fumble. Less entertaining than a game of Twister gone awry. Since the giants were coming through last, well, if we didn't clear the area, it would become a crushing situation. Next time we did this, I'd have to rethink our order. Big dudes first. Dainty drow and elves last.

Only Agnus and Clarence didn't come. Agnus could have, but he wasn't thrilled by the idea of giving up the best time of the morning when the sun poured through the window of the bedroom of the farmhouse. I called it sunbathing. Agnus called it basking in his glory and illuminating his divinity. According to him, you haven't lived until you've licked your junk under the warm light of the morning sun.

That was something I was determined to simply take his word for. No matter how much yoga I attempted, I'd never be able to pull it off, regardless. Not that I *wanted* to pull it off. But you know what I mean.

I could hear the crowds gathering outside. Cecil's voice echoed over all of the rest. It sounded like he was speaking through a megaphone. I couldn't make out a word he was saying. It's hard to make sense of anything that someone says through a megaphone. But I could detect the tone of his voice. He was rallying the crowd, and they were cheering as he spoke. Why? Because whatever he was saying, it sounded like people should be cheering in response. Honestly, he could have been shouting, "You should wipe back to front rather than front to back!" and the people probably would have screamed in enthusiastic affirmation of what he was saying, although his advice would be bad.

I'm sure that's not what he was shouting. He was probably talking about the evils of the government's alliance with Brightborn. How they were all that stood between the freedoms that America's forefathers fought for and tyranny. All true, of course. But it was nothing new, no actionable intelligence. Just rally cries meant to fire people up.

I suppose such speeches had their purpose. I'd given a few of them, myself, in the form of sermons. Sometimes people just need a little enthusiasm, a jolt of energy to reinvigorate their passions.

It sounded like Cecil was doing a good job. Little did he know that I was about to step through the doors right behind him.

"You ready to do this?" Layla asked, smiling slyly from the corner of her mouth.

I nodded. "Absolutely."

I pressed the bar that opened the door to St. Ensley's from the inside and stepped out onto the church's front steps. The crowd erupted in cheers. I wasn't sure how many there were. I guessed that the estimate Jag had given me was short.

Cecil scratched his head. He didn't realize I'd appeared behind him.

I rested my hand on his shoulder. He jumped. I laughed.

When he turned, his eyes went wide, and he embraced me. "You're here!"

I nodded. "I am. I thought our movement could use a little juice."

Cecil offered me the microphone. I declined it. I didn't have much to say. What could I say that he didn't? I did see a man in a wheelchair toward the front of the crowd gathered at the steps of St. Ensley's. He was dressed in camouflage and wrapped in an American flag.

I approached him. "Thank you for your service."

The man nodded. "Thank you."

"How were you hurt?" I asked.

"In Afghanistan. Took a bullet to the spine."

I placed my hand on the man's shoulder. I visualized his spinal cord full, complete, and functional as I channeled aether, the power of life, into his body. The man started wiggling his feet as tears fell from his eyes.

"Oh, my God. Thank you, Caspar!"

I smiled. "You'll need physical therapy to regain the strength in your legs."

The veteran nodded, wiping his eyes with his sleeve.

"A miracle!" Cecil shouted.

The people cheered. I doubted most of the crowd had seen what I did. I hadn't done it for any reason other than that I could. Call it compassion. I was just doing the next right thing. There was a man in need, and I was the only one who could help him. As I looked around, dozens of phones were all pointed at me. People would see what happened, and since some of those phones were probably live-streaming, it would only be a matter of moments before the government knew I was there.

Before Brightborn knew I was there.

It didn't frighten me for my sake. I was afraid of what would happen to these people. The crowd of good freedom-loving Saint Louisans and people who had traveled from elsewhere to support the march.

I decided to push the veteran in his chair. He wouldn't need it for much longer. But for now, until he built some muscle, he would.

"What's your name?" I asked.

"James," the man said. "I am honored."

I shook my head. "The honor is mine. You literally give your legs for our freedom. It is I who should be thanking you."

James nodded. "Still. Thank you."

I smiled as I pushed him in his chair. Layla walked behind me.

Then, the drow and the elf resistance, along with the giants, all gathered around. The giants moved to form the perimeter. If we were attacked, be it by Brightborn, the military, or even the police, they'd stand between the crowd and the authorities. I didn't know what was planned by the opposition, but I did know that shy of sniping us from one of the tall buildings around us or bombing us outright, which I couldn't imagine they'd do with so many good people marching through the streets, it would take some serious balls for anyone, riot police or soldier, to assault a giant.

As we marched down the street, things mostly remained peaceful. There were some police cars parked along the route, their lights flashing but their sirens silent.

None of them made a move to try and arrest me or anyone else. I was reasonably certain that if the government thought they could snatch me, they would. Still, perhaps they weren't trying anything because they feared stoking the fury of the crowd. So far, everyone was protesting peacefully. If anyone tried to attack us or arrest me, things could get nasty quickly. If the protest turned violent, that would only give our movement more attention. Our march would be featured on the national news. The last thing the government wanted was the optics of the police, or the military, attacking citizens who were simply exercising their right to protest, their freedom of speech.

Still, I was ready for anything. I had both my blades at my side. Layla and the other elves were armed with their bows, and their quivers were full. The giants carried their broadswords and axes—depending on each giant's preference. Again, marching with weapons might give the impression that the movement wasn't peaceable. But we wouldn't be the first ones to raise our weapons. We'd fight if we had to. If we needed to protect the people.

I glanced around and read the signs people were carrying. Some of them were rather clever.

Brightborn is the Black Death!

Freedom over Fear!

Caspar Heals. Brightborn Squeals.

Other signs weren't quite so positive, and I didn't agree with their messages.

Elves go home. Talk about xenophobia...

Humanity First! Not a message that would go far in terms of uniting the peoples.

It struck me that if anyone was to blame for these misguided messages, it was me. As Doris had told me, I'd focused most of my messages on the evils of Brightborn, the atrocities he'd committed on New Albion, what I believed he intended to do on earth as a tyrant. When you give people a message like that, even if it's true and the fear of what Brightborn intended to do was legitimate, people will respond in kind. Their signs, their protests, reflected a fear that I'd stoked.

Who was I to blame them for their misguided enthusiasm? Aside from my demonstration with the trees, before, I hadn't given them much of a positive, unifying message. Even if I had, would it have resonated?

Another sign disturbed me further: *Hosanna!*

It was what the Jews in Jerusalem had shouted when Jesus entered the city at the beginning of his passion week. When he came riding on a donkey, an image that reflected in part how Judas Maccabees had entered Jerusalem when he'd helped the people thwart the Seleucid king, Antiochus Epiphanes. Only, when Judas Maccabees entered the city, he'd come riding a war steed. Jesus, by contrast, rode a beast of burden. He'd had a different message, a different mission. He hadn't come to save the people from the Roman occupation. He'd come with a message of peace. In the end, he hadn't done what they'd hoped. He came to usher in a different kind of Kingdom, and the same people who shouted "Hosanna" in just a week would be shouting "Crucify him!"

Then again, I was no Christ. I was no Messiah. These people wanted me to save them from Brightborn, to rise against the elven king. So far, I'd played right into their narrative. I wasn't just mistaken. Unlike Jesus, who knew what he was about when he entered Jerusalem, I didn't have a clue what I was doing. A part of me had relished in the notion that I could lead an army, that I could fight back and slaughter Brightborn's legionaries. I'd tasted the thrill of battle. It tempted me. I liked the flavor. I wanted *more* even as a part of me opposed the very thing I desired.

I was hardly a blameless prophet. If they viewed me as a Christ-like figure, I feared I was the opposite. Was I closer to the embodiment of Antichrist than Christ? It was Brightborn who was promising false salvation.

Mingan had charged me to usher in a new order, something based on Annwn or Eden. I didn't have a clue how I was supposed to do that. More, what these people wanted wasn't a new order, a new peace. They just wanted their America back. They wanted the status quo. They wanted freedom absent of Brightborn's impending tyranny.

Certainly, that was preferable to Brightborn's vision for a one-world government. But there was a reason why Brightborn struck a chord with most of the world's leaders and many of the world's citizens. There were problems with the status quo world. There were issues, like climate change, that we as a race were failing to address. There were ongoing religious wars, senseless travesties like human trafficking and oppressive regimes.

All these things were only enabled by a world where the world's governments viewed one another as competitors, as antagonists. Hunger and poverty remained pervasive problems. Much of the world didn't even have clean drinking water. In our country, we were blind to much of it. We knew, in the back of our minds, about the suffering that went on elsewhere in the world.

But you know, out of sight, out of mind. So long as we had food on our plates, opportunities for work, shelter over our heads, and water in our pipes, we were mostly complacent.

Brightborn offered something different. Was it better? Certainly not. However, when the existing systems are failing, when suffering and oppression remain pervasive, people are willing to try anything other than what isn't working.

That was Brightborn's appeal. If all I offered was resistance, a movement to fight Brightborn, then I'd be nothing more than a knight for the old world, the way we've always done things, enforcing the broken systems of the past and present. I had to offer them something more. Something better.

Doris was right. Mingan was right, too. He'd told me what I needed to do but died before he could tell me how to accomplish it. What he told me was as useless as telling someone to go achieve world peace. Desirable, yes. But many people had visions of world peace without any realistic way to achieve it.

In truth, I couldn't promise the people a damned thing. Not unless I knew how to bring about the better future I wanted to initiate. So, I marched with the rest like a lemming, following the rest even as they imagined they were following me. Only while they cheered with exuberance, my heart was sinking into my bowels.

I felt like a fraud because in my mind, I *was* a fraud. Chosen one. Of what? An elven prophecy meant to unite the races, to unite and save the world? I was a man of faith. If I told Layla about my doubts, she'd tell me to trust the prophecy. Well, now my faith was waning. All I knew to do was fight. Fight against Brightborn.

But fight *for* what?

The protest reached the federal building. Cecil had more words, more platitudes shouted through his megaphone. Again, he tried to get me to speak. But I had nothing to say. So I declined. If you don't have something good to say, don't say anything at all. That was what I was taught as a kid in grade school. The same lesson applied now. Until I had something certain, a clear vision for what the world could become, I couldn't continue pouring fuel on the fire of these protests. So, I went through the motions. What else could I do?

CHAPTER SEVENTEEN

The crowd moved on from the federal building to the grounds surrounding the Arch. It was a spacious area. I remembered, back in 2008, attending a rally there for Barack Obama when he was running for President the first time. People had gathered there with their signs about change and their hearts full of hope. Whether he delivered on that or not was beside the point. The fact is that he had a message that resonated. Something different, something that people rallied behind. People were sick of how the government had operated before. He promised change they could believe in. I needed more than that. I knew, from my time in the ministry, that change for change's sake wasn't always beneficial.

While our rally wasn't as large as the crowd I remembered from 2008, we might have been the largest group who had gathered there since. But these people weren't looking for a change. They were looking to prevent it. At least that was the case until I could come up with something better, an alternative to the status quo, that would win them over. How was I supposed to convince them that I was going to bring the magic of some otherworld to Earth?

That I'd met an elf from centuries gone by, who'd returned from the dead and used to conduct druidic rituals in the Canadian forests? I doubted they'd find that message particularly persuasive. Hell, I didn't fully embrace it either, if only because I didn't have the slightest clue what it all meant.

I'd avoided speaking at St. Ensley's. I'd healed James, instead. I declined to speak at the federal building. How was I going to get out of making a speech a third time?

I wasn't. I had no idea what I'd say when Cecil handed me his megaphone. What could I say? I was standing in front of the oversized tree I'd sprouted and grown in minutes.

"Tell me, what did you come out today to see?" I asked, raising my voice through the microphone. "I recognize that most of you didn't expect me to come at all. Now that I am here, what is it you hope for?"

The crowd didn't respond. Perhaps they assumed I was asking a rhetorical question. Or, maybe, no one knew the answer. "We all agree," I continued, "that Brightborn must be stopped. But we have to ask ourselves, why is it that he has such influence at all? What ailment does our world suffer from that our leaders would be so ready to cede their authority to this otherworldly king?"

People were still listening intently. I wasn't sure if it was because they were considering my words or if they were confused.

"Today, we protest the President's alliance with King Brightborn. We are right to oppose it. We must make our voices heard. But it is not enough that we protest what our government does. We must also speak up against what our government has failed to do for years. We must speak out, and we must repent. For we've all had a part to play in the world we've made, a world ripe for this kind of exploitation.

"Today, we gather here, and we cheer those who would agree with us that the alliance with Brightborn must be broken. But we must also pause in somber reflection. We cannot go back to the way things were before. We need to do better."

"Caspar for President!" an unidentified man, somewhere in the crowd, shouted. Before I could respond, Jack, the veteran I healed, repeated the man's words. Before I knew it, the whole crowd had erupted into the chant, "Caspar for President, Caspar for President."

"I'm not a politician! I have no desire to be President!" I shouted through the megaphone. But my words fell on deaf ears. The chants were too loud. I might as well have been screaming into a vacuum.

The current President was two years into his second term. It was the season when people started announcing their candidacies. Perhaps they were just caught up in the spirit of the times. The problem, apart from my unwillingness to run for political office, was that even if I did stand and won, it would be too late. Brightborn wouldn't need two years to establish himself as the self-proclaimed emperor of Earth.

This wasn't a problem that could be solved through conventional politics. Still, I suppose, it wouldn't be the first time that folks had looked for a savior on Capital Hill. Why is it that people think politicians are the ones who will make the world a better place? They won't. They can't. Not really. They can do good things, of course, but bettering the world starts with individuals. Not political leaders. A better tomorrow isn't secured by a President. It's forged by the people. It can't be accomplished through policy positions and grand gestures.

The world changes when one person extends a kind hand to someone else, when someone places the needs of others above their own. *Real* change happens when we accept every liberty, every good thing, with gratitude rather than a sense of entitlement. When we exercise our freedoms not to do whatever the hell we want, just because we want it, but to make the world better for everyone.

I looked over the crowd as they repeated their misguided chant. Something in my ear started to ring. The power of aether welled up within me. The sound of the chants slowed, the tone of the concert of voices deeper. Everything around me appeared to move in slow motion.

There was a bang. It sounded like thunder.

A bullet moved through the air; it was targeted at my head. Everything had slowed down so much that I was able to step aside and avoid the sniper's attempt at assassination.

But the moment I moved out of the way, the world returned to its regular speed.

Everyone screamed.

I turned around.

The bullet had hit Cecil in the middle of his chest.

I ran to him and pressed my hand to his chest. I visualized his wound healing, but the bullet, when it struck, had stopped his heart. I couldn't help him. I couldn't heal him.

He was dead.

CHAPTER EIGHTEEN

I didn't know how I'd done it. It was as if aether itself, the elemental spirit within me, had taken over and either slowed down the whole world around me or given me such speed that time slowed. Whatever the case, someone had tried to kill me. They had killed my friend instead.

I gathered aether and air and took off into the sky. I flew like a missile toward the top of one of the buildings that stood in the distance, the place where the sniper was perched. I knew he was there. I saw it all happen.

I screamed as I flew toward him. I gripped my blades as I charged the sniper, dressed in all black, and I plunged my second blade into his body. With rage, I gripped the hilt of my second blade and twisted it in the sniper's chest.

I returned Aerin's blade to its sheath on the left-hand side of my waist. I reached down and removed the ski mask that the sniper was wearing.

It wasn't an elf. It was a man. A soldier, most likely. I looked into the sky and screamed. I took off again and flew straight toward the federal building. Gathering fire, I released a torrent of flames at the building and engulfed the whole thing in an inferno, a pillar of fire that stretched from the ground all the way to the clouds.

It took all the energy I had. The world started to spin around me. I lowered myself to the ground.

My knees buckled beneath my body, and I collapsed as everything went black.

Wake up, Caspar, Aerin said, her voice piercing the darkness.

I opened my eyes. I could barely move. I could hardly lift my head. I saw Layla standing over me. She fired an arrow, then another one. I clenched my fists, trying to muster a little energy. I heard gunfire—rapid-fire, like machine guns.

I turned my head. The giants had their weapons drawn. They swung their blades and axes at the soldiers who came after them. The giants' skin was so thick the bullets were bouncing off them. Nevertheless, they screamed in pain as they were hit. The bullets had to hurt like hell even if they didn't pierce their hides.

The drow were running around, using the giants as shields as they cut down the soldiers. Two drow who had taken bullets lay in pools of their own blood.

I struggled to process the carnage. "What's happened? How did this…"

Layla saw that I was awake and knelt next to me. "The military was waiting. They were ready for a fight. We're holding our own, barely."

"I need to get back into the sky," I said.

"You can't," Layla said. "You don't have the energy."

I grunted as I struggled to get to my feet. I looked around and saw bodies everywhere. Protesters, fallen beside their makeshift signs. A few of the elves, the members of the resistance, had fallen, too.

"We can't fight them off like this," I said.

"I agree," Layla said. "But when you were out, we couldn't portal out of here. Not with Trixie gone."

I nodded. "I can cast a fairy gate. It's a different kind of magic. It doesn't take the same energy. But we need to get everyone close."

Layla nodded. "Everyone on Caspar!" she shouted.

The giants backpedaled, shielding the drow and elves who were fighting beside them. We didn't have the numbers to win. Not without the full use of my abilities. If only I hadn't wasted all my power on burning down that damned building.

I hadn't even thought about how many people might be inside. Not just soldiers. Probably very few of them were military. Good people. Workers who did nothing wrong. People who had government jobs but didn't have a thing to do with the President or his decision to align with Brightborn.

My stomach churned. "My God, what have I done?"

"We'll talk about that later," Layla said. "Right now, you have to get us out of here!"

I nodded. I formed a fairy portal and connected it back to the junkyard ranch. We wouldn't be safe there. We needed the caves that Elrand had talked about before. Lord, I could only pray he hadn't been killed in the battle.

I pulled the portal down over all of us. The hard pavement beneath my body became soft ground, covered in grass.

I looked around. I saw Elrand, sitting cross-legged in the grass. I sighed in relief. With his unique abilities and knowledge, he was an asset we couldn't afford to lose. I looked around. Jag was still alive, although he had a gash on his right arm. I walked over to him, pressed my hand to his wound, and healed him.

"I'm sorry, Jag."

Jag frowned. "You're sorry? Why? You just healed me. I should be saying thank you."

I shook my head. "I mean for doing what I did. If I hadn't attacked that building…"

Jag looked at me dumbly. "They tried to assassinate you. They killed Cecil. They were already waiting for a full-scale assault. They would have attacked the second after they took you out. When you'd no longer be a threat."

"Still, there were likely innocent people in that building."

Jag nodded. "Some people got out alive. The building was made of stone. The flames didn't catch inside right away."

I nodded. "Some people, but not everyone."

"No. Not everyone," Jag said.

"And that's my fault."

I heard a snort behind me as Brag'mok approached, picking a bullet out of the skin on his right shoulder. "Damn bullets. The things really sting."

"You're comparing getting shot to a bee sting?" I asked, raising an eyebrow.

Brag'mok shrugged. "Not what I meant. But I imagine it's similar to what you'd experience. Bees and wasps can't sting us at all."

"I'm glad you're all right."

"We were expecting a fight," Brag'mok said. "That's why we were here."

I sighed. "Yeah, but this one could have been avoided."

"Maybe not," Brag'mok said. "They were trying to remove you from the battle before they attacked."

"See," Jag said. "That's what I just said. He thinks it's his fault for blasting that building with flames."

Brag'mok placed his massive hand on my shoulder, engulfing half my chest and back with his palm. "If you hadn't done that, the rest of the army might not have attacked. When the sniper failed, they would have likely retreated to regroup. When you attacked, they saw you were out of commission, and that's when they showed themselves."

I sighed. "I still put you all in danger, and not all of our side made it."

"Such are the costs of war," Brag'mok said. "Though I suspect for one such as you, who has not grown up in a war-torn world, such losses are more shocking."

"Without my full strength, they had an advantage," I said.

"Which is why they proceeded with the assault," Brag'mok said. "But you came to just in time. Now we know what they were planning. I suspect they'll attempt the same thing again. Take you out first, then wipe out the rest of us."

"How many people died out there?" I asked.

Brag'mok shrugged. "I don't know yet."

"We lost about a dozen," Jag said. "Two drow, the rest belonged to the elven resistance."

"Too many," I said. "How many of the protesters were caught in the crossfire?"

Jag's head fell. "A lot. Too many to count."

I clenched my fists. "They're going to frame this whole thing as if I was the terrorist since I attacked that building."

"I doubt the news outlets will mention that they tried to kill you first," Jag agreed. "I suspect they won't even mention Cecil's death. They'll lump him in with the rest. All the people caught in the crossfire when the noble military came to rescue them from you."

I snorted. "Sounds about right. I'm sure that's how they'll try to spin this."

CHAPTER NINETEEN

We couldn't stay at the junkyard ranch. Elrand knew of an uncharted cave somewhere near to the hut and stone circle where he'd lived in exile back when I first met him. The problem was that Trixie wasn't here. The other fairies didn't hang out near us without her around, so the only way we could go there was the old-fashioned way. At least the first time. After that, I could create portals to bring everyone with us.

This would be the third place I'd relocated us to in as many days. I doubted it would be our last. I *hoped* it wouldn't be. The only way we'd end up staying there indefinitely was if we lost the war, if Brightborn became somehow invulnerable, or if we never found him.

If Aelfrich knew where he was, we'd find out. Fairies can make themselves practically invisible. Trixie could hover a couple of feet from the elf and he'd never know it.

The giants helped me clear the debris off my Mitsubishi Eclipse. I'd left it at the junkyard ranch when we'd fled to the Canadian forests. It wasn't hard to hide a car in a junkyard. First, we'd covered it with a tarp to prevent the paint from getting scratched. Then, we'd piled various items all around and over the car to obscure it from view. Unless a scavenger decided to go digging through our piles of trash, the chances of anyone finding my car were slim to none.

I'd hidden the keys under the floorboards in the farmhouse. They were right where I left them, beneath a loose board in the corner of my bedroom. I don't know why I worried they'd be gone. Aside from the mice, there weren't many creatures with enough strength to move my keys that could get in there. I was more worried that the car wouldn't start. It had been a few months. Sometimes when a car isn't used in a while, the battery loses its charge.

After the giants uncovered the car and I removed the protective tarp to examine the car and ensure it wasn't damaged, I climbed in, inserted the key into the ignition, and fired it right up.

If that hadn't worked, we would have had to teleport to Elrand's old place. From there, he said the cave was a half day's hike. Too much time, given that the rest of the camp was vulnerable with me gone. It wouldn't take long before someone came looking. Sure, the place was veiled by fairy magic. But since there was a distinct possibility Brightborn and company knew we were there, we couldn't guarantee that the junkyard ranch would remain hidden long enough for me to get everyone out of there.

We had some time. A military fly-over wouldn't cut it. But it wouldn't take long before boots on the ground made their way to the junkyard. Unless they just decided to bomb the place for good measure. Since Missouri was home to Whiteman Airforce Base, where they kept the B2 Stealth Bombers, they could easily obliterate the junkyard if they wanted to.

Of course, there were people who lived in the vicinity—albeit a mile or two away. Despite our efforts to make sure Brightborn found out where we had gone, I doubted they'd bomb us without concrete intelligence to indicate that we were there.

We didn't have to get to the cave itself. I'd take Elrand's word that it would provide suitable shelter for a group of our size. We just needed to get to a place where I could teleport everyone. Worst case scenario, if the junkyard came under attack, Jag would call or text. We'd pull over, and I'd teleport to the ranch. I hadn't recovered enough energy yet to fight, but I could at least teleport them to the side of the highway and buy us some time. Ideally, though, we'd find a spot within a reasonable walking distance from the cave. A place under the cover of trees to reduce the likelihood that anyone would see us and report our location to the authorities.

I was also banking on the hope that my burner phone hadn't been identified by the government. I was careful not to access any of my accounts through it. All I used it for was communicating with Jag and Layla, who had burner phones of their own. The only thing we'd done with the phones that might be at all traceable was using them to upload our broadcasts to the resistance. Jag insisted that he'd sufficiently hidden the IP addresses and bounced our signal around the globe so that they wouldn't be able to trace the origin. I had to trust him on that account.

Somehow the elves had found us in Canada, but since we didn't have cell service there, I was pretty sure the phones weren't to blame for betraying our location. It was more likely that Brightborn had focused his search for us on the ley lines and located us in the forest. It had taken him a few months to track us down, after all.

Elrand and I took off down the Interstate. We weren't on the highway for long before we took smaller single-lane state highways. I used cruise control to stay near the speed limit. My car wasn't all that unique, but it was likely that since the car was registered in my name that the authorities would pay attention to any white Eclipse that matched the 2010 body style. Still, I didn't want to draw any extra attention to us, and even a regular traffic stop could give us up.

Thankfully, we didn't see any police on the drive. The roads we were traveling were so remote that I doubted we would. Still, I continually scanned the sides of the road, looking for any patrol vehicles that might be keen to investigate if they spotted my car —or any car like mine.

Elrand had me turn left on another asphalt paved road. No cops. A lot of deer and several squished armadillos populated the roadside. Armadillos used to be rare in Missouri. However, over the last couple of decades, they'd become so numerous that they'd become quite the nuisance. Most of the ones I saw were probably hit by farm trucks intentionally.

We turned right down a gravel road. By the looks of it, the county hadn't graded the road in some time. The middle of the road was covered in weeds. My car barely sat high enough to make it without bottoming out. Had I thought about it, and we'd had the time to siphon the gas from my Eclipse, we could have taken the truck that Jag had repaired. Of course, there was no guarantee that the old truck would survive the trip. The last thing we needed was a breakdown on the side of the road.

"There's an old barn up ahead," Elrand said. "Hasn't been used in years. You can hide the car there."

I nodded as I saw the barn, around a hundred feet or so off the side of the road. The drive leading to the barn was in even worse shape. I winced as I heard overgrown weeds and twigs scratching the sides of my car as I drove toward the barn and pulled into a small opening on the side that faced away from the road.

The whole place smelled like rotted wood and mildew. If it didn't look like the barn was a hundred years old and had been in disrepair for some time, I would have been afraid that it might fall down on top of us. "How far is the cave from here?"

Elrand pointed across a field to a tree line. "There's a trail over there that we can follow. It's probably a thirty-minute hike at a brisk pace."

I nodded. "This will do. I don't think anyone will find us out here."

Elrand nodded. "I'll wait here. I'd suggest not teleporting everyone into the barn. Those giants have heavy feet."

I chuckled. "Yeah, they do. I don't know how that thing is still standing, but it looks like it's weathered more than a few storms over the years."

I formed a fairy portal, envisioning a space in the bedroom of the farmhouse. It wasn't likely anyone would be standing where I emerged.

Agnus was the only one in the room, and thankfully, he wasn't where I appeared. Otherwise, I'd have inadvertently merged my body with his. I'd endured my fair share of "Casper the Friendly Ghost" jokes growing up, even though the cartoon character and I spelled our names differently. Caspar the Cat, though, wasn't a moniker I was eager to earn. Presuming, of course, that merging our bodies didn't kill us both instantly. That was more likely than the prospect that we'd become a single hybrid man-cat if I teleported into him.

"You ready to go?" I asked.

Agnus looked at me and narrowed his eyes. "Go where?"

"We aren't safe here. We're moving into a cave in the Ozarks."

Agnus huffed. "A cave? Seriously? We've moved from a city apartment to a junkyard to a camp in the forest, back to the junkyard, and now to a cave?"

I shrugged. "Yeah, I realize we aren't exactly moving up in the world."

"I think you might be reverting to Neanderthal."

"If we're really devolving, well, maybe you'll emerge as a Saber-Toothed tiger eventually," I said.

"Don't be dumb, Caspar. I'm a common tabby. I highly doubt I evolved from a Saber-Tooth."

I laughed. "You never know."

Agnus followed me out of the room. I found Layla, Clarence

at her side, gathered with the surviving elves and drow. The giants were huddled together about twenty feet away, picking at the bullets at each other's backs like gorillas harvesting bugs from each other's fur.

"We found the cave," I said. "Is everyone ready?"

A cave? Clarence asked. *I love caves!*

"You would," Agnus piped up.

Clarence growled a little.

"Well, at least some of us are looking forward to our new living arrangements," I said.

Agnus pawed at my leg. "Don't forget the litter."

I nodded. "Let's get everyone there first. Then I'll send our stash of supplies."

"I'll gather everyone together," Layla said before grabbing my hand. "How are you doing?"

I sighed. "I've been better. Honestly, the anger that overcame me when they killed Cecil... It scared me."

Layla nodded. "I bet. But you didn't kill him. You didn't launch the military assault against us. They were planning that before you burned the hell out of that building."

I nodded. "I know. Still, people died in that fire."

"War sucks," Layla said. "No matter what, there is always collateral damage."

I bit my lip. "There wasn't any reason to attack that building. It was pure passion fueled by fury. I'm sure that they already have images of that building in flames broadcasting on all the news networks."

Layla nodded. "Don't worry about that. If Trixie finds my father, we can hopefully avoid any more battles like that."

"I hope you're right," I said.

Three military helicopters were flying overhead. They couldn't see us through the veil Trixie had cast, but they were coming. I didn't waste any time. I cast a portal. Everyone went through it. I dispelled the portal and cast another one over our supplies. I portaled them into the old barn where my car was parked. Then, I jumped through the portal.

CHAPTER TWENTY

The supplies were safe in the barn. We'd have to come back for them later. Depending on the cave and how much space we had, I could teleport them there once I had a good image of it in my mind's eye that I could use to connect a fairy portal to.

Elrand led us down the trail that would take us to the cave. The trail was small. We had to go single-file. I laughed a little as the giants, who were right behind me, Layla, and Elrand, grunted as they had to duck under branches, breaking some of them off with their axes and swords as they did their best to clear enough of a path to make it through.

Jag walked with Rina and the drow. They'd been involved romantically for several months. It was an odd relationship. Jag was what you'd call a man's man. Rina, like the other drow, believed in and practiced female supremacy. How their romance worked was an enigma I hadn't quite figured out. Still, Rina was hot. Jag was clearly into her—obsessively, so. Despite his masculine pride, she had him wrapped around her little finger.

Who was I to judge? I had been married to Aerin in addition to being married to Layla. I rejected polygamy on principle but had briefly been a part of a polygamist marriage. I suppose in times such as these, a lot of conventions are thrown out the window. We were all finding our way in this new world, one where giants were now allied with their former enemies and the drow were now following the lead of one they'd exiled as he led us down a trail so we could all live together, or at least camp together, in a cave.

The path we were taking traversed several steep hills. There is a reason why the Ozark mountains are still classified as mountains despite being dwarfed by comparison to the Rocky or Appalachian mountains. Sure, hiking our way to Pike's Peak might have been a more rigorous climb, but that didn't mean this was easy, especially since I was still exhausted. I'd recovered enough energy on the drive that I could make it, but just barely.

We approached a small hole in the side of the hills that was surrounded by rock.

"You can't be serious," Gronk grunted. "You expect us to fit through there?"

Elrand shrugged. "I imagine you can make it on your hands and knees."

I chuckled. It was going to be a difficult trek into the cavern, even for me. I'd have to hunch over to avoid banging my head on the top of it. The giants were going to be miserable. I could only hope that none of them suffered from claustrophobia.

"Think you could spare a little fire?" Elrand asked. "To illuminate the cavern?"

I nodded. "A small flame shouldn't take much energy."

I connected my will to the element of fire and formed a small ball of flames over my hand. With so many of us crawling through the opening to the cave, I'd have to find a place inside where I could stand to keep the place lit. I was glad I managed to produce enough light. Without it, I probably would have bonked my noggin against the rocks more than once.

The crevice leading into the cave was smooth and slick with compressed mud and wet rock. Elrand was right, though. Despite the small opening to the cave, once we made it through about twenty feet of a small tunnel, the whole place opened up into a massive cavern.

I wasn't going to be able to keep my fire burning indefinitely. We'd have to build some fires inside to see.

One step at a time. Literally. Otherwise, I was likely to slip and fall.

Once Elrand and I were inside, I had to go back to help everyone else make their way through the entrance.

"The caves are larger beyond this cavern," Elrand said as we stood in the opening. "There are several corridors off this cavern that lead to miles of interconnected caves."

I nodded. "Very cool. Who would have thought something like this even existed here?"

"In any other state, this cave would probably be a tourist attraction," Elrand said. "In Missouri, where caves like this are a dime a dozen, hardly anyone knows this place exists."

"Good for us," I said. I squatted and shone my light through the small cave. The giants came through on their hands and knees. They were muttering curse words I'd never heard. From their tone, they were probably comparable to "shit" and "fuck."

Layla had Agnus in her arms as she came through behind the giants. The look on Agnus' face was unforgettable. His eyes were wide, and his ears lay flat against his skull. He wasn't a happy camper, but at least as a cat, he could see in the dark better than most of us. That wouldn't prevent him from bitching about it once he got over the shock of the experience.

Until I'd sufficiently lit the cavern, I wasn't about to risk attempting any fairy portals to bring people in or out of the cave. The last thing I wanted to do was portal someone into a wall or, worse, down a deep hole.

It wasn't the first time I'd camped in a cave. Back when I was a boy scout, we used to have a yearly campout in a cave that wasn't too different than this one. Since we went camping twelve months out of the year, we usually reserved the cave trip for one of the hotter months of the year when a steady seventy-degree temperature inside the cave would give us refuge from the scorching summer heat. Like this cave, that one also had a network of tunnels that we often explored. Back then, though, we wore helmets and carried flashlights. Now, we had neither but needed both.

There was a lot we needed that we didn't have. The supplies we'd purchased before were meant for surviving in a forest, not a cave. Still, it was all we had. After what we'd been through in the city, we couldn't afford another supply run. Not with images of me destroying a federal building airing on every news network nationwide.

I'd easily be able to teleport between the cave and the barn. Bring in supplies wouldn't be a problem. Getting everything else we needed was another matter altogether. Helmets were out of the question. We'd just have to endure a few goose eggs on our noggins. What we really needed was firewood. We didn't want to smoke ourselves out, either. The cave was spacious enough that it shouldn't be a huge issue. If it came to it, I could invoke the element of air to clear it out.

I decided to take Brag'mok with me to gather wood, if for no other reason than that he could hold a lot more than I could. That meant fewer fairy portal trips back and forth.

Brag'mok and I trekked through the woods, gathering all the deadfall we could find. He held his arms out, and I loaded him up.

"So, what's the plan?" Brag'mok asked.

"I don't know," I said. "Hope Trixie comes back with some information on Brightborn's location, I suppose."

"What if Aelfrich doesn't lead her to him? What then?"

I sighed. "Then we'll have no choice but to fight. Eventually."

"We can't fight the whole world, Caspar. Today's events proved that."

"I know," I said. "I fear I just made things a lot worse."

"If we fight, we have to attack first."

I nodded. "We'll have to strike hard. Use every power at my disposal to set any battle to our advantage."

"You're right, you know," Brag'mok said. "If we can get to Brightborn and take him out, we'll win the war. At least we'll achieve what we're setting out to accomplish."

I grabbed a broken tree limb and heaved it into Brag'mok's waiting arms. "But after that, you realize, there's no going back for me."

"Going back to what?" Brag'mok asked.

"My life," I said. "No matter what happens, I'll still be remembered as the one who burned down that building. If they arrest me, imprison me, even give me the death penalty. Well, I'll deserve it."

"You can't let that happen," Brag'mok said. "You realize that Layla will die too if they execute you."

I grunted. "I know. Which means my only chance to save her will be to live my life on the run."

"You restored magic to New Albion before," Brag'mok said. "You could do it again. You could leave Earth behind if push came to shove."

I sighed. "Yeah, maybe. But I still feel like I'm supposed to do more than just defeat Brightborn. There has to be more to all this. The prophecy. What Mingan said before he was killed. If I have to leave Earth, I need to leave the world a better place than it was before."

"Without Brightborn, it will be a better place," Brag'mok said.

I shook my head. "It has to be better than it was before anyone even knew elves existed. Brightborn is right about one thing. Humanity is a broken race. We've treated our planet with disdain. We've waged senseless wars. I have to wonder how much better will the world be when Brightborn is gone if humanity is left to go on as before."

"Just because Brightborn is right in part about humanity, it doesn't follow that he's right about the cure," Brag'mok said.

I nodded. "Maybe he can do what he promised. What if he does unite the world, save it from the trajectory of destruction? Would it be better to live in a restored world under tyranny or in a dying world with liberty?"

"You aren't suggesting that we should roll over and let Brightborn take over, are you?" Brag'mok asked.

I took a deep breath as I gathered a few more sticks. "No. I mean, I don't think so. But who am I to stand against him when I've proved myself no better than any other human?"

"That's not true, Caspar. You were chosen for a reason."

"You warned me before that I might lose myself in war. That I might become like Gronk, craving bloodshed and battle."

"But even Gronk is fighting on our side," Brag'mok said.

"Is he fighting for us, for this world, or is he fighting to avenge the defeat of the giants on New Albion?" I asked.

"Can't it be both?" Brag'mok said.

I nodded. "I suppose so."

"All of us are broken, Caspar. You lost yourself in a moment, but what was it that fueled your rage?"

I bit my lip. I could still see Cecil's lifeless body, shot by a bullet intended for me. "That was supposed to be me. I was the one they meant to kill. Cecil died because he followed me. I didn't save him. I couldn't save him. I moved out of the way of that bullet and allowed him to take a bullet for me. How can I live with myself after that?"

"So you attacked because your friend died for you?" Brag'mok asked.

I shook my head. "I blasted that building because I was a monster. The same monster who let Cecil die, who was too cowardly to take the bullet."

"Did you know that the bullet would hit him?"

"No. But I moved out of the way. My magic welled up within

me, and everything slowed down. I moved because I didn't want to get shot."

"No one wants to get shot, Caspar. And, again, you weren't the one who pulled the trigger."

"But if I hadn't moved, Cecil would be alive," I said.

"And the rest of us would have died in the battle that followed. Cecil's death didn't just save you. His sacrifice saved all of us. If you allow his death to make a monster out of you, as you put it, you only cheapen his death."

"But he didn't have to die," I said.

"But he did die, and by his death, you survived to save the rest of us. If you dishonor his death by losing yourself, by becoming the monster that Brightborn would like to convince the world that you are, then his loss was meaningless. But if you honor his sacrifice, if you remain the man Cecil followed to his death, then he died a hero. His death will be remembered, and his sacrifice will be cherished forever."

"Maybe," I said, shaking my head. "If we win this war."

"We will," Brag'mok said, smiling at me through his underbite. "It's why we still follow you."

"Even though I'm broken?"

"I told you already," Brag'mok said, "we're all broken. We all have wounds and flaws."

"But not everyone gets pissed and burns down buildings full of people," I said.

"It was an error in judgment," Brag'mok said. "A costly error, no doubt, but you have a choice. You can see it as a warning of what you could become if you let this rage, this lust for battle, consume you. Heed that warning, find yourself again, and prove to all of us that we are not following you in vain."

CHAPTER TWENTY-ONE

Brag'mok and I took three trips back and forth between the woods and the cave. We had enough wood to illuminate the cavern after I channeled a little magic to ignite the campfires we'd built. We'd need more wood eventually. For now, though, we were good. As good as we could be given the circumstances.

I sat down in front of one of the fires next to Layla and put my arm around her.

"How are you holding up?" Layla asked.

"I don't know," I said. "But I know I have to do better. I can't let rage consume me like that again."

"I'm glad you see that now," Layla said. "Remember the last prophecy? The one given to the elves?"

I nodded. "We make our own destiny."

Layla rested her head on my shoulder. "It's still true, you know. All is not lost."

"I don't know if the people will follow me again. After what happened... After so many people died."

"Maybe, maybe not," Layla said. "I think you need to give the people credit. A lot of people died, but a lot more survived to tell

THEOPHILUS MONROE & MICHAEL ANDERLE

the tale. They know that it wasn't you who killed all those people. It wasn't you who fired the first shot."

I sighed. "I don't think a lot of people will be eager to protest the government again after that."

"The government launched an attack on its own people," Layla said. "If anything, the people have more reason than ever to protest the government."

I shook my head. "But they won't. They'll be too afraid to resist, and I can't blame them."

"Only faith can overcome fear, Caspar. You just need to give the people something to believe in again."

"No one should put their faith in me," I said.

Layla smiled. "Then give them something bigger than you to put their faith in."

I took a deep breath and stared at the fire. "Those flames, they're almost hypnotizing."

Layla nodded. "There's something peaceful about a fire, isn't there?"

"Earlier, I used fire to destroy. How can an element that has so much power to devastate also be so calming?"

"You could say the same thing of all the elements," Layla said. "Water can kill. But we also need it to live."

I was reminded of the duality of all things. "Air, too. We breathe it in. We need it to survive. But it can become a tornado or a hurricane."

Layla rested her head on my shoulder. "All five elements are within you, Caspar. With such power comes both life and death. The power to wage war and also the power to heal."

"I've spent my life preaching a message of peace and hope," I said. "Now, I'm using the power I've been given to fight a war."

"Why do you think you were the one chosen by the prophecy, Caspar?"

I shook my head. "I don't know. I really don't."

"This isn't the first time you've had to fight your demons," Layla said.

I bit my lip. "When I drank, I was a monster. It wasn't until I hit bottom, with a broken marriage and my ministry on the rocks, that I found the strength to overcome my addiction."

"You've done this before," Layla said. "You can do it again."

I stared at the fire again for a few more seconds. I rested my hand on Layla's leg. "The first step was to admit that I was powerless over alcohol."

Layla put her hand on mine. "You found strength by admitting your powerlessness, your weakness."

I nodded. "Ironic, right? I had to realize that I needed to rely on a power greater than myself to overcome my problem."

"Then perhaps it's time that you do that again," Layla said. "I know how addictive battle can be. My world back on New Albion was a place where such an addiction overwhelmed us all until we destroyed our home. It's not weird that once you had a taste for battle and bloodshed that you wanted more."

"I can't fight that urge," I said. "That desire. That craving. It's too much for me. I'm powerless."

Layla nodded. "Then stop trying to fight it. Recognize it, and look to the faith that saved you before. It will save you again."

I smiled. "I wish I could go to an AA meeting right now. I really need it."

Layla cocked her head. "Where is he going?"

"Who?" I asked.

"Elrand. He just got up and walked into one of those corridors without any light at all."

"He's powerful. He can make his own light."

"Maybe," Layla said. "But it's still strange. What do you think he's looking for down there?"

I shrugged. "He likes to go off to be alone. Even back at the junkyard ranch, he used to sit on heaps of garbage for hours, separate from the group."

"I think you should follow him," Layla said.

"If he wants to be alone right now, that's his prerogative, Layla."

"If he wants to be by himself, he'll tell you as much," Layla insisted. "Still, he knows this place better than any of us. Maybe it's nothing. But I have a hunch that he wants you to follow him."

"A hunch?" I asked, raising my eyebrows.

Layla chuckled. "Call it a woman's intuition."

I chuckled. "Well, far be it from me question a woman's intuition!"

"Damn straight!"

I laughed. "All right. I was going to try and get some rest. I could use it. But if you insist…"

CHAPTER TWENTY-TWO

I followed Elrand into the dark cavern, a small ball of fire floating in my open palm. A bat whizzed past my face, and I almost peed my pants. Good thing I didn't. Doing laundry would be a problem. Though now that I thought about it, I imagined I could use my magic to wash my clothes if push came to shove. The element of water, mixed with detergent, followed by the element air to dry it out. Maybe, someday, if I survived all this, I'd give it a shot.

Pee in my pants or not, there wasn't any way to stay clean in this cave. I had to wonder if what I thought was cave mud spread on my pants and caked on my shoes consisted of a significant portion of bat guano.

Elrand must've known I was following him. He had no light at all. Not that he couldn't cast it himself. He wasn't as powerful as I was, but I'd seen him wield minor fire magic before. Since we were encapsulated in stone, I imagined he could use the cave to channel and amplify his magic in a similar way to how he'd used stone circles.

My light illuminated the whole cavern as I approached him from behind, casting a large Elrand-shaped shadow on the floor in front of him.

Still, he kept moving. He didn't so much as turn his head to acknowledge my presence. Maybe Layla was right; there *was* something strange about the way Elrand was acting. He knew I was following him. He *wanted* me to follow him. But at the same time, he didn't seem to care. He maintained a steady, average pace. He wasn't in a hurry. He wasn't taking his time, either. He moved with purpose but without any particular urgency.

I picked up my pace, careful not to slip on the slick cave floor, and jogged to the drow who'd used to be my father-in-law. Or was he still? When a spouse dies or gets her soul trapped in a sword, does your relationship with your spouse's parents dissolve at the same time? I suppose it's a matter of choice. There aren't any laws about it. If I wanted to look at him as a father-in-law, I could. He certainly saw me as a son-in-law, but in truth, I'd only been married to Aerin for a few weeks before she sacrificed herself and trapped herself in her blade. Elrand and I barely knew each other. Hell, he only knew his daughter a little better than he knew me.

"Where are you going?" I asked as I approached Elrand from behind.

"I'm glad Layla got the message to you," Elrand said.

"The message?" I asked.

"I told her to ask you to follow me. I needed to take you to a private place where we could speak."

I snorted. "She said it was her intuition that told her I should follow you."

Elrand chuckled, his eyes still fixed ahead. "I told her to be cryptic about it. I didn't want anyone else sneaking up behind us."

I scratched my head. "What's going on, Elrand?"

"Just a little farther ahead," the drow said. " There's a small cavern to the right side of this tunnel where we should be free to speak."

I looked behind him, moving my hand to direct the light down the tunnel through which we'd come. "I don't see anyone."

"These caves are made of stone," Elrand said. "Limestone in particular can channel all kinds of magic. It's easy to use and easy to access. I do not want our conversation to leave an impression in the stone that others might later extract."

"Like when we saw the vision of Taliesin in the stone circle at the North Pole?" I asked.

"Precisely," Elrand said with a nod.

Elrand placed his hand on the side of the tunnel. He pulled himself up, gripping a cranny in the rock, and on his belly pushed himself into a small hole in the wall.

I cocked my head. "You want me to follow you?

"Mm-hmm," Elrand grunted as he pushed himself through the constrictive tunnel.

I sighed and climbed up behind him. I couldn't maintain my magic well while also using my hands to climb. When I extinguished my flame everything went dark. I had to feel my way through behind Elrand, listening carefully to make sure I kept my distance and avoid a sandaled foot to my face.

I felt the tunnel drop off, and I heard Elrand land on the floor not far in front of me. I extended my hand into the opening and recalled the power of fire.

I gasped. The room was brilliant. The whole cavern was lined with crystalline structures. It reminded me of Superman's fortress of solitude, except these crystals were various colors. Pinks, yellows, blues, and even a few greens.

I slid out of the hole and tucked my feet around my body as I jumped down and landed about three feet from where Elrand was standing.

"This place is gorgeous," I said.

Elrand nodded. "Mostly quartz. Also some amethyst and agate. This is basically a giant geode."

"It doesn't channel magic like limestone?" I asked.

"It channels magic quite powerfully," Elrand said. "But it does not retain the impressions, the memories, that limestone or granite can."

"How'd you find this place?"

Elrand smiled. "When I was exiled, I came to Missouri for more reasons than the gateway to New Albion. There are ley lines all around the world, but here in Missouri's vast network of caves, the ley lines of earthen magic are more like a spiderweb of magical power."

I cocked my head. "Are you suggesting that this cave *is* a ley line?"

"Of a sort," Elrand said. "I've spent years exploring these caves, discovering the secrets that only the ancients before us ever knew."

"The ancients?" I asked. "You mean the druids?"

"There were other ancient peoples who wielded the magic of the earth, Naayak," Elrand said. "Here, it was the Osage tribe that was most in tune with the latent power in these lands."

"They taught you how to access this magic?" I asked.

Elrand nodded. "In a matter of speaking. The tribal peoples today have mostly forgotten the power their ancestors once embraced. They did not teach me directly. But the stones, the caves, all have tales to tell."

"The limestone," I said.

"Yes," Elrand said. " I've learned from them in the same way we invoked the memory of Taliesin. I learned what I could through observation."

I cocked my head. "So you know what the ancient Osage knew?"

Elrand laughed. "What I know barely scratches the surface of what the ancients here were once in tune with."

"So that's why you wanted to bring us here?" I asked. "It wasn't just a hiding place?"

"It is a hiding place of a sort," Elrand said. "But it is more than that."

"So what is it you needed to tell me? What you couldn't tell me in front of the rest of the group?"

"An operation like that military assault takes time to organize," Elrand said. "They knew we were coming. I don't think it was luck that Brightborn found us in the Canadian forest, either."

I scratched my head. "What are you suggesting, Elrand?"

"Forgive me for the cliche, Naayak. But there is a traitor in our midst."

I grunted. "Are you certain?"

Elrand nodded and extended his hand. He was holding a small crystal, not unlike the crystals I'd used to create the spires at the North Pole and, later, in the Canadian forest. I opened my hand, and he placed the crystal in my palm.

"Is this another spire?" I asked.

Elrand shook his head. "The crystals have more utility than that. They contain instructions, ways that magical energy can be channeled and directed to manifest. If that purpose is to build a spire or another structure, the crystal will direct it accordingly. If, however, the crystal is designed to channel magic into a direct line of communication from one person to another…"

I bit my lip. "Layla had crystals like these when we first met. They worked like a telephone. It's how she reported back to her father on New Albion before we knew what his real plans were."

Elrand nodded. "Then you know that these crystals can communicate not only across vast distances but even between worlds."

"Right," I said. "Do you think someone used this one to talk to Brightborn and tell him our plans?"

"I'm certain of it," Elrand said. "If you were to channel a little aether into it, Brightborn would pick up on the other side."

I grunted. "How do you know that?"

"Because when I found this crystal, I tried it myself."

I stared at Elrand blankly. "So Brightborn knows that we know someone in our ranks is sharing intelligence with him?"

Elrand shook his head. "I did not respond when he answered. But it was him. I have no doubt."

"Where did you find this crystal?" I asked. "Do you know who it belonged to?"

Elrand shook his head. "During the assault in Canada. I stayed behind to help gather the people and supplies for transport when we were luring the elves to us. If it was in the spire where the resistance lived, I'd say it belonged to one of them. If it was with the giants, while it's hard to believe that any giant would work with Brightborn, even that would be a reasonable conclusion. The same goes if it were found with the belongings of my fellow drow. But I found this one hidden in the ashes of one of our fires."

I bit my lip. "If aether would open it to communication, what would happen if fire magic were cast onto it?"

"You were the one who started the fires in our camp," Elrand said. "Naturally, I had the same question. I came to learn that any of the elements have the same effect. However, when the crystal is consumed with the element of fire, it doesn't merely open a channel to communicate. I believe it works like a homing beacon, a magical GPS of a sort."

I gripped the crystal in my hand. "That would explain how the elves found us in the Canadian forest. But how do *you* know that's what it does?"

"I don't know for certain," Elrand said. "But when I channeled fire into the crystal, it was shortly after we arrived back at the junkyard ranch. Shortly before we left to join the protest."

I cocked my head. "We left a few legionaries alive to tell Brightborn where we were, but are you telling me that you alerted him as to our plans?"

"Not intentionally," Elrand said. "I'm sorry, but I suspect that is how he learned we'd be at the protest. It's how Brightborn was able to mobilize the assault against us. And it's also how he knew to come looking for us again at the junkyard ranch after the battle."

"But this thing isn't working now, right?" I asked.

Elrand shook his head. "It is dormant. Whatever power I lent to it has been used."

I sighed. "Whoever this belonged to, I doubt this is the only one they had."

"I share that doubt," Elrand said. "The magic of the crystal won't be able to escape in these caves. It will behave as if it is operating. It will glow and channel the magic, but the limestone will absorb the power emanating from the crystal before it can escape and reach Brightborn."

"That's not bad news," I said. "If there is a traitor here, they'll surely try to contact Brightborn again. You said that limestone can absorb magic, like memories or events from history. If someone tries to use another crystal like this, will we be able to extract that information from the cave?"

"Theoretically, yes," Elrand said.

I sighed. "We can't just start searching people. That would raise red flags and alert the traitor to our suspicion."

"I agree," Elrand said. "But if the traitor uses such a crystal, the limestone will not only contain a record of the magic that the crystal used to communicate to Brightborn. It will also record the incident, the memory of what happened. Our best chance is to wait for the traitor to betray us again. When they do, we'll be able to identify the guilty party."

CHAPTER TWENTY-THREE

According to Elrand, we could use the crystals in the geode to extract any magical data—if you could call it that—in any of the surrounding limestone. We planned to meet there every morning and night to examine whatever may or may not have happened. We had to check often. If the traitor *did* attempt to reach Brightborn, but Brightborn didn't respond, they'd likely suspect that the cave was dampening their signal. We didn't want them to know that their efforts wouldn't work in the cave. We wanted to catch the traitor.

There were only a few people I could eliminate from my suspicions. Whoever it was had a magical affinity. That meant Jag definitely wasn't the traitor. I knew Layla wasn't, either. I couldn't eliminate the possibility that a giant was a traitor. They'd be familiar with the same technology that Layla had used to communicate with her father before, the crystal comms devices.

However, if a giant was betraying us, all I could figure was that Brightborn must've had him by the balls. Metaphorically, of course. A giant wouldn't side with the king who'd wiped out most of their race unless he had leverage against him. Still, the chance that a giant was the traitor was slimmer than it was for anyone else. The drow didn't regularly use magic. They were enchanters.

The elves of the resistance, however, were the most numerous of our population, and all it would take was *one* of them to be a secret Brightborn loyalist to pull it off. They could wield magic, and they were accustomed to the technology that the traitor was using. All signs pointed to an elf. Since Layla was their queen, and I was a thousand percent sure she wasn't the traitor, she'd have to keep her eyes open. She couldn't even tell Illarion. He didn't strike me as the traitorous sort, but I didn't have anything more than a hunch, and certainly not a woman's intuition, to prove his innocence.

As I stepped back into the main cavern where everyone was gathered, the smell of smores struck my nostrils. The giants were gathered around the fire as the drow were teaching them how to turn common graham crackers, chocolate bars, and marshmallows into a delectable snack.

"Oh!" Gronk moaned in ecstasy as he took his first bite. "Why didn't we make these before now?"

He skewered another marshmallow and started to roast it as other giants joined in.

"*Dreg shlammers!*" Gronk exclaimed, yanking his skewer from the fire, the fully engulfed marshmallow in flames.

Rina laughed and blew it out for him. "Some people prefer them that way. It's fine."

Gronk stuck the marshmallow right into his mouth, bits of it smearing across his bottom lip as he tasted it. His eyes rolled back in his head as he moaned a second time.

Now, I realize that there weren't many giant women left, but even with few available partners for mating his reaction to the marshmallow seemed inappropriate. Though, it only seemed that way. If he was aroused, at his size, it would be more than obvious. A mental picture that I'd never before entertained popped into my head, but I quickly dismissed it from my mind. *That* was one thing I hoped to never see.

Jag pulled a perfectly roasted marshmallow from the fire, squeezed it between two prepared graham crackers with a Hershey chocolate bar on one of them, and fed it to his drow girlfriend.

"Thank you, Jag," Rina said. "I'll take another."

I shook my head. Jag wouldn't eat smores. Not unless someone invented a way to make marshmallows out of whey protein. But if Rina wanted one, well, Jag was ready and willing to serve her desires. I doubted those desires were limited to smores—another mental image that I tried to avoid entertaining.

I suck at secrets. I've never been a good liar. Knowing that someone was pretending to be a part of the crowd roasting marshmallows around one of the small fires, that the traitor was laughing and telling stories, made it hard to have any fun with anyone. I suspected *everyone* except the aforementioned few who I knew couldn't be responsible for betraying us.

Something else didn't add up. I hadn't had time to digest what had happened in the city. But as I sat watching giants roasting their marshmallows over the fire, it struck me that the sniper who tried to kill me would have also killed Layla. Until now, we'd presumed that Brightborn wouldn't kill me because he knew it would kill his daughter. Based on the knowledge that the elves who showed up in the Canadian forest were trying to abduct her, it didn't make sense that Brightborn would order my assassination. Less than a father's love for his daughter, Brightborn saw Layla as a pawn, a tool, a weapon that he could use to help further his agenda.

Then again, what if the sniper wasn't trying to kill me after all? Not every bullet kills. Maybe they were trying to wound me. If I was hurt and lost enough blood to lose consciousness but not so much to die, Layla would still live. An elf could heal me after Layla was taken and she'd survive. Hell, if one of the elves in the resistance was the traitor, there was a reasonable chance that one of *them* could have healed me, and by so doing, it only further made his case that he, or she, was aligned with me rather than Brightborn.

I shook my head as I thought about it. Things were rarely what they seemed to be when Brightborn was involved. Perhaps the sniper was under orders that didn't come from Brightborn at all. If that was the case, I had to suspect that Brightborn was pretty pissed at whoever had ordered the shot.

I'd probably never know, for sure. No matter who was responsible, they wanted me incapacitated. Either by bleeding me to the point of losing consciousness or by killing me outright. Strangely enough, it would be *better* for us if the sniper was trying to kill me. A rift between Brightborn and the military would be a good thing. There wasn't much sense trying to figure it out.

I didn't have enough facts to favor one theory over another. That didn't mean it wasn't worth thinking through. Considering the possibility that Brightborn *did* want me shot and healed by the traitor, it made sense that the traitor was probably near me at the time. Ready to heal me, to keep me alive until the military defeated us and they were able to secure Layla.

Who had been near me at the Arch? Cecil, obviously. But from our group? Layla was near me. So was Brag'mok. Illarion wasn't far from my position, but most of the other elves and the drow were marching as a part of the crowd. The giants were marching along the perimeter to protect the protesters just in case what *did* happen might happen. Jag was near me with Rina and three of her drow bodyguards who never left her side.

I sighed. Again, I was speculating. Even if I suspected the people who were near me, I couldn't rule out the possibility that it might have been any common elf, or giant, or drow. The only way to identify the traitor was to wait and do as Elrand and I planned.

How long could I wait? Trixie could be back at any time.

Would she be able to find us here? I might have to step outside of the cave periodically to shoot off some random magic like a flare so she'd know where we were. But once she found me, what would I do if she had found Brightborn? I'd vowed that I'd never lie to the people who were following me, but how could I reveal the truth if there was one among us who was on Brightborn's side? If the traitor warned Brightborn we were coming, we'd be walking into a trap.

I either had to discover the traitor before Trixie arrived. Or I'd have to go after Brightborn alone.

CHAPTER TWENTY-FOUR

Apart from Elrand, Layla was the only one who knew that Brightborn had a spy among us. I knew it wasn't Jag, but I didn't tell him. The fewer people who knew, the less risk that someone might inadvertently alert the traitor that we were on to them. It wouldn't take much. An awkward, suspicious stare. A strange question. If Jag knew, he'd want to help. God bless him, he had his heart in the right place most of the time. He wasn't your stereotypical "all brawn, no brains" bodybuilder. He was intelligent. But he also had a big mouth at times, and he lacked in tact. He didn't do *anything* subtly. If anyone would spill the beans, albeit inadvertently, it would be Jag.

That didn't mean I didn't need Jag. We needed him to keep tabs on what was going on with the government, to check on the news and see what people were being told and how they were responding. I had a phone, and so did Layla. No one else did—at least not that we knew.

Even if someone was concealing that they had a hidden phone, they couldn't use it in the cave. Cellphone signals didn't get through to the cave any better than magical crystal communication devices. Since we didn't get a cell signal in the Canadian forest either, it was clear why the traitor had to resort to using communication crystals to reach Brightborn. Since there was only one way in or out of the cave, if anyone tried to sneak out to either use a phone or a crystal, they would be seen and immediately identified as a suspect.

Of course, as Elrand had pointed out, whoever the traitor was probably didn't know that the cave would prevent the crystal from working. Either way, if the spy attempted to contact Brightborn again, we'd know about it.

Jag and I went down one of the tunnels off the main cavern before I opened a fairy portal to take us to the barn. I didn't want to make a show of coming and going from the cave. I also wasn't inclined to use that narrow tunnel to come and go, especially since the risk of hitting my head in that tunnel was significant. Jag was taller and larger than me, so the risk was even higher for him.

Jag pulled out his phone. "Not much battery left. I've been keeping it turned off to preserve the battery."

I nodded. "You can charge it from my car if you need to."

"It looks like I have enough charge left for now. Depending on how long we're stuck here, I might need to take you up on that soon." Jag scrolled through his phone, furrowing his brow as he examined a few articles.

"What is it?" I asked.

Jag shook his head. "Looks like there's quite a bit of backlash against the government's intervention at the rally. Some are disputing whether you were the one who blew up that building or if the military was responsible."

I bit my lip. "No one got what I did on camera? You'd think with so many phones, someone would be recording."

Jag shrugged. "I'm sure those videos are out there. But when you blasted that building, the flames didn't pour from your hands. It was like they rose up from the earth. As easy as it might be to assume you were responsible, one could make the case that something else on the ground caused the explosion."

"So people aren't blaming me for it?" I asked.

"I didn't say that," Jag said. "It just looks like there's an argument from some media outlets who are disputing that you might have been trying to stop the fire rather than set it."

I sighed. "I'm not sure if that's good news or bad news."

"What do you mean?" Jag asked. "The fact that some of them are defying government efforts has to be promising."

"Except it's not true," I said. "I *was* responsible, Jag."

"You didn't send the military in to attack peaceful protesters," Jag said. "Cecil's wife is also making quite a stink, making her rounds to the various networks and blaming the President for the sniper who killed Cecil."

"Let me see," I said.

Jag handed me his phone. I clicked the play button that was imposed over an image of Shanda, Cecil's wife.

"I don't blame Caspar Cruciger," Shanda was saying. "He was there to inspire us, to encourage us to exercise our freedom of speech. The fact is, the administration didn't want him to speak. They tried to assassinate him and killed my husband instead. Someone must be held accountable."

I bit my lip as I listened to Shanda's plea. The host pressed her on a second question. "Didn't Mister Cruciger assault the federal building after the shots were fired?"

"He went after the sniper. I know that much. But if you want my opinion, it was a bomb that went off on that building. If anything, I think Caspar was trying to stop it before his powers failed."

I shook my head as I listened to the interview. It helped my case. But it wasn't true. Not entirely. She was right to blame the President. She was wrong to exonerate me. "Jag, I don't know what to make of this."

"Look," Jag said. "People are still rallying in support of you.

People are defending you, and more people are starting to question the President and the wisdom of his alliance with King Brightborn. That can't be a bad thing."

I snorted. "I suppose you're right."

"Of course I'm right," Jag said, slapping me on the back. He meant it to be encouraging. He nearly knocked the air out of me.

"But this still isn't uniting people," I said. "It sounds to me like people are more divided than ever over whether I'm a hero or a terrorist."

Jag shook his head. "Would you rather they be united in condemning you, Caspar?"

I shrugged. "They wouldn't be altogether wrong if they did. Look, Jag, if I'm really standing with the truth, I can't let falsehood like this stand. Even if it does shed a more positive light on my role."

"You aren't lying," Jag said. "People are looking at the facts and drawing their own conclusions. It isn't dishonest to allow things to play out. If people think you blew that building up out of anger, it will only hurt our cause."

I sighed. "Rigorous honesty. That's a part of my twelve-step program. I have to avoid deceit, I have to take responsibility for what I did, and I have to try and make amends however I can."

Jag snorted. "Do you realize how selfish that would be, Caspar?"

I frowned. "Selfish? How could telling the truth be selfish?"

"Look, you and I know that what you did was out of anger," Jag said. "It was uncalculated. But our enemies *planned* to take you out, to attack our army and the protesters. You might have acted recklessly in the heat of the moment, but if you own up to that, it will distract from the real truth."

"What is the real truth, Jag?" I asked.

"That the travesty that occurred in St. Louis was the government's doing. It was down to the President's misguided pro-Brightborn policy."

I shook my head. "I can't find peace in my soul if I'm living a lie, Jag."

"Would you have peace in your soul in exchange for giving tyranny a greater foothold over the world?" Jag asked.

I sighed. "I don't know. I mean, I know you're right. But if I don't deal with this the only way I know how to, I can't guarantee that those urges, that rage, won't overtake me again."

"What's done is done, Caspar. What would you do to try and set the record straight?"

"Let me shoot a video. Send it to the networks."

Jag shook his head. "Every time we broadcast something or send a file, we run the risk that we'll be traced."

"I thought you were bouncing your cell signal around the globe?" I said.

Jag nodded. "I am, but I'm an amateur compared to the computer experts working for the government. If they work at it hard enough and long enough, they'll be able to identify the tower that I originally sent the file from."

"Then we portal into the city somewhere," I said. "Maybe my old church or St. Ensley's. We send the video from there."

Jag took a deep breath. Then he tapped at his phone a few times. "I can't let you do that."

"If you don't do it, I'll record it on my own phone and do it myself."

"Your burner phone had a prepaid plan. I just canceled it."

"Dammit, Jag!"

"I'm sorry, Caspar. I know you need to sort things out with your conscience. But I can't let you put us at risk to do so. If you need to confide in someone, go talk to your minister friend. Hell, go to an AA meeting if you think you can do it and get out of there without being caught. But whatever you do, I can't let you risk our lives and the vitality of this resistance movement because you feel guilty."

I nodded. "Tell Layla I'll be back shortly."

"What are you going to do, Caspar?"

I sighed. "Don't worry. I'm not going to go spill the beans to the media. But I do need to get this off my chest. I'll be at Holy Cross, my old church. Then, I'll be back."

CHAPTER TWENTY-FIVE

I appeared as I had before in the chancel in my old sanctuary where I used to preach. I looked around. Doris wasn't there this time. I could only hope that Philip was around. If not, I would have to go back to the cave and try again another time.

I entered the door to the vestry behind the chancel. From there, I could enter a hallway that led to the pastor's study. I approached Philip's door—what used to be *my* study door—and knocked.

"Come in," Philip's friendly and familiar voice said from inside.

I smiled. I was lucky I'd caught him in the office. I grabbed the doorknob and opened the door.

Philip's eyes widened when he saw me. "Caspar! What are you doing here?"

I sighed. "I just need to talk. I'd go to an AA meeting, but what I have to say is information that would be a burden for anyone to carry. I don't want to put that on a bunch of recovering drunks."

Philip smiled at me kindly. "Well, at least you don't have any qualms about putting that burden on me."

I shook my head. "I'm sorry, I didn't mean…"

He waved a hand. "It's fine, Caspar. It's why I'm here. Paul wrote that we should bear one another's burdens and thereby fulfill the law of Christ."

I nodded. "The sixth chapter of Galatians."

Philip smiled. "Why don't you take a seat?"

I pulled a chair out from the opposite side of Philip's desk. I half expected he'd sit down in his office chair and talk to me across his desk. Instead, he wheeled his chair around to my side of the desk.

"Does this have to do with what's all over the news?" Philip asked.

I snorted. "I thought you didn't watch the news."

Philip chuckled. "I try not to. But when an old friend is the subject of half the stories, I can't tune it out entirely."

I nodded. "Well, in addition to bearing one another's burdens, in James, we're told to confess our sins to one another."

Philip nodded. "As you know, according to my ordination vows, whatever you confess is under the seal. No one else needs to know."

I bit my lip. "A lot is being said by a lot of different people. I haven't seen much of what's being reported, but I've seen enough to know that the truth is up in the air."

"Do you want to tell me what happened?" Philip asked.

I nodded. "This whole conflict that I've been put in the middle of, it's put me in situations where I've done things I never thought I could do. I have killed people, Philip."

"In the fire at the federal building?" Philip asked. "If it means anything, they're saying that nearly everyone got out."

I nodded. "That's good to know. But it's more than that. I did set that fire. That wasn't the beginning of it all. I'd say it's when I hit bottom. Now, I have to deal with the guilt that's been welling up inside my soul. It's changing me. I feel like I'm losing myself."

"I'm here to listen," Philip said.

"Before the incident downtown, I was in battles. I killed others with my sword."

"Acting as a soldier, most theologians agree that you are not thereby guilty of the sin of murder."

I nodded. "I'm aware. But death is still contrary to God's desire. War is still a symptom of sin and brokenness. When I killed in those battles, a part of me *liked* it, Philip."

Philip cocked his head. "You *liked* it? What do you mean?"

I sighed. "I hated it at the same time. But there was a thrill, a feeling unlike anything I've ever known when I took a life. It's addicting. I've found myself craving more violence."

Philip nodded. "Put your hand to your chest."

"Why?"

"Just do it," Philip said.

I placed my hand over my heart. "What do you want me to do, pledge my allegiance to the flag?"

Philip shook his head. "Not that, Caspar. Tell me, what do you feel?"

"I feel my chest," I said. "I feel my heart beating in my chest."

"You're still made of human flesh, are you not?" Philip asked.

I nodded. "I am."

"Do you believe what the Bible says about the flesh?" Philip said. "About the things that proceed from the broken, and fallen, human heart?"

I quoted from the book of Romans. "I know that nothing good dwells in me, that is in my flesh. For I have the desire to do what is right, but not the ability to carry it out."

Philip nodded. "Jesus said that what comes from the human heart are all kinds of evil, murder, adultery, fornication, theft, false witness, and slander."

I sighed. "I know the verse."

"You're not unique, Caspar. You may have unusual abilities. You have responsibilities, a calling that requires much of you. But in the flesh, in your heart, there's nothing about you that is any more or less evil than what plagues all of us."

I shook my head. "After that sniper shot my friend, I killed the sniper in anger. Then, without even thinking, I blasted that building to hell."

Philip nodded. "If I were in your situation, I don't know if I would have done any better, Caspar. Last I checked, I have human flesh, too. My heart longs for the same sinful things that yours does."

"But you haven't ever killed someone," I said.

"I'm not in your position," Philip said. "The sin in our flesh and in our hearts manifests in different ways depending on our circumstances, our personalities, and a number of factors. But I sin, too. Regularly. More often than I'd like."

I nodded. "I know we're all sinners and fall short of God's glory."

"None of us are worthy of whatever God has called us to," Philip said. "I'm hardly worthy to preach in this sanctuary to anyone. You aren't worthy to fulfill whatever prophecy it is that you've been called to. But do you know what I've learned through the years?"

"What's that?" I asked.

"God has a penchant for using broken vessels to do amazing things, and he chooses flawed people exclusively. He's never called a perfect person to do his will."

I shook my head. "But your sins aren't as big as mine."

Philip laughed. "You know better than what you're saying, Caspar. The size of one's sin doesn't matter. No sin is bigger than the expanse of God's grace and his love for you."

"I don't even know who I am anymore," I said. "I feel like I've lost myself."

"If anyone would save his life," Philip said, quoting Jesus again, "he must lose it."

"I feel like I'm walking in darkness."

Philip nodded. "When we are navigating the dark night of the soul, when things seem the bleakest, we're all the better prepared to be illuminated by the light."

"I don't know where to find the light," I said. "It's like I'm so deep in darkness that the light is a million miles away."

"The light is not yours to find, Caspar. It is a gift. It's there for you to embrace. When you close your eyes, it will always seem dark. All you need to do is open your eyes and see what's already yours."

"Which is what, exactly?" I asked.

"That you recognize the darkness is the first sign that you are ready to receive the light," Philip said. "Too many people walk in darkness but think they see. They never look for the light that's shining all around them because they refuse to acknowledge the darkness. You can walk across a dark room with false confidence. You might step on a Lego."

"Ouch!" I said, chuckling.

"Why would you walk in darkness when the light switch is there, and all you have to do is reach out and turn it on?" Philip asked.

My eyes stung. "Then how do I turn the light on again? What if I'm in an unfamiliar darkness, in a room I've never been in before, and don't know where to find the switch?"

"Then allow the Lord to turn it on for you," Philip said. "If you walk by the Spirit, Paul said, you will not gratify the desires of the flesh. There is freedom from the burden you feel, Caspar."

"Sometimes walking by the Spirit is easier said than done," I said.

"I agree," Philip said. "But I'm here to tell you that those who confess their sins will be forgiven. For our God is faithful and just, even when we've been faithless."

"I do confess my sins," I said, tears falling from my eyes. "I've failed to live the life I was called to."

"You are forgiven, Caspar," Philip said. "Now, set your feet on the path of the Spirit. You do not need to return to bondage again."

"But even a dog often returns to its vomit."

"And the dogs eat the crumbs that fall from the master's table," Philip said. "We are all beggars."

"That's true," I said, nodding my head.

"I can't tell you who the people of this world will tell you that you are," Philip said. "This world tells us that our identity is the product of our actions. That's not true, though. If it were, if we were honest, we'd all be lost. You have a different identity. Not one that's the result of your deeds or sins, but one that's been given you by grace. The Bible says that all of us are sons of God, and as his children, we are heirs of his inheritance."

I wiped my eyes. "Some people say I'm a terrorist."

Philip shook his head. "That's not who you are. Tell me, does the world define you, or does God?"

"God does," I said, nodding.

Philip nodded. "Then the evidence doesn't matter. The things you've done and the accusations or labels that people put on you aren't your identity. All that matters is the person that God has called you to be, who he's helping you become. It's up to you whether you walk according to the flesh and what this world says or if you walk by the Spirit. Your flesh testifies against you, that's true. But the testimony of the Spirit is greater than the testimony of your heart."

"Then what do I do next?" I asked. "How do I lead this movement? How do I fight against tyranny and injustice without losing myself again?"

Philip smiled. "I can't tell you what the next right thing to do is, Caspar. But I do know that if you're walking by the Spirit, you'll find your way."

CHAPTER TWENTY-SIX

Before I went back to the cave, I decided to go visit Shanda, Cecil's wife. She and their daughter Grace had recently moved into a new house. Once Grace could walk and attend regular school, Shanda had been able to work. Cecil had gotten a new job too, and they didn't have to channel all their money into medical expenses for Grace. Cecil had told me that I'd done more than heal his daughter. It had saved their family. That was why he was so loyal to me. Why, despite everything people were saying about me, he led the charge to rally people in support of my cause.

And he'd died for it.

What kind of shithead would I be if I didn't at least visit his family? He'd invited me to his housewarming party after they'd moved in. At the time, I was so wrapped up with all this elven prophecy stuff that I didn't make it. Now, I regretted missing it. But at least I knew where they lived. I could visit them now.

Since I'd never been there, I couldn't travel by fairy portal. I sure as hell wasn't going to ride the metro. Can you imagine what kind of hoopla that would cause? Shape-shifting was one ability I didn't have—if it was an ability that was even possible to attain. Still, it's an ability I'd often wished I'd had. Not seriously, of course. In the same sense that I used to pray as a child that God would give me the powers of Superman. Just a fantasy.

Of course, when it came to Superman-like powers, it seemed that my naive prayer had been answered. Sort of. I could fly. I could cast fire, although not from my eyes. I didn't have freeze-breath, but I could do some pretty cool stuff with water. Maybe if it was cold enough outside and I added air to it I could do something similar. While I wasn't invulnerable like Superman, I did have other abilities he didn't. I could heal. I could teleport. All I needed was some spandex, a pair of underwear I could sport on the outside of my tights, and a cape.

Maybe shape-shifting to ride the metro was off the table. However, since I *could* fly, that was my best option.

Would people see me soaring across the city? Probably. Would it get the attention of the people who wanted me dead? Most likely. But I could fly a few circles around and soar high enough to avoid unnecessary attention.

I'd recovered most of my energy since the debacle downtown. I hadn't slept much. I'd tried to get a little shut-eye in the cave before Jag and I headed out to check the news that morning. Not enough. Guano-covered cave floors are even less amenable to sleep than popped air mattresses on the exposed subflooring of an abandoned farmhouse.

Still, I had enough energy for a short flight across the city, provided I didn't have to dodge any missiles on the way. Given all that had happened recently, there wasn't anything I could rule out as a possibility.

I flew as high as I could while still breathing. Too high, and the air gets too thin. Plus, while it didn't trouble Superman, the pressure in the ears can be quite painful. Superman had the advantage of invulnerability, but he's not the only superhero who flies. The comic creators, it seems, don't think much about the pesky problems associated with flight.

So far, so good. No military helicopters or jet fighters in

pursuit. No missiles. I wasn't sure if I even showed up on radar. I was probably too small. Though, maybe not. My knowledge about such things was informed almost entirely by television and movies. I had to stay alert, just in case.

Flight was a taxing endeavor. It was freeing in a sense, but it took a lot of magic to keep a human body afloat and hurtling through the air. However, it was also relaxing in the same way jogging in the park was. It was usually peaceful when I wasn't worried about being blown out of the sky by a missile, but I almost always broke a sweat despite the constant influx of air blowing across my body.

I made my way to where Cecil's family lived. I had a general familiarity with the neighborhood. I didn't recall the exact address, but I knew the car his family drove, and he'd shown me a couple of pictures of the house when he first bought it. So, I was looking for a maroon mini-van parked in front of a small, brick-faced house.

If I went to the wrong house, I'd probably freak someone out, considering that my picture had been circulating on the news channels. Depending on their perspective. Some people thought I was a hero. Others believed I was a terrorist. I imagined there weren't a lot of people with opinions in-between.

I found a van that looked like the one Cecil drove. I hoped they still had the handicapped license plates from when Grace was chairbound. Since most of the members of Holy Cross had been elderly and the topic had come up a few times, I knew that the permanent disabled placard in Missouri was good for four years. While they couldn't use it anymore, I hoped they still had the plate on their van.

Sure enough, the van I spotted had the plates I was looking for, and it was parked in the driveway of a brick-faced house. I'd already lowered myself near the ground to get a look at the van's plates. I only needed to drop myself a couple more inches, and my feet touched the ground.

I stepped up the front door and rang the doorbell. The West-minster Chimes sounded from within the house. A few seconds later, Grace opened the door. Her eyes were red from tears, but for a brief moment, she appeared excited to see me.

"Caspar!" Grace said.

I opened my arms, and she wrapped hers around my body.

"I'm so sorry," I said.

Shanda appeared around the corner. "Thank you for coming, Caspar, but it's probably not safe here."

I nodded. "I know, but it wouldn't be right if I didn't at least stop by to offer my condolences. That bullet... It was intended for me. That Cecil took it instead, well, it would be wrong not to honor that."

Shanda nodded and wiped her eyes. "They think you're a terrorist."

"I know," I said.

"But they shot at you!" Shanda said. "*They* were the murderers!"

I nodded. " I saw what you said on the news. When you defended me."

"People need to open their eyes and see who the real threat is. It isn't you! It's this joke of a President and that elf king!"

Shanda had moved fairly quickly from the first stage of grief —denial—to the second stage. Anger. She still had three more stages to go through. Though in my experience, not everyone hits all of them, and most go through some stages faster than others.

"Do you have anyone to talk to?" I asked. "Any support?"

Shanda gestured to her kitchen. "People keep sending flowers. I don't know what I'll do with all of them."

I nodded. "I get that. It can be overwhelming. People want to do something nice, but..."

"Sometimes it's just too much," Shanda said.

I pressed my lips together. "Well, at least they haven't over-whelmed you with casseroles yet."

Shanda rolled her eyes. "You haven't looked in our refrigerator. I think I have six different casseroles right now. Would you like some before you go?"

I bit my lip. "I don't know. I'm not sure I should. I mean, you said it wasn't safe for me to be here, and I agree. I don't want to put you in danger."

Shanda waved her hand. "Surely a little green bean and french-fry casserole is worth the risk."

I chuckled. "Well, yeah. Depending on who made it."

"It was brought here by that sweet lady from your old church. What was her name, Doris, was it?"

I smiled. "If it's Doris' green bean casserole, you may be right that it's worth the risk."

I followed Shanda into the kitchen. Grace followed close behind. She pulled out three plates and retrieved one of several casserole dishes stacked in her refrigerator, and scooped some of what I'd once called "the green beans of heaven" on each plate. Considering that green beans are far from my favorite, the delectability of this particular dish spoke volumes about Doris' cooking ability.

One of the perks of being a minister, particularly of an older congregation, is a virtually unending supply of home-cooked dishes. If it wasn't leftovers from the latest pot-luck, it was often something brought to church and left in the refrigerator with my name on it. It was no wonder, no doubt aided by my workouts with Jag, that I'd lost so much weight since my former denomination gave me the boot.

We had a nice but quick meal. We kept the conversation light. I'd learned through years of consoling the bereaved that sometimes just being present for someone is better than offering senseless platitudes. People believe what they believe. Being told that their loved one is in a better place, while perhaps true, doesn't do anything to assuage the pain of the loss. Some things can't be made sense of or explained. Sometimes tragedies are just tragedies. There's no way to rationalize the agony away. But being with someone who cares, someone who in some way knew the one who was lost, even if not nearly so intimately, lets a person know that their grief is okay, that they aren't alone in their mourning. It doesn't do a thing to take away the hurt, but it makes it a little easier to go through.

CHAPTER TWENTY-SEVEN

I portaled back to the barn near the cave. Jag was still there, leaning on my car.

"What are you doing here?" I asked. "I figured you'd be back inside the cave by now."

"I might be flexible for a big guy, but I'm still a big guy. I was going to give you one more hour before I sucked it up and crawled through that tunnel again."

I snorted. "How did you know I'd come back here? I could have just portaled straight into the cave."

Jag shrugged. "I figured you'd want to grab some supplies. It was a gamble. Besides, sitting in here with service gave me some time to do a little more exploring on the net."

"Anything new?"

"Sure," Jag said. "My favorite supplement company just released a new andro."

I cocked my head. "Andro? Isn't that the legal steroid that baseball players were using back in the day?"

"I don't know about that," Jag said. "All I know is that this stuff has come a long way. Gives me a killer pump in the gym. Maybe I'll pick some up if I ever get to go to a gym again."

I bit my lip. "I thought you said your muscles were all natural."

"They are," Jag said. "Andros stimulate the body's natural production of testosterone. Besides, if everything comes from the earth, isn't everything natural originally? What else would it be? Supernatural?"

I scratched the back of my head. "I guess that's true now that I think about it. But I think people usually think if something has to be manufactured in a lab then it isn't natural in the sense that you couldn't pick it off a tree or grow it in a garden. It isn't naturally *occurring*."

Jag narrowed his eyes. "So if you use a fertilizer to stimulate the growth of a garden, does that mean the garden isn't natural?"

I shrugged. "I don't know. Isn't it just semantics, anyway?"

"This supplement is like a fertilizer for the body. Keeps the testosterone surging naturally even if you're an old fart."

I snickered. "An old fart like me? I hate to tell you, but I'm still in my forties."

"Yeah, that's old," Jag said.

"No, it isn't! Forty is the new thirty!"

"Says people who are over forty."

I cocked my head. "So there was some new steroid you want to try."

"Supplement!"

"Whatever," I said. "Is there anything new about things that matter? You know, about me?"

Jag raised an eyebrow. "You think your situation matters more than the size of my pectorals? I'm offended."

"Well, yes. I do."

"I'm screwing with you, Caspar."

I nodded. "I know. But have there been any more developments?"

Jag tapped his index finger on the screen of his smartphone. "Not exactly about *you*. A few things relevant to the war at large. You know, if we can call it a war."

"The government probably doesn't see it that way," I said. "We're too small, and we don't represent a nation or anything like that. Still, when people are being targeted and killed to achieve an objective, a government interest, I'd say that's a war."

"I don't disagree," Jag said. "Interestingly, a senator, that guy from Kentucky, is making quite a stink about the President authorizing an act of war against American citizens without so much as consulting Congress as to the necessity of waging an assault on domestic grounds."

I nodded. "Well, that particular senator is pretty vocal about the dangers of executive power. I think he has a point. We engage in warlike acts all around the world now by presidential order. But since we don't declare it a war, we don't call it a war, so who needs congressional approval?"

"Walks like a duck, quacks like a duck, it's a duck," Jag said.

I nodded. "Exactly. That's the point that the senator you mentioned and others are making. Just because we don't declare the wars we conduct around the world as such, it doesn't change the reality. Saying otherwise is nothing more than a semantic trick to bypass the constitution."

"Possibly. He isn't the only congressman who is pissed. Some people are accusing the President of treason."

"All from the opposite side of the aisle?" I asked.

Jag shrugged. "Well, they are the only ones using that specific word. But it sounds like even the President's own party is growing more concerned with his actions."

"This might work to our advantage," I said. "If there's political pressure on the President, he'll hesitate to act on behalf of Brightborn until things simmer down. If people are talking about not just impeachment, but treason, he'll have to be careful about fighting us or anyone else with the military on American soil."

"I think the protesters might have won a small victory on that front," Jag said. "If the protest put pressure on the President that prevents him from doing Brightborn's bidding for political reasons, then it succeeded. Even if the protest only temporarily forced the president's hand to distance himself from Brightborn."

I nodded. "He'll still be working with Brightborn, I suspect. But he'll have to be more careful about what he does publicly. That means if Trixie finds Brightborn and we go after him on American soil, we might only have to worry about fighting his legion rather than fending off the US military at the same time."

"I'm sure that the military will be supporting him in some way," Jag said, "even if they can't engage in an all-out assault on us for political reasons."

"Of course, all of this could change again tomorrow. Things are moving rapidly. Different parties look to be manufacturing their facts to try and interpret the events that occurred in St. Louis differently." I sighed. "We can only hope that Trixie will find us soon. Speaking of that, I need to fire off some magic so she's sure to find us when she's ready."

"What are you thinking? A pillar of fire?"

I chuckled. "I'm not exactly leading the Israelites through the wilderness to the promised land."

Jag cocked his head. "Aren't you? In a matter of speaking?"

I bit my lip. "I don't see the parallel."

"Think about it," Jag said. "You're supposed to restore that elf's land, bring its power back to Earth. What was it you called it?"

"Annwn," I said. "Or just Eden. That's easier to say."

Jag nodded. "Right. Eden. So, you unite a divided people who are lost in the wilderness, bound to serve as slaves under a foreign king, and you bring them to a sort of promised land."

I sighed. "I'm not Moses. But yes, I see the connections you're trying to make. Be that as it may, right now I just need to use magic, any magic, and it doesn't need to be anything impressive. Anything that will get Trixie's attention."

"Like what?" Jag asked.

I smirked as I touched the element of water within me. I gathered small droplets of water from the humid air and formed a bulb of water right over Jag's head. "Like this!"

I released the water and it splashed right over my friend's mohawked dome. His eyes went wide, then he squinted as the water ran into his face. His jaw was dropped in shock; I'd taken him off-guard.

"Caspar! You booger!"

I clutched my gut as I laughed hard. "I'm sorry! I couldn't resist!"

Jag smirked. "I suppose I'll just have to get my revenge the next time we work out together."

I bit my lip. "Work out? Yeah... I don't know. Maybe I'll start again tomorrow. Or the next day. Whenever I'm done saving the world."

Jag smiled, water dripping from the tip of his nose. "I'll get you back eventually."

I smiled. I called forth the power of air and blew it hard right into his face. So hard that it made his cheeks flap. I laughed so hard I snorted.

"Caspar! What the—"

"I was doing you a favor," I said, giggling through my words. "You were wet. I just wanted to dry you off."

Jag narrowed his eyes. "How do you think Layla will react when I tell her you just blew me?"

I almost choked on my tongue. "I can't believe you just said that!"

Jag smiled. "I've been in a lot of locker rooms, Casp. If you want to start a prank war, I might not have magic to use, but I have my tricks."

I portaled Jag and I back into the cave. Not much had changed since we left. At least I was in a better frame of mind. Talking to

Philip had helped me find my spiritual footing again. Visiting Shanda and Grace had helped me deal with Cecil's loss, and at some level, come to grips with the fact that his death wasn't entirely my fault.

Learning that the President was under a lot of political pressure and he wasn't likely to come to Brightborn's aid if we went after him was a positive development. Plus, now that I had cast some magic near the cave, I was hoping Trixie would come back and find us. Of course, even though she was a fairy, it wasn't a given that she'd find her way from the barn to the cave. Still, she'd recognize my car, and she'd know we couldn't be far away. I'd just have to hop out there periodically to see if she was out there looking for us.

I could only pray that she'd be back soon with information about Brightborn's location. This was an ideal time to attack. Before the traitor, whoever it was, warned him. While Brightborn was unlikely to have military aid, he'd probably have some protection. Maybe from the military. Maybe from the secret service. Hard to say. But I could handle that sort of thing with magic.

What I couldn't do was fight a war with the world's most powerful military with a small force of giants, elves, drow, a human, and a couple of talking animals.

Enough time had passed since I left that I was due to meet up with Elrand in the geode cavern again. I wasn't sure if I hoped the traitor would have revealed himself or herself by now or if I preferred not to know. It was one of those things that I couldn't *not* pursue—the knowledge of a spy in our midst was driving me batty—but it was also the sort of situation that in the past I'd just prefer to pretend didn't exist.

Back in the day, alcohol had helped me pretend unfortunate circumstances weren't what they were. Even after I stopped drinking, I sometimes used denial and distraction to procrastinate dealing with inevitably bad news or difficult situations. I found Layla first. If I went straight to meet with Elrand without first checking in with my wife, it wouldn't go over well.

Layla smiled at me the second she saw me. "You look different, Caspar. You look better."

"I'll update you on the news later," I said. "I visited Philip, and I went to see Shanda and Grace. I'll just say, while I'm not totally sure I've overcome the problem, the obsession with battle, I think I've found myself. I feel more grounded if that makes sense."

Layla nodded. "Of course it makes sense. If you weren't chosen by the prophet because of your faith, because of your ability to overcome whatever plagues you, I couldn't begin to guess why you were the one who fulfilled the elven prophecy."

I nodded. "I don't know if it matters to tell the truth. God once spoke through the mouth of an ass."

Layla scratched her head. "Like Jim Carrey did in that *Ace Ventura* movie?"

I laughed. "I didn't say he talked *with* his ass. He spoke through a donkey. It's a story in the Old Testament."

"Ahh, that kind of ass."

I chuckled. "Yes. That kind of ass. The point is, throughout the Bible, God chose the most unlikely people imaginable at every turn to do great things. I suppose, with all my flaws, I'm just one more example of someone chosen to do something bigger than myself."

"I'm glad you're doing better," Layla said, kissing me on the cheek.

I nodded. "I need to go meet up with Elrand. We'll talk more later, okay?"

I headed down the small corridor that led to the geode room where I was supposed to meet Elrand. He was already in the room.

CHAPTER TWENTY-EIGHT

"Any news?" I asked Elrand.

"I haven't checked yet," he said. "The impressions left behind in stone are not indelible. Every time they are viewed, they fade. I won't attempt to extract a vision from the cave alone. If an accusation is going to be made against anyone, it requires more than a single witness."

I nodded. "Smart. So, how do we do this? Just like at the stone circle? Channel all the elements into the whole cave, or should I shoot them in different directions?"

"When the stone circles retain and project a vision from the past, the colors of each of the elements contribute to the vision," Elrand said. "You have the primary colors contributed by water, fire, and aether. The others add hues to the image. While the colors might not match the original image perfectly, the stones help focus the elements each to produce the image precisely."

"When we saw the memory of Taliesin casting the elven prophecy, we cast something like a cone of the energies that swirled together," I said.

Elrand nodded. "Each element must settle into the stone in isolation. The energy that forms the memory contained within the stone will extract what is required from each of the elements to produce the hologram."

"Do we need to be in the part of the cave wherever the event happened?" I asked.

Elrand shook his head. "With the crystals in this geode, we can focus the image from anywhere in the cave and view it here."

"All right," I said. "Well, if you're ready, I suppose I am as well. Just channel each of the elements into the cave walls?"

Elrand nodded. "Try to send them into different sections of the wall, like when we used the five stones in the circle."

"Then, how do I find what we're looking for?"

"Rely on aether," Elrand said. "You should be able to sense anything that has occurred within the cave that was charged with magic. Or, at least an attempt to use a magical device like the communication crystal."

I nodded. I gathered the five elements to the forefront of my consciousness. I'd gotten more efficient at channeling them together. At first, trying to wield more than one at a time was a challenge. Now, while I could channel each of the elements together and separately, it was still a rather tiring experience, even with the small doses of magic needed to coax the limestone to reveal the visions imprinted within it.

At least it wouldn't be as exhausting as soaring through the skies and blowing up buildings. Good thing, since if the vision didn't reveal anything, I'd be doing this two times a day until we either caught the traitor or Trixie showed up and I'd have to leave the traitor to remain at large.

I allowed the five elements to escape my hands, one at a time. The flow, if you could call it that, wasn't really fast. I was standing within a ball of crystal. As I released fire into one of the walls, the crystals on that wall all turned red. I pivoted clockwise and released water. Those crystals turned blue. I continued spinning and casting each of the elements. Earth turned some of the quartz green, air left some glowing white, and with aether, a golden glow consumed a few crystals before it started to spiral around the cylindrical room.

The stone circle had formed a cone of energy. This was like standing within a crystal ball. Except, it wasn't a ball hewn from a single crystal, and we weren't examining it from the outside looking in.

All the colors started to swirl together. I reached out to aether, trying to sense something, anything at all magical. Something that would indicate, perhaps, that Brightborn's spy had tried to use a communication crystal.

I felt a tingle as my elemental energies interacted with the memories retained by the limestone in the cave. It felt like magic.

A figure appeared in the room. At first, it was just a shadow. As the colors collided and crystallized the image, however, it was clear that whoever was using the crystal was shrouded in a black cloak. The figure was smaller than a giant. That meant, at least, we could eliminate for sure the giants as suspects. The cloak, though, wasn't distinctly drow or elven. It was one of the dozens of parkas we'd had in our supply from our time at the North Pole. Since the cave was a cool seventy degrees, some of the elves and drow had me retrieve them from our supplies to wear at night.

Subtle, blue energy emanated from the hand of whoever it was behind the cloak. Would the traitor be able to tell that the message wasn't escaping the cave? These visions didn't contain audio. They were purely visual. The traitor was speaking to the crystal, but even attempting to rotate the image by engaging the power of aether, I couldn't get a view of the person's face. Whoever this was must have known that we could have been trying to spy on her. I guessed, based on the size of the hand that held the crystal, that it must've been a female. If it had been a male, I'd be able to eliminate the drow as suspects. Since it was likely a female, the traitor could be one of the drow or any of about half of the elves.

"Do you think it's possible that it could be a drow?" I asked. "These crystals are devices used by the elves."

Elrand nodded. "It's certainly a possibility. The drow are also accustomed to using enchanted objects. While it would be more likely to expect a New Albion elf to use a device like this, whoever this spy is could have been given the crystals she's been using by the elf king."

"Maybe if we keep watching, we'll figure out who it is," I said. "They have to get out of that parka eventually."

Elrand shook his head. "To refocus the view and follow it to elsewhere in the cave, you'd have to recast the magic."

"I can do it," I said. "Casting in stone circles isn't as exhausting as casting outside of them. It's the same here."

"But you won't be able to ensure that you're connecting to the same person," Elrand said. "Without a magical spike you can detect to orient you in the vision, you'll be looking for a needle in a haystack. Not just trying to survey every location in the cave but examining every minute in every location since we arrived. Is the information you're seeking there? Probably. But Caspar, if you spend all your time in here looking for the spy and you can't be available to address other things, you'll be granting them a victory. While you're trying to watch what the traitor might have done before, she will be free to do whatever she intends to do next."

I sighed. "Then what do we do?"

"Keep our eyes open. Come back here again, every morning and night, and see if we can pick up on any additional visions. All we can do is hope that at some point, the traitor is sloppy and reveals herself."

CHAPTER TWENTY-NINE

I made my way back to the rest of the group. They were still huddled around the campfire. When I'd left, most of them had been spread out around three separate fires. The giants with their fire, and the elven resistance and the drow, each with fires of their own. Now, everyone was gathered together.

I found Layla and sat down beside her. "Any news?" she asked.

"Sort of," I said. "Nothing definitive."

Layla's eyes darted around as she ensured no one was listening to us too closely. She kept her voice hushed. "Any clues who it is?"

I nodded. "Not a giant. Definitely female. But she was wearing one of those parkas. I couldn't get a good look at her."

Layla sighed. "That could be one of about a hundred people, elf or drow."

I bit my lip. "Exactly. At least we can rule out all the dudes."

Layla shrugged. "Maybe. I mean, we've been assuming that this spy is working alone. What if she isn't? What if there's more than one, and they're conspiring here together right beneath our noses?"

I grunted. "You're right. I hadn't thought of that."

"Still, it's likely that if there is more than one traitor, they're of the same race," Layla said. "I'd still suspect someone of the resistance is most likely. They were brought here by my father. They lived side-by-side with the loyalists. It would have been easy for my father, before he knew the resistance would end up aligned with us, to plant some loyalists in their group."

"I agree," I said. "That's the most likely scenario. I just don't think we should risk eliminating anyone as a suspect until we can rule them out definitively."

Jag and Rina, holding hands, walked over to us and sat down. "How goes it?" Jag asked.

I nodded. "Nice to see everyone gathered together."

"I agree," Rina said. "I thought it would be nice if we all gathered as one."

"This was your idea?" Layla asked, raising an eyebrow.

Rina nodded. "I figured the elves and giants wouldn't likely initiate something like this. You know, since they used to fight one another. If anyone was going to bring us together, other than Caspar, I figured it would have to be me."

I smiled. "Well, I appreciate it. We used to gather like this as a troop when I was in the scouts. We used to do sketches and such."

"Sketches?" Layla asked.

"Like little skits or plays," I said. "Funny scenarios, usually just a minute or two long. There were some classics that we recycled over and over, with different kids playing the various parts. Then, there were new skits that the kids made up on the fly. They weren't always good, but sometimes there were so bad that they were nonetheless entertaining."

"Any word from Trixie?" Rina asked. "Jag said you tried to get her attention back at the barn."

I laughed. "Did he tell you how I did it?"

Jag looked at me with wide eyes, shaking his head. "We don't need to go into that."

I smiled. "Not a big deal, Jag. It wasn't *that* embarrassing."

Jag sighed. "He cast some water over my head and dropped it on me."

"That's so mean!" Layla said, laughing.

"Funny, though!" Rina added.

"Then he gave me a blow job," Jag said.

Everyone went silent. "Shut up, Jag. I used air to blow-dry his face after I got him all wet," I said.

Layla giggled. "You had me worried there for a minute."

Rina rolled her eyes. "My Jag, always with his mind in the gutter. Always wanting something he'll never get."

I raised my eyebrows. "So you guys don't...you know..."

"Please," Rina said. "In our culture, we don't do that. The men service *us*."

"No reciprocation?" Layla asked.

"Why?" Rina asked. "It's an honor for a male to pleasure a woman in such a way."

I snorted. "Well, to each his own. So long as you're happy, Jag."

Jag nodded. "We come from different worlds. We have different expectations. But we're willing to compromise and find a middle ground."

"Yes," Rina said. "He does what I say. I give him a treat. We don't usually give our men treats, so I'd say that's a compromise."

"I'm not a dog!" Jag protested.

"Good thing!" Rina added. "I'd never let a dog do what you do!"

"All right," I said, laughing. "Too much information. For what it's worth, Aerin never expected me to behave as a male drow might. She respected me."

Rina rolled her eyes. "That was Aerin. Since you were the chosen one, I suspect she was able to look past certain conventions. Not sure how she did it. I mean, it's not uncommon for a drow to have several husbands. But to share a husband with another woman and an elf, no less?"

"She didn't share me," I said. "Aerin and I never consummated our marriage."

"Their connection was more political than romantic," Layla added. "She respected the love that Caspar and I have for each other."

Rina raised her eyebrows. "She sacrificed much for all of us."

I tapped the hilt of my blade to make a point. "She's here, you know. She can hear what you're saying."

Rina nodded. "Maybe she is. I mean, I don't have any reason to doubt that what you're saying is true. Do you think I could speak to her through the blade?"

I shook my head. "It only works between us because of the bond that formed between us when we were married. Aerin thinks our binding was completed when I took the blade. Swinging the blade, with her soul inside, functioned the way consummating our marriage would have if we'd ever...you know..."

Rina nodded. "It would be nice if there was a way for us to hear her. She was our princess, after all. When we lost some of our warriors in the city, she would have known what to do. We need to give our fallen the proper rites."

I bit my lip. "I hadn't thought of that. But you're right. When drow fell in battle, that was very important to her."

"Why didn't you bring back our fallen with you after the battle?" Rina asked.

I sighed. "I'm sorry, Rina. If there's any way I can recover them, I will."

"To be fair," Layla added, "he barely regained consciousness in time to save all of us and get us out of there. None of us would be alive right now if he hadn't done that."

"I'm not saying I'm not grateful," Rina said. "But at some point, our sisters will need to be put to rest properly."

"I understand that," I said. "I honestly didn't even know who had been hurt and who hadn't been when I portaled us out of that fight. If I had known, I would have brought them with us."

Rina nodded. "Well, I just wanted to make sure you hadn't forgotten how important it is to us that our dead not be left behind."

I nodded. "I understand. I don't know how, but I promise if I can find out where the bodies were taken, I'll see if I can figure out how to get to them. But I won't risk any other lives to do it."

"And if we get news on my father's location," Layla added, "that has to take priority."

Rina nodded. "Of course it does. I wouldn't expect anything less."

CHAPTER THIRTY

"That's some kind of nerve," Layla said, shaking her head as Rina and Jag walked away.

"What do you mean?" I asked.

"To put that burden on you, to worry about their dead, when we're facing such unfortunate odds in this war already."

I shrugged. "I can't fault the drow for wanting to mourn the fallen. If we stop mourning those who die, we'll forget the value of life."

"I understand that," Layla said. "But in war, there's rarely time to mourn."

I bit my lip. "Perhaps that's why so many wars last as long as they do. We measure wars and battles by body counts. But when a person becomes a number rather than a life, it's easy to minimize the loss. Think about it. What's the difference between a battle when, say, a hundred men die or a hundred and one?"

"Doesn't sound like a big difference."

"Tell that to the family of that one," I said. "For them, it's a huge difference. Every single life lost represents a whole family unsettled, an emotional wound that will never totally heal."

Layla nodded. "I have a few of those wounds myself."

"Your father?" I asked.

Layla nodded. "But it's different for me. His death might help to heal the wounds he's caused. I mean, he was responsible for my mom's death. He's hurt so many people. The giants, especially. At least if he's finally dead, I'll know he can't hurt me or anyone else ever again."

I nodded. "I get that. Even then, it's not wrong to mourn."

Layla huffed. "I don't know if I can bring myself to mourn if my father dies."

"You can mourn that he never lived the kind of life he could have had," I said. "How he missed what might have been, the relationship with you he should have had, in exchange for his pursuit of power. You can mourn and feel sad that he became what he is. I know this much. No matter what he thinks he'll accomplish if he succeeds, no matter how happy he'll think it will make him if he finally takes over the whole world, I suspect he'll discover that what he pursued wasn't happiness at all. Some of the world's most powerful people are also the most miserable."

"And some of the poorest people, strangely enough, are among the happiest."

"Also quite true," I said. "That's because happiness isn't something you achieve. It's something you recognize. It's not something you find on the outside by accumulating wealth or power. It's something you find on the inside when you discover peace and serenity in the heart."

"Are you happy, Caspar?" Layla asked.

I bit my lip. "Sometimes, I admit, I forget that. But when I think about all that I have to be grateful for, how can't I be happy?"

"What are you thankful for?" Layla asked.

"I'm thankful that I have my health," I said. "I have enough food to eat and clean water to drink. I'm grateful that the air we have is still breathable. I'm grateful for the people in my life—especially you, Layla."

"And Agnus?" Layla asked, smirking.

I laughed. "Yes, I'm even thankful for my cat. The point is, we have a choice to number all the things that we want to be miserable about in life or to count our blessings. Which list we keep will determine how happy we'll be."

Layla nodded. "How'd you get to be so wise?"

I snorted. "I'm not. I'm just really good at bullshitting. How'd I do?"

"Shut up!" Layla said, laughing.

I smiled. "We still need to figure out who this traitor is."

"And perhaps more importantly," Layla added, "why it is they'd betray us at all?"

"What do you mean?" I asked.

Layla shrugged. "Anyone who has lived with us for any time at all should be able to see a big difference between you and my father. If someone is betraying us, they must have a reason to take his side."

"Everyone has reasons for what they choose to do," I said. "Doesn't mean their reason is a good one."

"Well, let's hope we find out soon. If Trixie returns with information about where we can find my father before we identify the traitor, I don't know how we'll be able to mobilize against him."

"I've already thought about that," I said. "If Trixie comes back, and we can't identify the spy, I'll have to go after your father alone."

"Alone?" Layla asked. "I don't think so. I'll be going with you."

I shook my head. "You can't, Layla. It's you he's trying to get, and it's not fair to ask you to play a role in killing your own father. I don't want to kill again, but now I know that I can do it for the sake of the war without allowing it to consume me. At least, I think I can."

"You had better not go after him without letting me know you're leaving," Layla said.

I grabbed Layla's hand and held it tight in mine. "I could never leave without saying goodbye."

I glanced across the cavern to where Jag was sitting with Rina. He was obviously infatuated with her. He raised her hand to his lips and kissed it gently. She didn't react much at all to his obvious display of affection. I was worried about him. It wasn't that drow women couldn't love their husbands. But for most of them, if they chose a man, it was a practical matter above all else. They chose men who could offer them something of use, perform work that might benefit them, or because they were good "stock" and would likely produce desirable children. Love was a secondary concern.

I scratched my head. "What do you think Rina is getting out of her relationship with Jag?"

"I don't know," Layla said. "Why do you ask?"

"It strikes me that she doesn't seem nearly so into him as he is into her," I said.

Layla shrugged. "She might break his heart. I imagine, since there weren't any drow men around, she just thought he'd be fun to play with."

I bit my lip. "Maybe. That could be it. Or perhaps it has something to do with Jag being my friend."

"What are you suggesting?" Layla asked.

I shook my head. "Maybe I'm cynical, but Jag was the one who told me about the protest that was being planned. He's the one who suggested we go there. I thought it was a good idea, but what if it wasn't his idea?"

Layla took a deep breath. "You aren't suggesting that Rina is the traitor, are you?"

I shrugged. "I don't know. I can't imagine what her motive would be. But it would make sense of some things. Namely, how Brightborn knew so far in advance to prepare his assault on us at the protest. Think about it. We decided to go there on the spur of the moment."

Layla nodded. "Even if the traitor told my father right away, it would have taken some time to put together such a complicated plan, to get a sniper in place, to have the forces in place for the attack."

I nodded. "Unless having us attend that protest was the plan from the beginning. The spy didn't *tell* Brightborn we were going to it. She convinced us through Jag that we should go."

"An interesting theory," Layla said. "But you need to be careful. If you're wrong, this could blow up in your face."

"I can ask Jag about it," I said.

"That's what I'm saying. If he thinks he loves her, he'll be blind to the possibility that Rina might be a traitor."

I nodded. "Then I'll have to ask my questions carefully. We need to find out if she was the one who let him know about the protest or if she had any strong opinions suggesting we should go to it."

"Before you do that, you should probably talk to Aerin about it," Layla said. "She might have some insights. She knows Rina a lot better than we do."

"All right," I said. "I'll do that. Then, after that, we need to find a place to curl up and go to sleep. I think I've had maybe two hours of sleep in the last three days."

Layla kissed my cheek. "I'll be here waiting for you."

CHAPTER THIRTY-ONE

I rarely went anywhere without Aerin's blade at my side. Not because I expected a fight all the time—although it was always a possibility. I carried the blade almost constantly because even though I could only hear or speak to Aerin when touching the blade, she could still listen in on anything that happened near the blade. If I wanted her advice, she'd know pretty much everything I was thinking the moment I touched it.

I ducked into one of the corridors that spider-webbed off of the larger cavern where everyone was resting. Those who weren't asleep were well on their way.

I hoped to join them soon after I had this conversation. I wasn't about to risk it inside the cave, not even deep down a corridor. There were too many people and too much risk that someone could overhear me. Especially since these caves had such strange acoustics.

I went far enough down the corridor that I was out of view from anyone in the main cavern, and I cast a fairy portal to the barn. At this hour, I could have gone anywhere, even my old church. I wasn't sure if anyone was living in my old apartment. I thought about going there just so I could show up and sing *Old*

Apartment by the Barenaked Ladies. Someday, if I ever wasn't the headline for *America's Most Wanted*, I'd probably try it just for kicks. Tonight I was inclined to take as few risks as possible and stay as close to the group as I could.

For extra security, I got inside my Mitsubishi Eclipse. I doubted anyone was hiding in the piles of rotted hay or outside the barn doors, but given that we were dealing with a spy I was a little paranoid that she could be listening in at any time. After all, I wasn't certain that Rina was the traitor. Even if she was, I couldn't be certain that she was working alone.

Climbing into my Eclipse with a sword attached to my waist was a comedy of errors. Every time I tried to sit down, gravity would pull the tip of the sheath down, blocking me from sitting. I had to "clear" the blade like someone might move a dress when taking a seat. I suppose Mitsubishi didn't design the vehicle with samurai in mind.

I touched the hilt of Aerin's blade.

Rina isn't a traitor, Aerin piped up before I even had a chance to introduce the question I had in my mind.

"Are you sure? The shoe fits. It would explain why the military was so prepared for us when we went to that protest."

Rina might be a lot of things. She can be stubborn. She might even be taking advantage of your friend. But she'd never betray the sacred cause.

"The sacred cause?" I asked.

The drow have recognized for centuries that it was our place to identify and support the Chosen One. When you completed the trials, every drow was duty-bound to defend you and do whatever it takes to ensure you fulfill what the prophet predicted.

"Still, she's made it clear more than once that she doesn't totally trust me," I said. "Since I'm the only one who can hear you speak."

Even if she doesn't trust you or questions your motives and actions, she would still do whatever it took to ensure you fulfilled the role given you. Even if it meant working in spite of you.

I snorted. "In spite of me? What do you mean by that?"

Face it, Caspar. You've made some poor choices. People have died, in part because of your decisions. I'm not saying that Rina wouldn't undermine you. But if she does, she's doing it for your good. She wouldn't betray you to Brightborn.

"But *someone* is making contact with Brightborn. They're using a crystal to communicate with him."

I'm not saying that there isn't a traitor. It's possible. But if it was Rina who you saw in that vision, and she was communicating with Brightborn, it wasn't to betray you.

I sighed. "If Rina is talking to Brightborn, and she's trying to negotiate something, why wouldn't she just tell me?"

Maybe she doesn't trust you yet. Perhaps she fears that you'll react to whatever information she has irresponsibly.

"I guess I couldn't blame her for that. So, you're saying I need to earn her trust? But how can I do that when I'm not sure *she* can be trusted?"

Do you trust me? Aerin asked.

"I do."

Then believe me when I tell you that you can trust Rina.

CHAPTER THIRTY-TWO

When you're a minister, you make some strange connections and develop some unusual relationships with interesting people in the course of being a part of people's lives at their most vulnerable moments. When people were sick or dying, I forged relationships with dozens of doctors, nurses, and hospital personnel. For obvious reasons, I knew almost all of the funeral directors. I also had a unique relationship with the law enforcement community. I'd had members in my church who were on probation. I'd had members who were victims of crimes and had ministered to people in the community who were later arrested. I know a lot of people who'd been arrested, both because I was a minister and because I was a part of the recovery community. While most of the people in AA who had significant time in sobriety hadn't had any run-ins with the law recently, many of them had serious encounters with law enforcement in the past.

So what would happen to the bodies of the drow, and the other elves, who'd fallen in the battle? They didn't need to be identified. The cause of death wasn't in question. No investigations needed to be performed. That meant they wouldn't likely go to the coroner. I knew that much from my contacts in law enforcement over the years. These were bodies unlikely to be claimed. The government would want to go to minimal expense to dispose of them. They didn't often bury bodies like that. It took up space and cost more than cremation.

Thankfully, due to my connections with funeral directors, I knew the one who handled most of the cremations for the city. I couldn't be totally sure that he'd have the bodies, but it was worth a shot. If he did, and I could bring them back to Rina, it might go a long way toward convincing her to tell me the truth. Aerin said, after all, that if she wasn't telling me what she was up to, it was probably because she wasn't sure she could trust me to act wisely on her information. This might not prove to her that I made the best decisions. However, it *would* show that I was mindful of and sensitive to the drow's needs. It would be a step toward hopefully building some trust. More than that, it would serve as an olive branch that I could offer when I asked her if she'd been communicating with Brightborn.

The mortician I needed to reach out to wasn't the most personable mortician I'd dealt with as a minister. Many of them are both morticians and funeral directors. They embalm and cremate bodies, on the one hand, and then they engage the bereaved and plan services on the other. Some morticians work better with the dead than the living. Dealing with mourning is difficult. To do it day in and day out takes something of a gift, not just sensitivity but also a degree of intestinal fortitude. Not everyone can be empathetic to such intense emotions on a regular basis without allowing it to affect them personally. It takes a special person. It also takes a special sort of person to work with dead bodies on the regular. That's why there are very few people well-suited to be morticians *and* funeral directors.

Morty was the sort of mortician who excelled at working with dead bodies but didn't do well with people experiencing grief. Of course, Morty wasn't his real name. It was a nickname. I think his real name was Dennis. No one called him that, though.

Every time I saw him, I'd called him Morty. That was how he'd introduced himself to me, so I stuck with it.

He worked in a funeral home downtown. Morty just didn't deal with the living. He spent all his time in the basement, applying makeup to the deceased so they'd look like themselves, pumping some full of chemicals to preserve them for burial, and cremating others.

Most of my funerals were conducted at my former church. From time to time, the family would choose to have the service at the funeral home. At the very least, they had the visitations there. It wasn't the only funeral home and mortuary I'd worked with, but I'd been there enough that I supposed at this time of the night I could portal myself there and, hopefully, not inadvertently emerge from my portal in someone's body—living or dead.

If I knew Morty like I thought I did, he'd probably be working late into the evening, especially if he had the bodies from the battle downtown to deal with. I could only hope that he had the bodies I was looking for and that he hadn't cremated them already. A lot of people had died in that battle, but most of them were protesters caught in the crossfire. They were people who had families, who'd have funerals in their own churches or the funeral homes of their choosing. They wouldn't be sent with the unidentified and unclaimed that usually went to Morty.

I cast a portal, visualizing the service room in the funeral home. I could only hope they hadn't remodeled in the year or so since I'd last been there. So far, so lucky. I hoped my luck would persist. What were the chances? It was a shot in the dark, but it was a shot worth taking. What was the worst that could happen? Morty saw me and called the cops? I'd portal out of there and go back to the cave facing the same problems I had before.

Hopefully, that wouldn't happen.

I heard banging coming from the basement. I wasn't sure what was causing the banging. The banging was replaced by buzzing, the sort that you might hear when power tools were in use. He wasn't doing woodworking. He wasn't crafting an armoire. He might have been cutting through an arm, though.

I bit my lip. I'd never had the strongest stomach. I was fine with dead bodies—*after* they were dressed and made to look like wax mannequins in their caskets. In their more natural, gruesome state, though, not so much.

I followed the hallway that led to a stairwell and an elevator—a casket-sized elevator—that led to the mortuary. I decided to take the stairs.

The stairwell smelled faintly of formaldehyde or whatever chemicals were used for embalming these days. It was a strange custom. Most people knew that if you buried a body deep enough, or you had them sealed in vaults, there wasn't any real risk of disease seeping into the ground. The chemicals were meant to preserve the body. Some Christians thought it was a good idea to preserve the body for the day of the resurrection prophesied by the Bible. As if God couldn't just remake people from their ashes. The whole practice struck me as being more aligned with ancient Egyptian mythology concerning the dead. In truth, the death industry was a business like anything else. The grieving often had life insurance money to spend on a funeral. The cynic in me suspected that embalming and the large catalogs of fancy caskets—including those lined with memory foam for the comfort of the deceased—were a way to exploit the grieving, to give them a sense that they'd laid their loved one to rest in luxury. As if the dead person cared.

At least it gave people like Morty a job. Who knows what he'd do otherwise. He'd probably go into something with computers. A job that didn't involve dealing with living human beings.

I stepped into the room, and the smell hit me like a ton of bricks. It reminded me of the time we'd dissected pigs in my sophomore biology class. Except the stench was stronger.

Morty was dressed in a long gown. He wore thick, black gloves and had an eye shield and mask over his face. He set down his saw next to the body of whoever it was he was busy chopping into bits and stared at me in surprise. "Caspar?"

I waved awkwardly. "Hi, Morty."

"We're closed," Morty said.

I snorted. "I didn't know you had regular operating hours. Do you still serve breakfast before ten AM?"

Morty cocked his head. He didn't get the joke. I figured taking it a step further and asking for an Egg McMuffin wouldn't resonate.

"What are you doing here?" Morty asked. "Aren't you supposed to be in jail?"

I bit my lip. "Hopefully not any time soon. I came to see if you had the bodies of the drow. There were two of them who fell in the battle."

"The dark-skinned elves?" Morty asked.

I nodded. "That's them."

Morty gestured to a pile of body bags stacked against his wall. I doubted that was the way he was supposed to be dealing with the bodies. But if these were unwanted, unidentified bodies, who was going to complain? Especially if they were about to be cremated.

"Are they in there?" I asked.

Morty shrugged. "If I have them, that's where they're at. You're free to take a look. Still, I'm contracted to cremate them."

"If they're there, I need to take them with me," I said.

"I don't know if I can let you do that," Morty said.

"Morty, come on. Their people want to mourn them. If the government wants you to give them ashes, surely you can come up with some. It's not like anyone could tell the difference."

Morty shrugged. "All right. Well, that will save me some time tonight. I have ten bodies to process."

"Ten?" I asked. "All from the battle downtown?"

Morty shrugged. "Some of them, yeah. Others were homeless people. Overdoses, more than likely."

"That's sad," I said.

Morty shrugged as he picked up his saw again. "Pays my bills."

"What are you doing with that guy's body that requires a saw?" I asked.

"Arm was mangled in an accident. I have to manipulate it to look normal in the casket."

I grimaced. "Good luck with that."

Morty nodded. "Now, go fish!"

"Go fish?" I asked.

"Yeah, haven't you played that game before?"

I snorted. "I get the reference. It's a strange way to think about sorting through a stack of bodies."

"I could say it's a game of pick-up stiffs," Morty quipped.

I swallowed a chuckle. "Yeah, that would work, too. Anyway, thanks, Morty."

"Perhaps I'll see you again soon," Morty said.

I shrugged. "Well, I'm not working in the church anymore."

"No, I mean on my table. The way it sounds, you'll end up here sooner than later."

I cocked my head. "Yeah, good seeing you, too, Morty."

I unzipped three body bags before I found one containing one of the drow. I almost shouted, "Eureka," but that would have been weird. So I kept my mouth shut and pulled her body aside, zipping her back up. I looked at two more bodies, probably homeless addicts, then I found the second. Luck had finally turned my way.

I wouldn't say I'd struck oil or struck gold. Finding a couple of corpses isn't most people's idea of luck. But in my situation, it was what I needed. I pulled both bodies into a corner. I waved at Morty, and he saluted me. Sort of weird, but whatever.

I formed a fairy portal and took the bodies back with me to the cave.

CHAPTER THIRTY-THREE

I'd teleported into one of the corridors off the main cavern. The body bags held most of the stench within. Still, it seemed best to leave them to the side. I set some fire ablaze in my palm to illuminate the tunnel and made my way back to the main corridor. I wanted to find Rina. I looked around the drow area. She wasn't there.

Maybe she was sleeping with Jag. By sleeping, I hoped I was being literal. I certainly didn't want to walk in on them.

I found Jag curled up in the fetal position, his massive arm tucked under his head as a pillow and a blanket draped across his body. Rina wasn't there.

I tapped Jag in the back a few times with the toe of my shoe. "Hey, Jag. Wake up."

He didn't move.

I sighed. I hated trying to wake up people who didn't want to be awakened. When it's another dude, you're extremely limited. It wasn't like I could tickle him awake without it getting weird. Of course, I couldn't do that with most women, either. I could only get away with that with Layla.

There isn't a good way to wake someone up that isn't weird.

Or annoying. So I duplicated my little prank from before and dropped a blob of water over his face.

Jag grunted and rolled over. "Dammit, Caspar!"

I smiled. "It was either that or tickle your tootsies, and I didn't want to get your foot stink on my fingers."

"What the hell do you want?" Jag asked. "We're trying to sleep."

"Just wondered if you know where Rina was. I got her something... Well, a couple of somethings."

"You getting my girl gifts, now?" Jag asked. "Am I going to have to kick your ass?"

I snorted. "If you think two dead bodies is a romantic gift, then okay."

Jag as up. "You found them?"

I nodded, smiling. "I couldn't believe it, myself. But yes."

Jag looked around in confusion. "I wonder where Rina went. She was cuddled up right here just... I don't know; however long ago it was I went to sleep."

"I didn't see her with the other drow, either," I said.

Jag scratched her head. "She likes to have a little time to herself sometimes."

"How long has she been going off by herself?" I asked. If she was calling Brightborn, it made sense.

"It started after the whole North Pole debacle," Jag said.

I nodded. "If she comes back, let her know I'm looking for her, will you?"

Jag nodded. "I can do that."

I paused before leaving. "Oh, one more thing. Strange question, but did she tell you anything about how she felt about the protest downtown? Before we went there, I mean."

Jag cocked his head. "Yeah, actually."

"What did she say?" I asked.

"She tried to insist that I asked you not to go," Jag said. "But I disagreed with her. It's like she knew something was going to go wrong."

I bit my lip. "Thanks, Jag."

What if Rina *was* working with Brightborn, but she was doing it so she could lead him to believe she was on his side? Perhaps he had some leverage on her or had made her some promises. He'd told Aerin that the drow would have a special place as elves in his New World Order. Might he have offered the same to Rina? If so, perhaps she gave him the *impression* that she'd work on his behalf.

Aerin had insisted Rina would never betray me. However, maybe she was playing the double agent to earn Brightborn's trust, and she planned to use the information she managed to glean from him against him. But she couldn't show her cards too soon. She must've known that Brightborn *wanted* us to go to that protest. Could she have possibly known it would end the way it did? I doubted it. She would have surely said something, refused to take the drow into an ambush.

But she *did* know that Brightborn had wanted us to go. She'd known he was planning something, and she'd tried to warn Jag about it. But what could she say without revealing that she had been talking to Brightborn? It was clear she didn't trust that we'd have the patience to let whatever she was planning play itself out if we knew she was talking to him.

I scratched my head. I wasn't sure where Rina had gone. I headed back toward the exit of the cavern, the small tunnel we had to go through. Elrand was sitting next to it, keeping an eye on the entrance and exit.

"Elrand," I said. "Did Rina leave, by chance?"

Elrand nodded. "A couple of hours ago."

"And you just let her go?" I asked.

Elrand shrugged. "What could I say to stop her that wouldn't let her know I was on to her if she happened to be the spy?"

I sighed. "I don't think she's a spy. But I think she is working with Brightborn as a double agent, trying to get information to use against him."

Elrand narrowed his eyes. "A risky endeavor."

I nodded. "Aerin insists she wouldn't betray us. I have to take her word for it. It adds up. She tried to tell Jag that it wasn't a good idea for us to go when he found out about that protest. Maybe she knew something."

"If she did, then she could have warned us," Elrand said. "She could have come clean."

I nodded. "Maybe she knew something was going to happen but she didn't realize it was going to be as devastating as it was."

Elrand nodded. "Perhaps. Well, if you hope to catch her, you should leave soon. She's been gone for a while."

I sighed. If she was on foot, she couldn't get far. I checked my pockets. Where the hell had my car keys gone? Did she seriously pickpocket me when we were speaking? I wasn't paying close attention. If she took my car...

"I think she took my car!"

Elrand winced. "Drow women can be sneaky. Trust me, I know all about that."

"I'm sure you do," I said. "Do me a favor and let Layla know I went after her, would you? I promised before I wouldn't go after Brightborn without saying goodbye first. Still, if things with Rina are more urgent than we anticipated, I don't know if I have time to spare."

"I'll do that, Caspar," Elrand said.

"Thank you." Rather than trying to crawl through the tunnel, I formed a fairy portal and connected it to the barn. Sure enough, my car was gone.

"Dammit!" I shouted, kicking at the dust.

"Damn what?" a high-pitched voice said, accompanied by a buzz.

I turned. "Trixie! You're back!"

"I am!" Trixie said. "I know where Brightborn is!"

CHAPTER THIRTY-FOUR

I didn't know where Rina had gone. Trixie didn't, either. Drow were experts at evading fairies. They'd done it for centuries, limiting their use of magic to enchanted devices. Still, it was curious that Rina left only two hours before Trixie had returned. Trixie said she'd been there a while but clearly after Rina left. So, the best I could figure was that they'd missed each other by mere minutes.

"So, Aelfrich led you to Brightborn?" I asked.

"Eventually!" Trixie said, enthusiasm in her voice. "Funny, though. I followed that elf all that time, and he only led me to the elf king minutes before the king cast a simple spell. I could have found him anyway!"

I bit my lip. "How long ago did he cast that spell, and what did he cast, exactly?"

"About an hour ago!" Trixie said. "Just as Aelfrich arrived. He's in a suite in super, super, tall tower thingy in New York!"

I smiled. "A high rise?"

Trixie laughed. "That's silly! No, it was a tall tower thingy."

I nodded. "Right. A much more serious way of looking at it."

"Anyway, Aelfrich got there eventually. I was like, well, what do you know? That little booger knew where Brightborn was all this time and didn't say a peep!"

"But Brightborn cast a spell when Aelfrich arrived?" I asked.

"Channeled it right into a crystal," Trixie said.

I bit my lip. "One of our own has been communicating with Brightborn through a crystal. I'm thinking she was trying to help."

Trixie shook her head. "The crystal had magic in it. Something I couldn't sense. Not like I can with regular magic. What Brightborn cast *through* it was something like aether but warped. Tainted somehow."

I bit my lip. "Any idea what the spell did?"

Trixie shrugged. "Like I said, it was *really* weird! I never saw anything like that here on Earth, and definitely not back on New Albion!"

I sighed. "Let's go into the cave. I need to talk to Elrand about this."

"Sure thing! But you know, we don't know how long he'll be there! This might be our only chance to get to him!"

I let Trixie take us back into the cave. She was more precise and efficient when it came to fairy portals because, well, she was a fairy. Trixie explained to Elrand what she's seen.

"What about the magic he cast gave you the impression that it was different than common aether?" Elrand asked.

"Aether is life, right? This was almost like the opposite. If Aether comes from the source of life, it was like whatever t his magic connected to was from some other source."

"Not the Tree of Life, but the tree of the knowledge of good and evil," Elrand said.

I cocked my head. "We're talking Garden of Eden stuff again?"

Elrand nodded. "You know the lore as well as I do. I know it from a different perspective. The tree of knowledge is often seen as a tree that grants freedom. Liberty. But it is a delusion. The will is free when it is attuned to life. Some protest; they imagine that limitation to the things of life and light is a form of bondage. But limitation is not the opposite of liberty. Sometimes, it is a lack of limitation that enslaves us the most."

I scratched my head. "I sort of get what you're saying."

"Think of it like this," Elrand said. "Gravity is a kind of limitation, is it not?"

"Of course. It prevents us from floating out into space."

"You might think without it we'd be free, but in truth, gravity allows us to live. Limitation is not the opposite of life. It is a prerequisite for life."

"So this other tree, the tree of knowledge, is something of the opposite?"

"It deceives us into believing that freedom comes through license," Elrand said. "By being able to do whatever one wishes at any time regardless of what's good, right, or beneficial. Without limitation, we find ourselves enslaved to an endless pursuit of something in nothing."

I nodded. "I think that makes some sense. Sort of."

"Tell me, Caspar. When you were a child, what did you want to be when you grew up?"

I smiled. "I wanted to be the next Michael Jordan."

Elrand laughed. "What if every child who wanted to be the next Michael Jordan became that?"

"Then I suppose his abilities would become the new average," I said.

Elrand nodded. "What did you discover when you *tried* to play ball like Jordan?"

I laughed. "I found that I'm clumsy, can't catch, can't shoot, and can't jump. I gave up on that dream pretty quick."

"You discovered a limitation. That limitation helped you discover yourself. You found what makes you, you."

"I think I'm still looking for that, in part," I said.

"We all are," Elrand said. "Most of us live life in discovery. But if we had no limitations, if we didn't have *different* limitations, we'd have a lot of athletes, a lot of pop stars, I imagine. We'd have few who do the important jobs necessary for a thriving world and society."

"I get that," I said. "But what does this have to do with what Brightborn did?"

"Somehow, he's extracted the power of the tree of knowledge from Annwn, from Eden," Elrand said. "The bloodshed in the forest must have done something to those lands. He has harnessed that power, and while it is alluring, while Rina might have had good intentions, he's used it to bind her will. Because what the tree of knowledge does is not grant freedom. It deceives us into a form of bondage, a will that only seems free but in truth always pursues only what it desires, not what is best."

"You think this magic took control of Rina, somehow?"

Elrand shook his head. "It's not mind control, exactly. Consider this. Your faith believes that when the first man and woman ate from the tree of knowledge, they introduced sin into the world."

I nodded. "More or less. That's right."

"Freedom comes when our affections, our passions, are bound to what is good," Elrand said. "The love of one another. Bondage comes when our affections and passions are unfocused, seemingly free but not. When we are allowed to cling to whatever feels good, whatever satisfies temporary carnal pleasures, it turns us inward, blinding us to others and the good we might do."

I frowned. "So you're saying that Brightborn used the power of passion, of sin, to somehow lure Rina? To control her?"

"To lure her, yes. To control her? Consider it a temptation. Will she be able to stand against it? To embrace what he offers is deceitful. It promises freedom but gives only misery."

I nodded. "I used to justify drinking that way. I'd say I'm an adult. I can drink however much I want! But doing what I wanted wasn't freedom. It was slavery."

"Then perhaps this was why you were chosen, Naayak,"

Elrand said. "This is the battle I fear you are about to face. Bright-born will not want to kill you. He'll want to offer you something, give you something, tempt you in some way. But if you accept it, you will lose."

"I won't take anything he has to offer," I said. "Whatever he says, I know it's a lie."

CHAPTER THIRTY-FIVE

I went to find Layla. I needed to hurry, but I told her I'd never leave without saying goodbye.

I leaned over and kissed her on the cheek. "I have to go," I whispered. "I love you."

Layla rolled over. Her eyelids parted. "Go?"

I nodded. "It's time."

"I'll come with you," Layla said.

I shook my head. "That what he wants. I need to do this alone. It's the only way."

Layla reached up and touched my cheek. "Whatever you do, stay true to yourself. Find a way to end this that doesn't change you."

I nodded. "I'll see you soon, okay?"

Layla grabbed me and kissed me softly on the lips. "You'd better come back to me."

"One way or another, I will. I promise," I vowed.

I stood and grabbed my second sword, then I glanced at Trixie and nodded. She formed the portal around me.

So many emotions flooded into my mind at once. It felt like I'd reached the end. I'd heard the shouts of Hosanna. I'd heard the cries to eliminate me from others. I'd done my best to rally this small army. They'd fought well when they needed to.

However, this was my chance to end it all. To stop the cycle of bloodshed. How would I do it? I didn't know. I'd meant what I said. I intended to come back to my bride. But how could I guarantee it?

I didn't know much about this magic that Brightborn had extracted from Annwn, from the tree of knowledge. I'd encountered magic drawn from the Tree of Life before, though. None of my powers could stand against it. Somehow I was supposed to *restore* that magic to this world. But how? All I knew was that Brightborn had tapped into a kind of magic that was the source of everything evil, everything broken, everything selfish and destructive. And somehow, I'd have to face it.

I didn't know what he had done to Rina. I had to save her, if for no other reason than Jag would kick my ass if I didn't. I owed it to her. Even if I didn't, no one deserved to be exposed to the kind of magic that Brightborn now possessed. How would he use it to accomplish his agenda? I didn't know, but I was sure he had a plan.

I appeared in a fancy suite at the top of a tower somewhere in New York. The whole place was lined with gold. Golden curtains. Gold-flecked paint on the walls. It was gaudy as sin, which was probably appropriate. I can't imagine more gold had ever been in one room since Solomon's temple storehouse, the same one he showed off to the Queen of Sheba.

Solomon, too, was gifted. Granted wisdom in excess of that of any man. However, wisdom didn't save him from temptation. There is no wisdom, no knowledge, that can stand against what tempts us. There's no dogma that you can learn, as if the faith was a textbook to master. The only way to stand against temptation is to recognize the fact that we are all spiritual beggars. We cling to faith, which at the end of the day is the trust a child has when his parents take him in their arms. When the baby receives everything he needs from his mother and father.

That was the kind of faith I clung to as I stared down Brightborn on the opposite side of the room. My swords were both sheathed at my sides.

Brightborn stood there, a darkness in his eyes. Whatever this magic he had absorbed was, it had made his pupils dilate to consume each of his eyes.

"You're messing with something you don't understand, Brightborn," I said.

"I understand well enough," Brightborn said. "Did you know that when you killed my men in that little camp you set up in Canada, their blood watered a seed from the otherworld? It sprouted a great, powerful tree. Now I hold all its magic at my command."

I shook my head. "You only think you have mastered it. In truth, it has enslaved you, Brightborn."

The elven king laughed. "With this power, I will compel the whole world to bend a knee to me, even as I have the acting ruler of the drow."

"What have you done with Rina!" I shouted.

Brightborn laughed. "I rewarded her with the honor of my bed. For she has served as my eyes and ears as of late."

I snorted. "She wouldn't betray us."

Brightborn smiled as he paced, his long, golden robe barely grazing the black tile on his floors. "You're right. She wouldn't. She thought she was using me, that she had the upper hand. But I played her all the while."

I shook my head. "She didn't want us to go to that protest. When you tried to kill me in the city."

"Kill you?" Brightborn asked. "I didn't intend to have you killed. Only to wound you and capture you, that I might welcome you and my daughter here as my rightful heirs."

"Your heirs?" I asked. "Heirs to what? I've fought against you every step of the way. Why do you think I'd want to take over this false empire you're trying to build?"

Brightborn smiled. "But you will. It's a shame you didn't bring Layla with you. I'd hoped this could be your coronation."

"You hoped?" I said. "You mean you expected me?"

Brightborn nodded. "I brought Rina here. I know you'd come for her. I knew you'd use the fairies to follow Aelfrich to me."

I shook my head. "Where is Rina, Brightborn?"

Brightborn smiled. "Patience, Caspar. I'll bring her out to you soon enough."

"I could strike you down right now," I said.

Brightborn shrugged. "Then do it."

I clenched my hand and channeled the element of fire into my fist. When I tried to release it, nothing happened.

"Dampeners," I said, shaking my head. "Just like Aelfrich's spire."

Brightborn laughed. "If you want to kill me, you'll have to do it with your blade."

I pulled my second blade from its sheath. The second I did, Brightborn raised his hand, and the fire I'd tried to channel blasted out of my hand and consumed the blade, burning so hot it melted the steel into a puddle of liquid me.

"Not with that blade," Brightborn said. "With your *other* blade."

"I won't kill you with this blade," I said.

"Why not?" Brightborn asked, smirking. "Are you afraid poor Aerin won't be able to overpower me when my soul joins hers?"

"She's stronger than you, Brightborn."

"Then strike me down, and we shall see."

I touched the hilt of the blade.

Don't do it, Caspar.

"Why not?" I asked.

It's not about me. It's about you. If you strike him, if you shed blood again, you'll lose yourself. It will give him a foothold.

"I'm not going to kill you, Brightborn."

"Then, how will you become my heir?" Brightborn asked, laughing.

"I don't want to be your heir!" I shouted.

"Look out of the window, Caspar," Brightborn said. "Tell me what you see."

I approached the window, fearing the worst. All I saw was the view overlooking downtown New York. I'd never been to New York, but everyone knows what New York City looks like. "I see a great city."

"Some believe it is the model city," Brightborn said. "It is here where the United Nations meets. That's why I'm here, of course. Some have called New York the capital of the world. I intend to make it exactly that. As my heir, all you see and more could be yours. This whole world could be yours."

I sighed. "What profit is it for a man if he gains the whole world but forfeits his soul?"

"I'm not the devil," Brightborn said. "I'm not here to bargain for your soul."

"No matter," I said. "I'm not interested in ruling a kingdom of this world. I'm only interested in serving a kingdom of love, justice, and righteousness."

Brightborn nodded and walked over to a large cabinet. Like everything else in the room, it was trimmed in gold. The handles. The hinges. Even the doors on the front were solid gold. He opened it and reached inside to grab two glasses. He selected a bottle and filled both glasses halfway.

"Why don't you take a drink with me?" Brightborn asked.

I scowled. "I'm more than five years sober. I don't drink."

"But you aren't who you used to be," Brightborn said. "The power within you, the elements, they can help you. Haven't you always wished you could drink like a normal person, without being consumed by addiction?"

"Of course I did," I said. "At least, I used to."

"It's possible, you know," Brightborn said, taking a sip. "The powers you have will protect you from the effects of the drink."

I shook my head to refuse the drink Brightborn handed me. "I know my limits, Brightborn. I won't put it to the test."

"Very well," Brightborn said, placing the glass intended for me on a crystal table in the middle of the room. "I can respect your resolve."

I nodded. "Yeah. Thanks. I guess."

"Then what if I were to promise you your freedom? The world thinks you are a criminal. A terrorist. With one phone call, I could change the narrative. I could have you seen as a hero, loved by all. Or, if you prefer, I could simply give you your life back. Would you like to preach again? You already have a church. What is it you call that place where you married Aerin and my daughter?"

"St. Ensley's," I said.

Brightborn laughed. "Yes, you named it after the dead fairy."

I clenched my fists. "He was my friend, Brightborn."

"My apologies, and my condolences," Brightborn said. "With your name cleared, you could preach to full crowds every week. I wouldn't interfere. I'll see to it that your messages are shared throughout the world. You could inspire hope across the globe."

"And what would I have to do for that?" I asked.

"Kneel, pledge your fidelity to me, and accept your role as my heir, as my son."

"While you oppress the world, force humanity to serve you?"

"Humans are meant to serve," Brightborn said. "They thrive in service. They spoil everything when they attempt to rule. I offer them freedom, Caspar. No longer will humanity feel compelled to rule, to dominate the world. Instead, they can live in a world healed from human exploitation. A world of abundance."

"Your track record suggests otherwise," I said. "You exploited the magic that kept New Albion alive. You took what was meant for life and used it to wage war."

"My intention was always to come here, Caspar. It was the orcs who stood against me. It was they who forced me to fight that I might come and redeem your world from your race's failings."

"I don't believe that for a second," I said.

"You are supposed to be the chosen one, are you not?" Brightborn asked.

I nodded. "I am."

"I will not live forever. As my heir, you can take over the rule I establish. If you wish, you can then grant all races equality. You can unite the races. This is how you were always meant to fulfill the prophecy."

I shook my head. "I don't think that's the way."

"You married my daughter," Brightborn said. "Why are you so convinced that I am your enemy?"

"Oh, I don't know," I said sarcastically. "Perhaps it has something to do with the fact that you murdered millions of giants on your former planet. Maybe it's because your former high priest refused to pass along the priesthood to one of your own. Perhaps it's because you forced me to kill a man back at Pruitt-Igoe. Whenever you've had your way, death and bloodshed have followed."

"Sometimes peace must come at a cost," Brightborn said. "Were lives not lost when this nation that you call home earned its independence? Have not thousands of Americans died to protect freedom?"

"Perhaps it's time that we seek peace through love rather than war," I said.

Brightborn laughed. "A noble sentiment, but naive. Still, it is you who forces both our hands. I am giving you the chance now to accept my peaceful emergence as the world's emperor. Every time I've shed blood since I came to Earth was when you opposed me. It was only when I was left with no other choice that lives were lost."

I shook my head. "You didn't have to attack the protesters the other day, Brightborn."

Brightborn shrugged. "I didn't. I allowed this nation's military to conduct that operation. What they showed you is the brutality that prevails when humans are allowed to govern themselves. Consider it but a demonstration of what will persist if humanity resists me."

"So if people resist you, people have to die?" I asked. "That's not a peaceful rule, Brightborn. Those people were exercising their freedom of speech."

Brightborn shook his head. "It didn't have to be like this, Caspar. But once again, you are forcing my hand."

"What are you going to do?" I asked. "Kill me?"

"Not you," Brightborn said. "Aelfrich, bring out the drow."

Aelfrich emerged from a golden curtain behind Brightborn. He had Rina in his grip. Her hands were tied, and her eyes were completely black like Brightborn's. Aelfrich had a dagger to her neck.

"You wouldn't!" I shouted.

"I won't," Brightborn said. "If you kneel and accept your position as my heir."

I clenched my fists. I couldn't use my magic. I had Aerin's blade, but could I take out Aelfrich before he slit Rina's throat? I couldn't move that fast.

A green orb appeared behind Aelfrich. It was Trixie! She hadn't left. She must have been hiding here the whole time. Aelfrich must have heard her buzz because he flinched. He turned and swiped at her with his dagger.

This was my chance. I grabbed Aerin's blade and charged Aelfrich. I was about to plunge the blade into him when Rina lunged at me, her eyes suggesting that she wasn't in full control. I pivoted my foot, trying to move out of the way.

As I did, Aerin's blade caught Brightborn under his chin and sliced through his throat.

Aelfrich took two steps back, a look of horror on his face as the elven king collapsed. He fell to his knees. He had a *smile* on his face as the blood poured out from the wound I'd inadvertently cut through his throat.

The blade tingled in my hand, a surge of energy consuming it. Then the usually radiant blade turned dark. A black haze, matching that in Rina's and Brightborn's eyes overwhelmed it. I tried to let go. I couldn't.

"Aerin!" I shouted.

Aerin is otherwise occupied, a voice said from within the blade. It was Brightborn's voice. I couldn't believe I'd killed again, and I'd trapped Brightborn in the blade...

Then, my hand sheathed the blade, but I didn't do it. Brightborn was controlling me.

The drow is under my power. And since she's bound to you, it seems, so are you. Now, together, we can fulfill my plan. Your power is in my control; my designs will all be fulfilled in you.

I tried to scream. Nothing came out.

"Trixie," my voice said—but it wasn't me speaking, "take Rina back home. I'll join you back at the cave shortly."

CHAPTER THIRTY-SIX

"Aelfrich," Brightborn said, speaking through me. "Upload the broadcast."

"Yes, my Liege," Aelfrich said.

What broadcast was Brightborn talking about? Certainly, he hadn't recorded our whole exchange. Even if he had, I can't imagine he'd want to share it. I tried to assert myself. I tried to rise up and reclaim my body. Aerin was in here, somewhere. Could we take him down together?

Brightborn followed Aelfrich into the room behind the curtain where Aelfrich had emerged from with Rina under his knife just minutes before.

Aelfrich pulled out a computer from beneath Brightborn's bed and fired it up.

"Go ahead and play it," Brightborn said. "I'd like Caspar to see it."

To see what? I asked, my voice echoing in my head but failing to escape my lips.

"You'll see," Brightborn said, the tenor of his voice more like my own than before. He was using my vocal cords, after all.

Aelfrich navigated to a video. Brightborn was featured front and center, wearing the same golden robes still adorning his dead body, though now soaked in his blood.

"Greetings, leaders of this world," Brightborn said. "I am delighted to inform you that the problem with the resistance has been resolved. Caspar Cruciger, who you know is married to my daughter, has had a change of heart. I urge you to pardon him of his former crimes and heed his voice as you'd previously followed mine. He is powerful. His agenda is now aligned with ours. Consider him my rightful heir. When he speaks, I speak. With his power at our disposal, our plans can now be expedited. We will heal this world. For those who oppose us, we must have heavy hearts, but we must also suppress any resistance. The fate of this world depends on our newfound unity. Peace cannot thrive so long as terrorists and resistors are tolerated. Strive to convert them, as I have done with the former Reverend Cruciger. If you cannot convert those who oppose you, detain them, and if it is your custom to execute traitors, you may follow your laws to that effect.

"As for me, you will not see me again. It has been the honor of my life to bring you together, but the power that this world needs to heal demands a sacrifice. I offer myself for the sake of this world. But know this. My life is laid down according to my will. It is a sacrifice that I gladly make for the sake of healing this world. What is one life, after all, for the sake of many? While I know this is abrupt and unexpected, I insist that in accordance with our treaty, you grant my son-in-law and heir, Caspar Cruciger, all deference and honor that you previously gave to me. I assure you, he is now fully aligned with our cause. Only with his power and the sacrifice of my blood can we fulfill our divine purpose. Only as one can we save this world and usher in a new era of peace under one rule—my rule, and now the rule of my son."

You piece of shit, I said.

Brightborn laughed. "I told you I could pardon you, Cruciger. Upload the broadcast, Aelfrich."

You had this all planned from the start? You meant for me to kill you?

"Consider it my Plan B. You were unwilling to yield, so I was left with no other choice. Needless to say, I was prepared for this particular inevitability."

What are you going to do with your body?

Brightborn smiled, looking in a mirror. It was creepy as hell to see my face smiling back at me. But the way my lips curled, the way my eyes glared back at me with the same darkness in them as was in Brightborn's eyes was different; it was distinctly *not* me.

Brightborn still held onto Aerin's blade. Could he ever let go of it? If he did, even as I lost contact with Aerin before, I should be able to reclaim my body.

So what's the plan? You hold onto Aerin's blade forever? Surely that will be an awful inconvenience.

Brightborn laughed. He didn't laugh like me. His laugh was a cackle, while I tended more toward a high-pitched bellow. "I told the truth in my message to the world's leaders. My body must be sacrificed, bound together with yours at the root of the tree of knowledge. Thankfully, now that I have access to your memories and your abilities, going there will be as simple as a fairy portal. After that, so long as my former body holds the blade and remains enveloped in the tree, and the tree's power remains with this body, I will retain control over you."

Where is Aerin! I screamed.

Brightborn snickered. "She's in here somewhere. To think, after all she and I went through, that we should be bound together in the end."

Aerin didn't respond. Was she really there? Perhaps she was choosing to bite her metaphorical tongue. How could she and I rally against Brightborn to reclaim my body? We couldn't conspire with one another without him knowing. We couldn't plan anything without him recognizing what we intended to do the moment we'd think it.

So what now, Brightborn? We take your body to the tree?

"Almost. First, we must retrieve Layla. Her power, the angelic power she wields, is required to seal the bond and ensure that I remain perpetually at the helm of your mind."

She'll never agree to that! I protested.

Brightborn smiled. "She will. When you ask her to do it."

I sighed. *You son of a bitch.*

Brightborn smirked. "Careful, Cruciger. You realize, by calling me that, you're referring to your wife as a granddaughter of a bitch? What will that make our children when we have them?"

You're disgusting! You're planning to have children with Layla?

"Why not?" Brightborn asked. "This body will not survive forever. I'll need a new vessel eventually. A proper heir to absorb my mind, each generation to the next, as my eternal rule over this world endures."

CHAPTER THIRTY-SEVEN

Brightborn had cast fairy portals when he was in league with Develin, the fairy king of the Unseelie court. Since he had access to my memories, he knew exactly where to go. Where to connect the portal and how to visualize its manifestation on the opposite side.

First, Brightborn created a portal and sent his body somewhere. I wasn't sure where he'd sent it. There wasn't any sense asking. It wasn't like he was inclined to appease my curiosity. After that, he cast another portal. This time, he connected it to my memory, to the caves where my people were hiding.

We appeared in the same cavern I'd used before when I cast fairy portals out of the cave. Brightborn had his hand firmly placed on Aerin's blade. He had to. But he also needed to convince Layla to join him in the Canadian forest.

I wasn't sure how late it was. It was still dark in New York when we'd left Brightborn's tower. It was only one time zone's difference in Missouri, and the central time zone was one hour earlier than the eastern time zone. If it was three in the morning in New York, then it was two in the morning in St. Louis. It wasn't a surprise that most everyone was still asleep.

Rina was back. She was cuddled up with Jag. I looked around. I didn't see Elrand. Where had he gone? He must've known Rina had returned without me. If Jag knew she was back, I doubted he'd let her know that the bodies were back.

Even if he had, I wasn't sure how much control that Rina had over herself. Her eyes, black like mine, would be hard to see in the dark cave. The only light we had was from a handful of campfires. Since our black eyes were the only visible sign that we'd been infected by the warped magic—call it sin itself if you like—drawn from the tree of knowledge, there was little chance anyone would notice as long as we were inside the cave.

I could feel everything that Brightborn felt. I had access to all my senses. I just couldn't *control* my body. Why did he have more command over what I did than I did? It was my body, after all. Surely there was a way I could take back control. Even as I thought about it, I knew that Brightborn would know what I was going to do before I did it.

He stepped into the man cavern without much fanfare. Everyone was asleep, after all. Even those who were awake wouldn't think twice about me coming and going at all hours.

As soon as Brightborn approached Layla, Agnus' head popped up from the opposite side. He looked at us, cocked his head as he sniffed the air, and hissed.

"Shhh," Brightborn said. "It's just me, buddy."

Agnus sounded off with a high-pitched, *"Meeeerrrrow!"*

Layla rolled over. "Caspar?" she asked.

"Not Caspar!" Agnus protested.

"What are you talking about?" Brightborn asked, glancing at Layla and chuckling. "I think he must've woken from a bad dream or something."

"I don't know who you are! But you are *not* Caspar!" Agnus screeched.

The ruckus was causing a stir. Jag and Rina woke up. The giants were stirring, but it would take them a bit longer to start moving. Getting a giant going after sleeping is a lot like getting a semi-truck moving up a steep hill from a cold stop.

Then I heard a roar. Clarence came bounding after us. Brightborn clung tight to Aerin's sword as he gathered up a little air magic and hurled it at the bear, sending him crashing into the cavern wall.

"Caspar!" Layla shouted. "What the hell is going on?"

"I was hoping you could tell me!" Brightborn said. "Why's the cat freaking out?"

"Because you aren't Caspar!" Agnus screeched.

Jag approached with Rina at his side.

Brightborn put his arm around Layla. "So, you're back, Rina?"

Rina nodded. "I am."

She was still out of it. Whatever magic Brightborn had cast over her had her in a daze. If only someone would shine a light, turn on their phone, make a torch from one of the fires, they'd see it in her eyes. It was in my eyes. Agnus was right. Of course, he could see in the dark almost as well as in the day. That must've been how he realized I wasn't myself.

"Layla," Brightborn said, grabbing her hands. "I need your help. I don't have time to explain."

"We'll come with you," Jag said.

"This is something we need to do alone," Brightborn replied.

Rina remained silent. If only Agnus would take a look at her and see it in her eyes. But Agnus had noticed Brightborn in an instant. Might it be that Rina didn't resonate the same change to Agnus that I did since she was only being influenced by the tree of knowledge's magic, while I was literally possessed by another person's consciousness?

I didn't know for sure. But whatever the reason, I knew that the hold on Rina wasn't the same. She was being influenced by the magic, but she wasn't compelled. She wasn't possessed. She could resist it. I could only hope she would tell them the truth.

"Where are we going?" Layla asked, strapping on her armor, her cloak, and grabbing her elven bow and quiver.

"Mingan told us what to do," Brightborn said. "Back in Canada. That's what I intend to do, now."

I would have sighed if I could. But I didn't have any control over my inhales or exhales. The fact that Brightborn could access my memories made his persuasiveness difficult to dispute. Only Agnus knew the truth, although he'd said nothing to give me the impression that he realized it was Brightborn who possessed me.

"Rina," Brightborn said. "I'm worried about Clarence and Agnus. Can you take care of them?"

Layla cocked her head. "The drow don't heal, Caspar. You know this."

"I just meant for her to check on them," Brightborn said. "By the way, Rina, when I get back, we can complete the funeral rites for the fallen. I've recovered the bodies."

"Thank you," Rina said. "I'll take care of the animals."

Rina scooped Agnus up. He wiggled in her hands, clawing the shit out of her forearms. Rina barely seemed to recognize it. It was like she didn't feel pain at all. If the magic within her was from the tree of knowledge, a tree that sent mankind on an endless pursuit of pleasure, perhaps the magic numbed the pain.

Agnus had scratched me a lot when he was a kitten. It didn't feel good, especially on the tender skin on the inside of a forearm. Ultimately, Brightborn was just trying to get the cat out of the way. Agnus might not have realized what was up, but he knew *something* was up. I could only hope that someone else went with her and checked on him. However, if Layla went with me, who was likely to come to his rescue?

In AA, we often began our meetings with the serenity prayer, praying that God would grant us the serenity to accept the things we couldn't change. In this instance, I couldn't change a damn thing. Was I supposed to just accept that? The prayer continues to bid us to have the courage to change the things we can. What could I change if I couldn't control my body? Absolutely nothing. The wisdom to know the difference, therefore, was in this instance a mere distinction without a difference at all.

Brightborn wrapped my arm around Layla and pulled a fairy portal over us.

We reappeared in the Canadian forest, in the place where Mingan had been killed. It was dark. The place was illuminated by moonlight. Where his body had fallen into the middle of the creek bed sprung a black tree. The trunk was black. The leaves, too. Only the fruit on the tree, which resembled large red and purple melons, had any color to them. They dangled from the branches, pulling them down on account of their weight.

"What is this?" Layla asked.

"The tree of the knowledge of good and evil," Brightborn said.

"Like the one from your Bible?"

Brightborn nodded my head. Then he grabbed Layla and kissed her deeply on the lips.

My stomach turned. *Dude! Get my lips off my woman. Off your daughter!*

Brightborn chuckled. "Would you like to have children?" he asked Layla.

"Sort of an odd time to ask," Layla said. "But sure, when this is over. What happened with my dad? Did Trixie take you to him?"

Brightborn nodded. "She brought us together. His body is already here."

Brightborn gestured at his body, which was resting against the base of the tree of knowledge.

"You killed him?" Layla asked, cocking her head.

Brightborn nodded. "It is done, Layla."

Layla shed a tear. I couldn't blame her. Yes, she hated her father. She resented all he'd done. But at the end of the day, he was her father. "I suppose he got what was coming to him. Are you, okay, Caspar?"

Layla looked at me—at Brightborn. Under the moonlight, the

color of my eyes was evident. She noticed right away. I could tell by the expression on her face. "Your eyes... Caspar..."

Brightborn laughed. "The power of this tree. I can feel it within me."

"The power?" Layla asked. "Caspar, what happened to you? You don't talk about power. You sound like..."

"I sound like your father?" Brightborn asked.

"Agnus was right," Layla said. "You aren't yourself. You aren't Caspar."

Brightborn laughed. He grabbed Layla and pressed her against the tree. He stood against it, channeling the dark magic within my body to force branches to sprout from the side, and a root from the ground, binding Layla in place.

"You look so much like your mother," Brightborn said, looking at Layla as the tree constricted its branches and roots tighter around her.

"Dad?" Layla asked, cocking her head.

Brightborn smiled. I could feel the way my lips curled. She'd be able to see it in the *way* he smiled that it wasn't me, confirming what she'd realized.

"It is me, daughter."

Layla's eyes went wide. "You just *kissed* me! You sicko!"

Brightborn laughed. "We must produce an heir. I have claimed this body as my own. To continue to govern this world, to maintain the era of peace I intend to usher in, I must have heirs into perpetuity. An heir from my own flesh and also descended from the chosen one, whose abilities I can retain across generations."

"You're disgusting!" Layla protested. "I'll never do that with you! What did you do with Caspar?"

Brightborn shrugged, then he looked at his fallen body at the base of the tree. "We swapped. What can I say?"

You fucking liar! I screamed.

Layla burst into tears. "You didn't! There's no way! If you killed him, I'd die, too!"

Brightborn shrugged. "As Caspar would have put it, when you two married, you became one in flesh."

Layla shook her head. "That's not how it worked. The rings that Aerin gave us bound is in *soul* rather than body."

"What is a soul, anyway?" Brightborn asked. "It seems you were mistaken. After all, he's dead, and you're still here. I have his body now."

Brightborn grabbed his dead hands with my living hands. He dragged his own body in a circle, leaving a circle of blood all around the tree. Before, there'd been a stream here. Rising waters. Now, on account of the tree, the creek bed had run dry. Like the tree had sucked up all the water, and now it was drawing on the blood that surrounded it.

"What are you doing?" Layla asked.

"Feeding the tree with my blood," Brightborn said. "When I consume the fruit nourished by my blood, my possession of this body will be sealed. It will be irreversible."

Layla screamed with rage. As she did, the purple power she possessed soaked into the branches and roots that were wrapped around her.

Brightborn laughed. "Yes, fuel the tree with your rage, daughter! Let it out!"

All of this coaxing, this tormenting on Brightborn's part, was meant to force Layla to release the celestial magic that coursed through her.

The purple of Layla's magic and the red of Brightborn's blood swirled together from the ground, enveloping the tree's black trunk. The colors continued to spiral up to the branches, soaking into the fruit of the tree. The very fruit, I presumed, that Adam and Eve once consumed. The taste that brought sin, death, disease, and brokenness into the world.

Brightborn was still clinging to Aerin's' sword with my hand. He raised her sword and cut one of the fruits that were now radiating both red and purple. He held it in his hand.

"The sword," Layla said. "Caspar's in there, isn't he? He killed you with it."

Brightborn shrugged. "Once I eat this fruit, the sword won't matter."

Caspar...

It was Aerin speaking. She finally found her voice.

"Silence, drow!" Brightborn screamed.

You must not allow this. You need to stop him.

But I can't! I cried.

You can! Aerin said. *You have to do it while your body is still your own. You just need to find yourself. You didn't kill him. He stepped into my blade. You didn't shed his blood. That guilt is not on you.*

"Enough!" Brightborn screamed.

"He is in there, isn't he?" Layla asked. "Both of them are!"

"Shut up!" Brightborn said. He started to raise the fruit to his lips when an arrow struck it straight through. The juices exploded out, dripping from my hand. Brightborn clenched my fist with a fury. He reached with Aerin's sword a second time to grab another fruit as he looked around to find who had fired on him.

It was Illarion with his bow. The rest of the resistance stood beside him with their bows drawn. They blasted the fruits in the tree with arrows, every one of them.

"*No!*" Brightborn screamed.

A flash of gold appeared on the opposite side of the creek and the drow stepped out, Rina now holding her bow. Elrand stood beside her on one side, Jag on the other. Then a third fairy portal appeared downstream, and the giants emerged.

"It's over, Brightborn!" Rina shouted. "You're surrounded."

Brightborn snarled, "How did you break my hold?"

Elrand smiled as he rested his hand on Rina's shoulder. "The magic you've brought from the otherworld can be resisted, Brightborn. All I had to do was give Rina the confidence to do it."

"With the spirits of our fallen sisters now at rest, I have the strength to resist you!" Rina shouted.

Brightborn sighed. "This tree will produce more fruit. My mission will be finished. All you've done is join me here to your own end!"

Brightborn raised his hand—the one not holding Aerin's blade—and a black cloud started to swirl outward from the tree. As it struck the elves, the drow, even the giants, they started to cough. Their eyes widened in horror.

Caspar, find yourself! Aerin shouted. *You know what to do!*

"Don't do it!" Brightborn shouted.

Whoever wishes to find his life must lose it, Aerin said.

If I do that... If I can even gain enough control to do it... Layla would die, too.

What is death? Aerin said. *There is no lie greater than that death is the end. It is an end. But it is also a beginning.*

"You can't take over!" Brightborn shouted. "You're weak!"

I am weak. I am powerless. But in my weakness, I find strength! I screamed back.

God, I prayed, *give me the strength!*

I felt a tingle consume my body as I regained control. My eyes must have changed. Layla saw it. She looked at me with love even as she winced in pain.

"Layla," I said. "I don't have much time. I don't know how long I can hold on. But this power, I can't stop it. It will kill everyone if I don't."

"Hold my hand," Layla said. "Do what you need to do. We will be together."

I nodded and kissed Layla deeply. Then I took Aerin's blade and thrust it into my gut, through my body, and into the tree.

I let go of the blade and grabbed Layla's hand. Tears were in her eyes. My tears blurred my vision. But she was right. We were together. She gasped. I felt my heart beat for the last time.

Then, nothing.

CHAPTER THIRTY-EIGHT

I opened my eyes and found myself lying in a field. Green grass grew all around me. Not just green. It was a brilliant green, more vibrant than even the best-kept professional baseball field. But this grass wasn't manicured. It was wild. It grew up around me, encapsulating my body.

Did I have a body? I felt like I did. I looked down. I had two legs. My toes wiggled. They were my toes. I hadn't been teleported into anyone else's body. I grabbed at my abdomen. I didn't feel a thing where the wound of Aerin's sword should have been.

Then I noticed that I was completely naked.

Fantastic. I suppose, if this was Heaven, it made sense. If Adam and Eve went in the buff in the Garden of Eden before sin came into the world, it should have made sense that we'd be naked in Heaven, too. I tucked my legs underneath me and stood. The air was pure. It vivified me in an instant. I might have been dead, but I felt more alive than ever before.

"Hey there, lover," a voice I knew said.

I turned. Layla stood there, her blonde hair flowing in the radiant light of whatever world we were in. There wasn't a sun in the sky. The whole place just radiated with light, as if sunlight was a part of everything.

"Nice to see you two," another voice said.

I turned, and Aerin was standing there in the flesh. I'd almost forgotten how beautiful she was. She wasn't my Layla, of course, but she was striking. Even more now in the afterlife than she had been in life.

"Wait," I said. "If you two are here…"

"My father must be here somewhere," Layla said.

Aerin snorted. "He probably got sent to Hell."

"You believe in Hell?" I asked, raising an eyebrow.

Aerin snorted. "I didn't. Not until we found ourselves bound to him. There has to be a hell for people like him."

Layla pressed her lips together. "There's a tree over there."

"The Tree of Life?" I asked.

"How am I supposed to know?" Layla asked.

All three of us approached the tree. It was the opposite of everything that the tree of knowledge had been. Had Brightborn brought the tree of knowledge from the otherworld? I didn't think so. I must have caused it when I'd shed blood on the sacred land, a place that connected Earth to this place—call it Annwn, call it Eden. All I could figure was that Brightborn's legionaries, who we'd left behind, had discovered it. Brightborn, seeing the opportunity, had seized its power.

What was it that the serpent had told Adam and Eve in the garden, according to the Genesis account of creation? "You will not surely die!"

Brightborn had been deceived in kind. He'd siphoned magic from the tree of knowledge, hoping he could manipulate it to live forever. In his body. In my body. In the bodies of children borne by Layla. Would it have worked if he'd succeeded in binding himself to my body? I didn't know. How could I know? But at least we knew that we'd stopped him.

The Tree of Life was golden—not the pretentious, lifeless gold that adorned Brightborn's New York loft. Rather, it was a radiant, blazing, gold like that of the sun itself.

I stared at it in awe. This was *the* Tree of Life. The one from the beginning. The way God had intended to provide for all mankind from the start. At least that was how I understood it.

It was hard to see why anyone would ever be tempted to eat of the fruit of the other tree. Perhaps, over time as it often happens, the wonder, the luster, of this great tree would wear off. There's an insatiable curiosity in the human spirit. They say that curiosity killed the cat. I didn't know about that. If it had, well, Agnus would have probably died eight of his nine times by now.

Still, it must've been true that curiosity killed humanity's chance at paradise. Not because it's wrong to be curious. Rather, because mankind failed to cherish the great gift of life, the gift of the Tree of Life, the gift of creation itself. They lost sight of the gift. They sought to own, to possess, to seize and control. They lost sight of gratitude and pursued power instead.

Something rumbled beneath our feet. I extended my hands to steady myself. Did I still have my powers here? I didn't know. Did it matter?

"Caspar!" Layla shouted, looking behind us.

The ground split apart.

Flames burst from the crevice as it expanded in every direction, forming a lake of fire.

The tree of knowledge, the one we'd seen in the Canadian forest, blasted out of the flames. The fire didn't consume the tree —rather, the tree fueled the flames.

I expected Brightborn to be within the flames, clinging to the tree or emerging like a dragon out of the midst of the lake.

Instead, I heard footsteps thudding behind me.

Layla, Aerin, and I all turned as Brightborn charged at us. Black energy, as before, radiated from his body.

What was he doing? We were already dead, weren't we? Did

he think he could kill us here? Then what? We'd be double-dead? Hell, I thought I knew how this stuff worked.

Sorry, bad choice of words. You know, given the situation.

I raised my hand. Did I have power here? Would it work?

I tried to invoke air.

Instead, I channeled green energy like Mingan had wielded against me back in the forest. Golden roots from the Tree of Life broke out of the ground and caught Brightborn by the ankle. It snuffed out whatever power he had taken from the tree of knowledge.

Layla, Aerin, and I approached him.

"It's over, Brightborn," I said.

"We're all dead, you idiot!" Brightborn shouted. "Look at what you've done!"

"Death is but the beginning of life," a voice said, and a familiar elf appeared seemingly out of thin air.

"Mingan?" I couldn't hide my shock.

The old elven druid nodded at me. "Indeed. There's someone else who would like to meet you."

Another man appeared. His face was kind. His beard, white. His narrow frame was robed all in white. He had a radiant, golden brow. If the light that filled this place came from any single source, it was from this man.

"Taliesin?"

The man nodded. I recognized him from the vision I'd seen in the stone circle at the North Pole, but now he looked more like an angel than a man.

"All life begins from another beginning's end," Taliesin said. "You may return to your lives if you wish. Or, you may return to the cauldron of rebirth. You can choose a new life, a new path, a new story."

"What about him?" Layla asked, glancing at Brightborn.

"He will be born again, as well. Though his next birth, I expect, will not be so bright."

"Will he come back as a worm?" I asked.

Taliesin shrugged. "Perhaps he'll come back as a cat."

I bit my lip. "He wants to be worshiped. It would fit."

Taliesin raised his hand. The roots from the Tree of Life curled around Brightborn's form then unraveled quickly, sending him flying through the sky.

Brightborn struck the tree of knowledge and fell into the lake of fire. Once it received him, the fire fizzled out, and the tree of knowledge disappeared. The ground healed, and green grass emerged to take its place.

"So we have the choice?" I asked. "I haven't fulfilled your prophecy yet."

"But the prophecy itself said your destiny was your choice, did it not?" Taliesin asked.

"How can I possibly go back?" I asked.

Taliesin smiled. "It seems that despite his efforts to destroy the world, the elven king has set you up in a unique position to unify the world."

I sighed. "I don't want to rule."

"Then don't," Taliesin said. "You don't have to rule to lead."

"I don't know if I can," I said. "If I have what it takes."

"Of course you do!" Layla said. "You just gave your life. Mine too, I guess, but you did it to save us, to save the world."

"That is the heart of the divine," Taliesin said. "Whatever you believe, whatever name you give the Almighty, one thing is certain. The God of all is a great giver. He gives of himself. He sacrifices for no other reason than that he loves his creations. This is the beginning of the world's redemption. It is the heart of the prophecy. It is the seed of the Tree of Life that you will plant in the world."

I bit my lip and turned to Mingan. "I thought you said I was supposed to bring Annwn, or Eden, to Earth?"

"I did," Mingan said. "But I did not tell you it would happen overnight, did I? A seed must be planted, in accord with the ways of the Tree of Life. Only then can it overgrow the deathly seeds of the other tree until darkness is overwhelmed and the ways of the world are reversed."

"So, what am I supposed to do?" I asked. "How *exactly* do I plant that seed?"

Layla looked at me and smiled. "I think you know the answer to that, Caspar. You'll do the next right thing."

CHAPTER THIRTY-NINE

Brightborn was gone. It was over. Would he be reborn as a slug, destined to be tormented beneath a wrathful twelve-year-old's salt shaker? Would he dwell indefinitely in perdition? I suppose it was six of one half a dozen of the other. He'd tried to seize eternal life for himself. He hoped to claim it by stealing my life, and the lives of the children Layla and I might one day have. He'd hoped to secure eternal power by lording this authority over others.

True power comes through service. By using whatever strength, whatever power, one has in service to others rather than in service to one's pride. Might Brightborn have saved the world? Could he have reversed climate change? I don't know. I'd have to figure it out even if it meant planting a trillion trees.

But I was getting ahead of myself. We were still in Eden. Layla and I walked, hand-in-hand, totally nude in the garden like Adam and Eve must have done. Aerin was naked, too. While I might have taken a peek in the past, I didn't see her in this place as an object of lust. I saw her as a beautiful creature. A reflection of the divine, an image that can be seen in every person if you have the eyes to see it. When I looked at Layla here, did I desire her? Of course. But in this place, we were not objects to be seized by the other. We were gifts to one another. She was a gift to me, freely given. I was a gift to her. Both of our bodies, freely given. Both of our bodies, freely received.

The book of Ephesians describes human marriage as a divine mystery, a reflection of the relationship God intends to have with us. For once, without the passions of the flesh in the way, I understood it. I desired nothing more than to offer myself to my wife. She desired nothing more than to give herself to me. Our focus was not on ourselves, on satisfying our urges or desires. Rather, we truly had an understanding of what marriage was supposed to be in the beginning.

"You don't have to go back," Taliesin said. "Not to the world you knew."

I sighed. "Of course I do. How can I live this life, this kind of heaven, this perfection, while I know that the world remains blind? While people persist in the way of the tree of knowledge, of exploitation?"

Taliesin laughed. "Indeed. I wouldn't expect you to wish to stay. For while you're here, when you know the heart that was intended for man and woman in the beginning, you cannot help but ache for the world as it persists today."

"It is beautiful," I said. "This desire to give of ourselves to one another. But I feel we must also give ourselves to the world."

"There was only one way for you to enter this place, to open the gate, and you found it," Taliesin said.

"To die?" I asked.

"To sacrifice," Taliesin said. "To give of oneself for no reason other than the love of others. Whenever you do that, whenever you love others more than yourself, Heaven is not far from you. Eden, Annwn, is awakened in your heart."

"So we can continue to live with this...I don't know how to describe it....this feeling?" Layla asked.

"Of course you can," Taliesin said. "Live in gratitude, live generously, give to others more than you hoard unto yourself. Place the wellbeing of others, even that of your enemies, above your own. When you do, while your feet might traverse on the broken Earth, your soul will remain planted in the fertile soil of Eden."

"And we plant this seed from the Tree of Life by doing the same? By showing this way of life to others?" I asked.

Taliesin nodded. "You do. What this place teaches us is not that we should neglect ourselves or despise ourselves for the sake of others. We cannot give freely unto others unless we truly receive the gifts that our Maker would have for us. We learned to give from the great Giver. For if we do not receive what we are given, we dishonor the Giver."

Layla nodded. "It's rude to turn down a gift."

"Indeed," Taliesin said, chuckling. "Imagine a world where everyone lived receiving every good thing with gratitude and loving others more than oneself in return?"

"There would always be peace," I said, "if everyone knew that kind of love."

"But all it takes is one who is selfish, one who intends to exploit the rest, to break the peace," Aerin added, speaking up for the first time.

"This is true," Taliesin said. "Which is why some have said it is better to suffer an injustice with patience than to seek vengeance. For when we seek to repay violence with violence, the cycle of love is broken. Justice is not, as some have imagined, when one gets what one is due for his or her wrongs. Justice is when everything is as it should be. When what was wrong before is made right."

"I think I'll stay here for a while," Aerin said.

I cocked my head. "Are you certain?"

Aerin nodded. "You and Layla deserve a life together. I will take my chances with another life at another time. When I can know love. When I can receive another and give of myself, as I should."

"When you're ready," Taliesin said. "You may be reborn."

Aerin nodded. "Or perhaps, I'll stay here until the end. We shall see."

"You are free to do as you wish, Aerin." Taliesin turned to Layla and me. "Caspar, Layla. Are you ready for your rebirth?"

I smiled and looked at Layla. "I'm ready."

"Me too," Layla said. "Where will we return?"

"You will return as you left," Taliesin said. "Here, time passes differently than on Earth. In a sense, this place exists outside the domain of time. However, it is fitting that you return at the time you left, for that is the moment when the world, when humanity and all the races, needs to hear your message the most."

Taliesin led us to a giant pool. It bubbled with green and golden energies, coursing with the original magic of this place—the magic of life itself.

"This was where life began," Taliesin said. "It is where all life begins. Only many forget their origin, their source."

"So, what do we do?" I asked. "Just jump in?"

"Let the waters, the magic, envelop your entire frame," Taliesin said. "Recall the last memory of your previous life. Cling to one another, and you will remain bound in spirit and soul throughout the course of your Earthly lives."

I nodded. Then I turned and gazed at Aerin. She looked at us, her eyes wide. There was a sparkle in her eyes I'd never noticed before, like flecks of gold sprinkled across her green irises. "Thank you, Aerin, for everything. For your sacrifice. For your guidance."

"For marrying my husband," Layla said, snickering.

Aerin laughed. "It was my pleasure. I'll miss you."

"We'll miss you, too," I said. "I hope, perhaps, one day we'll meet again."

"We will," Aerin said. "One way or another."

I nodded, then looked at Taliesin. "Thank you for your guidance."

"You were the one I saw from the beginning," Taliesin said. "Your battle is now over. But your mission has only begun."

I smiled. "I'm ready."

Layla grabbed my hand, and our fingers intertwined. A part of me wanted to cannonball into the pool. Whether these waters were the primordial cauldron, as some believe, or the waters of baptismal rebirth, I cannot say. Need it be one or the other? I decided against making a big splash.

Layla and I stepped into the water. It felt cool at first, but it did not chill our bodies. Warmth flowed from the waters, from the magic, into my flesh as I slowly entered the water.

I smiled at Layla. "See you on the other side?"

Layla nodded. She kissed me softly. "It is my honor to give myself to you, husband."

"And it is mine to be yours," I said.

We continued walking into the pool until the green and golden energies enveloped our bodies. I did not loosen my hold on Layla's hand. I didn't close my eyes.

Had anything changed at all? The warmth I sensed when we entered the water faded. I still held my breath as my feet touched the bottom of the stream. The rocks were sharp. I squeezed Layla's hand.

The current wanted to carry us downstream. We walked sideways and with the current until we reached the shore. The sunlight hit my face as I gasped for air at the surface.

I turned and watched as Layla took her first breath. We exchanged smiles.

We were home.

We stepped ashore.

Our people were still there. The tree of knowledge was gone. I already knew that the creek that had dried up was flowing again because that's where we had been returned. To the place where the tree of knowledge had stood, to the very place where we'd died.

The elves were gathered, the former resistance. The drow were there, too. Elrand smiled at us. Jag's jaw dropped. His eyes focused on Layla even as Rina elbowed him in the ribs.

"Sorry," Jag said.

"You've returned," Brag'mok said.

"It is as I said," Targigoth, the giants' prophet, told them.

"And as I said," Elrand added.

I snorted. We were back in our broken world. Even something so simple as who was going to take credit for predicting our resurrection reflected the pattern of this world.

I laughed. "It doesn't matter who predicted it. Or if no one predicted it at all. We are back. Brightborn is gone. The war is over, but our calling, our true purpose, remains to be fulfilled."

"Put some clothes on!" a familiar voice said from somewhere in the crowd.

Agnus slunk around from behind Brag'mok. He nuzzled my shin.

I reached down to grab him.

"Na-na-na-nope!" Agnus piped up. "Put some clothes on first. Then you can pick me up."

"Does anyone have something I can wear?" I asked.

"Layla, if you'd like, you can pick me up just the way you are," Agnus said.

I laughed. We were back. Some things hadn't changed at all, but for the first time in my life, I felt like I knew who I was. I knew what my life was supposed to be. Did I know for sure what I'd be doing in five years? Did I know what I'd be doing next week?

Not exactly, but that didn't matter. Who we are is more than what we do. It's more than our mistakes. It's more than good deeds. We are who we are at our core. We are our character. When we err, that doesn't have to define us unless we allow it to.

We can always find ourselves again. We can choose to embrace a vision of ourselves that is what we were meant to be. We can choose a life of love. And no matter what we've done, whatever path we've taken, it's never too late.

We can choose love. We can choose gratitude. We can choose the way of Eden.

CHAPTER FORTY

One Year Later

The meetings with the United Nations were painful. They were almost as bad as those church council meetings used to be. So many insecure people, everyone imagining that the other side was out to get them. Still, we'd made a lot of progress despite the uphill battles we'd faced.

I wasn't sure how pleased everyone was that I presided over the group. However, they'd all signed a treaty granting Brightborn the gaudy title of Emperor Supreme, along with the right to declare his heir. The last thing he'd done was tell the UN that I was to take his place.

The treaty also granted Brightborn more authority than I was inclined to exercise. So, I didn't. I believed it was best to encourage rather than enforce.

We were in the midst of a project to bring clean water to every country in the world. I didn't use magic unless I had to. I didn't want to rob the people of their chance to give, to sacrifice themselves for the betterment of others. I intended to lead by example.

People still wanted to bicker about their rights. They wanted to compete over resources. They sought power at the expense of others. All I could do was plant seeds. As Taliesin had told me, seeds take time to grow.

So, we focused on providing clean water. We focused on cleaning the air. I planted forests, but I also encouraged everyone to plant trees themselves. Magic can't do everything for us. We all need to play a part. We need to give of ourselves, expecting nothing in return.

That's what planting a tree does. After all, a little sapling or bare-root tree doesn't give us much at all. It offers no shade. It produces no fruit. When we plant a tree, we learn a little bit about the heart of God. To give, expecting nothing in return. To receive the profit of our efforts. Not because we have earned it, but because our labors of love have reciprocated love in return. When I plant an apple tree, and the tree offers me its first fruit, I eat it with gratitude. It is the way the tree does what it was created to do—to give, to provide love in its own way.

Strangely, I found planting trees teaches us a lot about how to live together. We must tend to one another's needs, not because we expect anything in return, but because we wish to see one another grow and thrive. In due season, our deeds of love will likely come back to us.

Layla and I had restored the old farmhouse at what used to be the junkyard ranch. I had ten bare-root trees growing in the back. I watered them once a week. Again, it was a labor of love.

I was eager to get back home. The US government had granted all the elves and the giants a path to citizenship. The British parliament offered them the same. Most of the world's governments agreed, should they wish it, that they could make a home in their countries. Most of them chose to move back to Missouri, near Layla and me.

The peoples were all united. There was still work to do. I'd never hammer people into a new way of living. I couldn't force anyone to love another person. All I could do was demonstrate love.

Elrand stepped into the room. He didn't usually interrupt the assembly unless there was a good reason. Based on the date on the calendar, I didn't have to guess what it was he had to tell me.

I got up from my seat. "I'll have to insist on a recess for the week."

"For the week?" the French ambassador asked.

I smiled. "Yes. At least one week. We'll resume seven days from today unless you're notified differently."

The room was abuzz with chatter as I followed Elrand out of the room. He was my counselor. Not a secretary. He was there to give his valued advice. I might have had a taste of Eden, but in this world, I was as susceptible as anyone to error. He was the voice I heeded whenever I needed a course correction. So far, he hadn't failed me yet.

"How far along?" I asked as we walked briskly through the hallway.

"Her contractions are five minutes apart."

I smiled. "Then we'd best hurry."

We ducked into my office, and I closed the door. Sure, most people knew what I could do, but I didn't want to show it off. Power is meant to serve others. Not to serve one's own glory. The more power I showed, the more people tried to make me into something more than I was. The more they tried to use me to serve their interests.

I formed a fairy portal and connected it to the master bathroom at the farmhouse.

Layla was in the inflatable tub that we'd purchased with Rina attending her. Who would have thought that, in drow society, Rina had served as a midwife? How could we turn her down when she offered to deliver our baby?

Agnus paced the room nervously. "Is it here yet? Is it here yet?"

I chuckled. "Go out and run around with Clarence. We'll let you know when the baby is here."

"What do you think it will be?" Agnus asked.

"A human," I said.

"I mean a boy or a girl!" Agnus said.

"We'll see," I said. Layla and I wanted it to be a surprise. I stepped over to the edge of the tub as Layla was on her hands and knees in the water. She lifted her head and gripped my hand as she moaned in pain.

"Almost there," Rina said. "I can feel the head!"

I smiled as Rina held a mirror under the water. It was an incredible sight. Our baby's head pushing through Layla's expanded...yeah...

"One more big push!" Rina said.

Layla was surprisingly quiet and calm. Not at all like in the movies or the medical shows where the women screamed bloody murder. She'd been practicing a hypnosis birthing method. Rina insisted it worked.

For the last several months, we'd been listening to recordings, over and over, about visualizing her opening. About how pleasant her "birthing time" would be. The program didn't like to use the word "labor." That implies work. This was supposed to be easy, natural, calm, or at least that's the frame of mind the program wanted us to believe.

So far, so good. Layla squeezed my hand as she pushed.

"The baby's coming!" Rina urged.

Sure enough, I watched in awe as our child emerged from Layla's body and into Rina's arms. Layla, carefully, rolled over and Rina placed our baby in her arms.

"It's a girl!" Rina said as the baby took its first breath and offered its first cry.

"She's beautiful!" I said. "Like her mom!"

We were both crying at this point—tears of joy. I stroked Layla's head as she held our baby in her arms.

"One more push," Rina said. "You still have to birth the placenta."

Layla nodded as she placed our baby in my arms. "Remember, I want to keep it!"

I smirked. Layla planned on encapsulating the placenta. Back on New Albion, they just blended it and ate it. Weird, right? Rina suggested encapsulation. Apparently, it helped with post-partum and a host of other things. It still seemed weird to me. However, when it came to decisions regarding childbirth, I'd learned quickly not to dispute what my wife wanted.

I looked down at our daughter. "I think she has your ears."

"Good!" Layla said. "I was worried she'd have weird, round, human ears."

I chuckled. For the first time, our baby girl opened her eyes. She looked at me. I knew that a baby's eye color could change, but her eyes were unique.

Green irises with flecks of gold.

"Layla," I said, "You have to see this."

Layla finished birthing her placenta. Rina held it in a bowl close to us. Layla's birthing plan included waiting for the last of the cord's blood to go to the baby before we cut it. She was all about the midwifery perspective. Now that we'd been through it, I couldn't deny it was quite a beautiful experience. Maybe not for everyone. But for us, it all went perfectly, according to plan.

Layla took our baby back in her arms. When our girl looked at her mother, Layla gasped. "You don't think... Could it be?"

I smiled. "I don't know. But I've only seen one person ever with eyes like that."

"And only in Eden," Layla said.

I nodded. "She said she'd come back when the time was right. I suppose it's possible."

"Then I suppose we only have one choice," Layla said.

"What is it?" Rina asked.

"Her name is Aerin."

We might never know for certain if our baby girl was the same Aerin we knew before. Had she been reborn as our child? It was possible. Even likely, perhaps. But I doubted she'd have her old memories. Still, every now and then, she'd make a coo, a gesture, something that reminded me of Aerin. Elrand even insisted that our girl looked just like his daughter, albeit lighter of skin when she was born. Either way, she was our daughter now. She was ours to love.

Thankfully, New York was never more than a fairy portal away. I could take care of my responsibilities there and make it back to Missouri every night.

I also resumed a preaching post at St. Ensley's. The last pew was dedicated to Cecil. It was where Shanda and Grace sat most weeks. Most of the pews had been purchased from other churches that had closed and repurposed for our new church. I'd purchased some of them from Holy Cross.

I couldn't believe that it had been six months since the church had closed. It had been seven months since Doris passed. I'd attended her funeral. Philip's message was perfect. I said a few words at her graveside service. In many ways, I think she saved my life. When I was lost, it seemed she always had the wisdom, the faith, to help me see through the shadows of the wilderness.

Many of my old denomination's churches were closing. It was sad, in a way. However, it was an inevitability. When being right becomes more important than being righteous, the decline is inevitable. The church was meant to be a vessel of love, to do what I was called to do, to plant seeds of Eden, to be God's presence in the world. There were many good Christians in that church. People who truly embraced the message of grace, the heart of God, the message of sacrifice. Some of my former parishioners were now members of St. Ensley's.

If you had to put a label on it, we were non-denominational. I didn't think about it much. We were a community of diverse peoples; humans, elves, drow, and even a handful of giants, who all knew that hope was a necessary ingredient to navigate a broken world. We all had different backgrounds. We didn't agree on everything when it came to spiritual matters. However, we were all seeking the path of love. We were seeking the heart of the divine.

I smiled at Layla as she held Aerin. Our baby was still too young to be a ring bearer. Rina was fine with Layla serving as her matron of honor with her child in her arm.

Technically, I was both the best man and the preacher. Not a usual arrangement, I suppose, but Jag insisted I be both.

It was an honor. Rina was insistent that I not read that passage from Ephesians about wives submitting to their husbands. I'd pointed out that the passage actually said to submit to *one another* out of love. Still, she'd chosen a customary drow reading. Jag had asked that I read from the thirteenth chapter of First Corinthians. Technically, in context, the passage had nothing to do with marriage, but it did speak profoundly about love. In that respect, it was totally appropriate.

All love, whether it be a love shared between spouses, or a love between a parent and a child, or even the kind of love we show to our neighbor or our enemies, is ultimately a love that proceeds from the heart of God.

At least, that's what I believe.

In the end, you can believe whatever you like. What matters the most is that you love one another. You live life with gratitude, and you never lose hope for a better tomorrow.

Jag stood up front. It had taken him a month to get a tuxedo that properly fit his massive shoulders and arms. I had to admit, he cleaned up quite nicely.

Rina looked a lot like I remembered Aerin had the first time I met her. She wore a traditional, colorful Indian dress from her culture. That's what the drow wore for formal occasions. It was quite beautiful. *She* was beautiful. Jag was a lucky guy. Almost as lucky as me.

I'd never felt so grateful. I'd lost a lot since that fateful day when I was stabbed by a giant holding the Blade of Echoes. B'iff was Brag'mok's brother. He was the first, I think, who taught me the real meaning of sacrifice. I'd never forget him. Others had given their lives, too. Even Fred, who had betrayed us, had sought forgiveness in the end. I gave it to him. His sins were not greater than many of my own. Who was I to harbor resentment against him? We'd lost others. The drow and elves who fought and died in the battle of the Arch—that's what we called it.

The American people had elected another President. A lot of people still put their hopes in the new administration. They'd soon learn that they'd never find a savior on Capitol Hill. They wouldn't find one in me, either. I might have been one chosen, once, to fulfill a prophecy. In truth, I hadn't completely fulfilled it. There were still divisions in the world.

However, we *were* growing more unified by the day. The more we learned to love without qualification, the more we opened our hearts and our ears to other people and their struggles, the more we learned to embrace a common future, a hope for a better tomorrow.

For Aerin, in our baby, I had to believe that a better tomorrow was possible. I'd do what I could to make the world a better place. That's all any of us can do. I wasn't perfect. I might have been for a moment, a brief moment when Layla and I walked hand-in-hand in Eden. We'd experience that again, someday. But until then, we'd live every day grateful for each moment. We'd embrace every sunrise. Every breath. Every laugh or giggle from our daughter. Every snarky comment from Agnus. Life was always supposed to be a gift.

Layla and I knew we'd face hardships and even tragedies. We might suffer from sickness. We'd age. Eventually, we'd die. But we were determined to count our blessings. To receive everything we had as a gift. Only then could we learn to live our lives as a gift to others.

Only then could we embrace a life worth living.

A life enveloped in love.

As I'm writing these notes we recently observed the twentieth anniversary of 9/11. At the time, I was in college. I hadn't went to seminary yet. I didn't have any formal theological education. Still, twelve days after those attacks a prayer service was held at Yankee Stadium. A minister of the denomination in which I'd eventually serve as a pastor offered a prayer. This prayer unleashed a controversy that lasted for the better part of the next decade in my former denomination. These disputes continued to rage when I began my formal theological training. They were always "in view."

Why would a *prayer* be so controversial? Because he prayed alongside people of other faiths. He gave the "impression" that we might worship the same God. Some called for this man's removal from office, his excommunication. But in the wake of an event like 9/11, when people were hurting and looking for answers, the last thing people were concerned about was whether or not the identity of the deity revered by Christians was the same as that revered by Muslims, or if his prayer displayed theological and doctrinal purity.

I must confess—as a young theology student in that same denomination I initially took a different position on that incident than I would today. Still, as I look back on that event, it reminds me of how callous we can sometimes be, how blind we can become in the name of "dogma," for the sake of "being right," that we miss something more fundamental, something at the heart of the human spirit. We all experience suffering in this world. It doesn't always make sense. It usually doesn't. But now that I look back on that event twenty-years ago it seems absurd that in the wake of such suffering so many of the people I looked up to at the time retreated into dogmatism, into a belief that "being right" or a purity of message was more important than embracing people with a living love, the kind of love that Christ demonstrated for those who suffered, even those who didn't quite understand who he was, or have their theologies perfectly in order.

One of my favorite theologies—as you might have guessed by his occasional quotation in these books—was Martin Luther. He once remarked that what makes a good theologian is a combination of prayer, meditation, and *struggle*. In the years since 9/11 I've endured my own share of struggles—much like Caspar, and many of them the same. I think Luther had a point. When we're acquainted with "struggle," or with "suffering" we grow closer to the heart of God. We gain compassion for others who suffer and struggle. We grow through struggle. Struggle also has a way of putting things like "dogma" into perspective. We all believe something. Faith has content. Still, if we think that we're closer to God just because we've intellectually mastered certain truths we've missed the heart of what (I believe) true religion should be. Pure religion, according to the book of James, involves becoming acquainted with those who are enduring affliction (James 1:27). Having the right answers, when you're suffering, doesn't remove the pain. Caspar reflects in these stories, on a couple occasions, that at a funeral he'd learned that the only comfort he could offer was his *presence*. Platitudes didn't help—even if they were true.

These days, my theology is a lot messier than it was when I was a minister. In truth, the content of my faith hasn't changed much. I've broadened my perspective a bit. I've also entered the bardic grade of the Order of Bards, Ovates, and Druids. I find that particular tradition more complimentary than contradictory with my core beliefs. Like Caspar urges, at the end of this book, I've started planting trees. Did you know you can get ten bare-root trees from the Arbor Day Foundation for a donation of only ten bucks? I've found it therapeutic. As Caspar observes, caring for something that offers very little in return (and doesn't talk back—differentiating trees from children which is another kind of creature I'm busy raising) helps us get outside of ourselves. I think it draws us closer to the heart of the Divine—however you define the God of your understanding.

Enough of that! Let these books speak for themselves. Take from them whatever you like and patch-work it into your own spirituality if you'd like. In the end, though, I hope you found these stories engaging, entertaining, and a little bit thought-provoking. I suppose we could have expanded these books further. But at this point I think Caspar has said everything he needs to say. He will still face challenges during the course of his life, for sure. The world at the end of this book hasn't been totally saved. But he's planting seeds. He's trying to make a difference. After all, to quote Martin Luther again who was once asked what he'd do if he knew the world was going to end tomorrow, he replied, "I'd plant a tree."

Thank you to everyone who has supported me as I've slaved away long-hours hammering out my manuscripts. Thank you to Michael, and the rest of the LMBPN team, who partnered with me on this endeavor. I look forward to whatever "fruit" the seeds of our partnership might produce next! Thank you to my wife and children who've always supported me. And thank you to everyone who has played a role in the course of my life, as I've endured my own struggles, as I've searched to define myself not only as a writer, but as a person. It's been a journey. It remains an adventure. And I can't wait for the next chapter.

-Theo

AUTHOR NOTES - MICHAEL ANDERLE
OCTOBER 1, 2021

First, thank you for not only reading this story but these author notes in the back as well.

I appreciate Theophilus ramrodding these stories, taking a core part of not only his considerations but his personal story, and adding those ingredients to make Casper's story that much more real.

Both of us realized we might have reviews that push back on the message in this series. However, both of us wanted to get the message out. Whether at the core it was for the same reason or simply adjacent reasons, I've never figured out.

In the end, both of us wanted to speak to the hypocrisy of beliefs going too far. Both of us grew up in Christian faiths of some sort (I was Catholic as a child, Southern Baptist as a teenager, and non-denominational as a young adult.)

And yet, I saw so much pain created by those believers around me and their dogma. I believed something was wrong.

For "them" to be right, there is a feeling that "others" need to be wrong. That is not true, by the way. Someone else being wrong doesn't make "them" right. It just proves one person has more wisdom and allowance for love (in my opinion).

We chose to place elves and orcs against each other, with millennia of beliefs encouraged by those who wielded power. What you see in the end is the corruption of belief by those in power.

The truth was always there, no matter what was believed.

Honestly, how much truth is still out there that humanity can't believe because of the corruption of those who held power centuries before me? I have no idea. However, I don't feel the answer is "none."

I can imagine my own feelings about justice not equating to law are probably partly accurate...and partly too many emotions.

My wife has a J.D. in law, so you can believe I bite my tongue to keep peace in the house at times. Am I wise? Not any wiser than any other husband who bites their tongue when their spouse has a different opinion. I *still* say stuff that I am very aware is going to push her buttons. I can't help myself. I'm human...and a guy. I'm probably doomed.

I think I'll blame testosterone. That's a legit reason, right?

Thank you for coming along for Casper's story. Theophilus and I agreed that everything with Casper was finished. We have closed this chapter and will go forth and produce a story that is perhaps not so personal in nature...but still a kick-ass book to read!

We have it working now, and I'll be excited to share more... when Theophilus is ready. I will say that the main character is deadly...*very, very deadly.*

I look forward to talking to you in the next series!

Regards,

Michael Anderle

ALSO BY THEOPHILUS MONROE

The Druid Legacy (Complete Series)

Voodoo Academy (Complete Series)

The Legacy of a Vampire Witch (Complete Series)

The Fomorian Wyrmriders (Complete Series)

The Legend of Nyx (Series in Progress!)

Nanoverse (Series in Progress!)

The Vilokan Asylum of the Magically and Mentally Deranged (Series in Progress!)

The Blood Witch Saga (Series in Progress!)

FREE BOOK OFFER: DRUIDESS

BOOKS BY MICHAEL ANDERLE

Sign up for the LMBPN email list to be notified of new releases and special deals!

https://lmbpn.com/email/

For a complete list of books by Michael Anderle, please visit:

www.lmbpn.com/ma-books/

CONNECT WITH THE AUTHORS

Connect with Theophilus Monroe

Website: www.theophilusmonroe.com

Social Media
https://www.facebook.com/pages/category/Author/
Theophilus-Monroe-Urban-Fantasy-Author-101469961530864/

Connect with Michael Anderle

Website: http://lmbpn.com

Email List: http://lmbpn.com/email/

https://www.facebook.com/LMBPNPublishing

https://twitter.com/MichaelAnderle

https://www.instagram.com/lmbpn_publishing/

https://www.bookbub.com/authors/michael-anderle

www.ingramcontent.com/pod-product-compliance
Lightning Source LLC
Chambersburg PA
CBHW020402110726
47899CB00006B/1826